ONCE BURNED

CAPTAIN MACKENZIE CALHOUN— IN HIS OWN WORDS!

I closed my eyes against the sight of the battle, but that didn't stop me from hearing their voices in my head. I could hear them calling. . . .

"Mac . . ."

The suddenness of the voice startled me, and it took me a moment to realize that it was inside my helmet rather than in my imagination. It was Kat Mueller's voice. She was remarkably in control, but I could hear the edginess in her tone. "Are you seeing it?"

"Yes."

"My God, Mac . . . what have we done?"

"The question isn't whether you're asking that, Kat. The question is whether the rest of the crew is. Where are you? Do they suspect . . . ?

"No. No, not at all. At least, I hope not. There's all sorts of rumors flying throughout the crew about what happened. The captain made that announcement about you—"

"And people know that it's not true?"

"Well . . . no. There's discussion about it."

"You mean they're not rejecting it out of hand?"

"Some do. A lot . . ." Her voice trailed off.

I shouldn't have been surprised, I suppose. I'd made no effort to really get close to the crew. I liked keeping my distance, wanted to maintain my loner status. Consequently, it had cost me. When it came down to the word of a beloved captain versus the actions of a suspicious newcomer and outsider, one should easily have been able to expect that reaction.

Nonetheless, it hurt. It hurt far more than I ever would have expected.

"Mac . . . are you still there?"

"Yes." I shook it off. "Yes . . . I'm here. . . ."

"Your air supply . . . How's that holding up?"

I checked my on-line systems and realized that I'd been paying no attention to it at all. That was probably not the brightest move on my part, considering I was hanging on to the outside of the ship. "It's running low. Eighteen minutes before I'm breathing my own carbon dioxide in here. Are you planning to beam me in?"

"That . . . could be a problem."

I suddenly started to feel icy, as if the vacuum of space was seeping through my suit. "A problem . . . How?"

"Lieutenant Cray doesn't want a repeat of your vanishing act. So he has security guards at all the transporter stations until further notice."

"Oh . . . perfect. How am I supposed to get back in? Crawl up a photon torpedo tube?"

There was dead silence.

And she said, "Well . . . actually . . ."

ONCE BURNED

MACKENZIE
CALHOUN
TOLD IN HIS OWN WORDS!

AS RECORDED BY
PETER
DAVID

THE CAPTAIN'S TABLE CONCEPT BY
JOHN J. ORDOVER AND DEAN WESLEY SMITH

POCKET BOOKS
New York London Toronto Sydney Tokyo Singapore

An *Original* Publication of POCKET BOOKS

POCKET BOOKS, a division of Simon & Schuster Inc.
1230 Avenue of the Americas, New York, NY 10020

This book is published by Pocket Books, a division of Simon & Schuster Inc., under exclusive license from Paramount Pictures.

ISBN: 0-671-02078-1

First Pocket Books printing October 1998

10 9 8 7 6 5 4 3 2 1

Printed in the U.S.A.

FIRST ENCOUNTER

YOU NEVER FORGET the first man you kill.

Man.

Well . . . that may be an exaggeration.

I was fourteen seasons at the time, a youth on my homeworld of Xenex. My father had died several seasons before that, beaten to death in the public square by our Danteri oppressors as a signal to all my people that we should know our place. It is my everlasting shame that I did not immediately retaliate. Instead I stood there, paralyzed. I can still remember my older brother digging his fingers into my shoulder, keeping me from attacking. That was what I wanted to do at the time. I wanted to charge from the crowd, leap upon the man who was inflicting such punishment upon my father, and sink my teeth into his throat. I wanted to feel his blood fountaining between my teeth.

Unfortunately, I was a child. My brother was probably concerned—not without reason—that I would be cut down before I got within twenty feet of my father's tormentor. So I stayed where I was, and watched, and wished the entire time that I could tear my eyes from my sockets, block out the cries from my father's throat.

Such a proud man, he was. So proud. What they did to him . . .

It fueled me several years later when I began my campaign against the Danteri.

There was a tax collector, a rather hated Danteri individual named Stener. A short, squat individual, he was, with a voice like a rockslide and a viciousness in attitude and deportment that made you cringe as soon as you look at him. He rode about on this mount, a large and hairy creature called a Pok that had been specially bred by the Danteri to be a sort of all-purpose steed. He always had several guards with him. On this particular day, he had three. They were massively broad, although it was difficult to get a precise idea of their build beneath their armor. They were not wearing helmets, however, possibly because it was hot and the helmets were sweaty. Instead their helmets were tucked under their arms. That would prove to be a costly mistake.

It was a very hot day, I remember. Very hot, the last day of a very hot week. Tempers were becoming ragged as it was, and whispers of my rabble-rousing were already beginning to reach the ears of the Danteri. At that particular time, though, they dismissed me as nothing they need concern themselves about. I was, after all, merely a loudmouthed teenager insofar as they knew. Perhaps more erudite than many, but nothing much more than that. Still, they saw the growing anger in the eyes of my people. The downward casting of glances, the automatic subservience . . . that seemed to be present less and less, and it very likely concerned the Danteri.

I was determined to give them more than cause for concern. I wanted to send them an unmistakable message. To let them know that my people would not tolerate their presence on my world any longer. To let them know that their torture of my father—rather than serving as a warning—had instead awakened the slumbering giant of Xenexian pride. And I wanted my hand to be the one that struck the first blow, that hammered the gong which would chime out the call to freedom.

Stener had collected the taxes in my home city of Calhoun, but he had very likely tired of the epithets, the curses, the increasingly aggressive sneers that greeted him. Nothing actionable or worth starting a fight over, but it very likely grated on him. He didn't know that I was following him, stalking him. He can be forgiven for his obliviousness. There were any number of scruffy, disheveled Xenexian youths around, so there was no intrinsic reason for him to focus on me any more than on anyone else. I stuck to the shadows, skulked around buildings, and whenever any of his men happened to glance in my direction, I managed to melt into the background, to disappear.

To a certain extent . . . it was a game. I was in the throes of youth, pleased with my skill and alacrity. As I paced them, keeping to myself but never letting them from my view, I felt an increasing sense of empowerment. Even—dare I say it—invincibility. That is naturally a very dangerous state of mind. Under such circumstances, one can become exceedingly sloppy. One should never underestimate an opponent, and I do not for a moment recommend it for anyone.

They reached the outskirts of Calhoun and still had

not spotted me. Had they then decided to return to their vessel and depart, they might very well all have survived. But they didn't. That was their greed, their own arrogance and sense of invincibility . . . as dangerous to them as to me. Stupidity is remarkably evenhanded.

Since they were certain that my people were too subservient to pose a serious threat, they decided to make their way to the neighboring, smaller village of Moute. Everything was happening spur-of-the-moment. Had I given the matter any thought at all, I would have gone into it with something approaching a plan. But I was flying on instinct alone, which was a habit that I would thankfully not continue to indulge in for my future dealings.

There was only one road between Calhoun and Moute, and I knew they were going to have to take it. Stener's Pok was moving at a fairly slow pace, and his three guards had to walk slowly to match it. As a result I had more than enough opportunity to get ahead of them. I moved with an almost bizarre recklessness, searching out and finding higher ground along the rocky ridges that lined the road. Ideally there would have been something with sufficient altitude that I could have sent an avalanche cascading down on their damned heads. Unfortunately the territory was fairly low, the ridges rising no more than maybe ten feet, so that wasn't an option. So I had to resort to other means to accomplish my task. I examined the stones beneath my feet and around me as I kept in careful pursuit, selecting those stones that best suited my purposes. The best were smooth and round, capable of hurtling at high speeds if thrown with enough strength. Believe me, the way I was feeling at that moment, my strength was more than sufficient. Such was the confidence I had in myself that I only selected three stones. It never even occurred to me that more might possibly be required.

I moved with speed and stealth, getting farther ahead until I was satisfied with the distance I'd put between myself and my targets. Crouching behind one of the upright outcroppings, I held one stone in either hand, and popped the third into my mouth for easy access. I listened carefully to determine if there was any useful information I could derive from whatever chitchat I might overhear, but there was no crosstalk at all. They rode in an almost eerie silence, as if they existed only to be my victims and otherwise had no lives up until that point.

The sun was beginning to descend upon the horizon, but it would still be quite some time until night. I had no interest in waiting until darkness. I wanted to see their faces clearly. I wanted them to know that even in broad daylight, there was still nowhere safe that they could hide. Besides, they'd be easier targets in the daylight. However, everything was going to depend upon my speed.

My back against the outcropping, I took a deep breath to steady my racing heart. I knew that the main thing I had going for me was the element of surprise. The moment that was lost, only pure speed could help me. I sprang from my hiding place and hurled the first rock, flipped the second rock to my throwing hand as I spit the third out. The first rock struck the closest guard squarely in the forehead. It knocked him cold. The second guard whirled around to see what had happened to his associate, but the second rock was already in flight and this one struck as accurately as the first. The third guard didn't even have a chance to turn; my last missile hit him bang-on in the back of his head. He went down without a sound.

It had all happened so quickly that Stener hadn't

fully had the opportunity to comprehend what was going on. His Pok was turning in place in alarm. It was everything that Stener could do to keep his grip on the beast. "What's happening? Who's there?!" he called out.

I admit, at the time I had something of a flair for the dramatic.

I leaped down from the rocks, landing in a feral crouch. My sword was still strapped to my back. Perhaps it was because of that that Stener didn't yet realize he was in any danger. The fact that three of his men had just been dropped in rapid succession didn't jibe with the unkempt teenager who was approaching him. He likely considered me some sort of prankster. "You, boy! Are you responsible for this?"

I took a mocking bow. "The very same," I said.

"These are my men! This is official business! How dare you—?"

"How dare you," I snarled back, quickly losing patience with the oaf. "How dare you and your people think that you can abuse my people indefinitely. Today begins the day we strike back. Today is the day we begin the long march toward freedom."

I unsheathed my sword, drawing it slowly from the scabbard on my back for maximum effect. It was that threatening sound, and probably the look in my eye, that made Stener truly comprehend that his life was being threatened. "Now, wait just a minute, young man," he said, but even as he spoke he tried to angle his Pok around, in obvious preparation for trying to make a break for it.

He need not have wasted his time. We were in a fairly narrow pass, after all, and it was no great trick to angle myself around and block his only real escape route. I brandished my sword in a reasonably threatening manner. Stener began to stammer a bit, his bluster become tangled with his concern for self-preservation. "Now . . . now wait just a minute. . . ."

"I have waited long enough already," I replied. "All my people have. We wait no longer. Today we strike back."

That was when a sword seemed to flash from nowhere.

My block was purely on instinct as I brought my sword up to deflect the blow. One of the guards I had struck—the one from behind—apparently had a harder head than I had credited him for. Perhaps it was a lesson I was being taught for attacking from the rear—a less than heroic tactic, I fully admit.

Our swords locked at the hilt. He was bigger than I was, and very likely stronger. But he was still slightly dazed from the blow to the back of his head. Even were I not the superior fighter, the fact that he was fighting at less than his best would have been more than enough to tilt the battle in my favor.

He tried to push me off my feet, but I disengaged my sword and faced him. He had put his helmet on, and it obscured his face, although his eyes seemed to glitter with cold contempt. He appeared to take the measure of me for a moment and then he swung his blade. Our swords clanged together, the impact echoing in the soundlessness of the place.

Stener was reining in his panicking Pok and attempting to send it back in the direction from which they had just come. I wasn't concerned; I was certain that I could dispatch my opponent and still catch up with Stener in time to kill him as well. Such confidence I had. Such confidence considering that I had never taken another life. The other two guards were unconscious only, as this one was supposed to be. Stener was intended to be my first blood, but my feeling at that moment was that the guard would do just as nicely.

He fought well, I'll give him that. For a moment or two, I actually found myself in trouble as his sword flashed before my face, shaving a lock of my hair off. I didn't even realize it until I found strands on the ground later. There were no words between us. Really, what could we have said? An exchange of names? Pointless. A mutual request for surrender? Beyond pointless. We both knew what was at stake, both knew that there would be no backing down. This was no coward I was facing; he was willing to die to do his job. Likewise, he must have known that I would never have staged the assault if I had not intended to see it through.

A parry, another parry, and I fell back. He smiled. He probably thought he had me, since I was retreating. He didn't understand that I was simply watching him expend all his "tricks" as I studied his method of attack, his offensive skills. They were, I quickly discerned, limited. I knew I could take him. I waited for the best moment, and eventually it presented itself. I appeared to leave myself open and he went for the opportunity. I blocked the thrust and my blade slid up the length of his sword, off, and then my blade whipped around and I struck him in the helmet with such force that I actually shattered the head covering. Understand, my sword was not some delicate, polite saber. This was a large blade, four feet long, heavy as hell. In later years, I'd be capable of knocking an opponent's head from his shoulders with one sweep. But I was still a young man, and hadn't quite "grown in" to my weapon yet. Nonetheless, the impact caved in the side of his skull.

Just that quickly, his body was transformed from something of use into a sack of bones with meat surrounding it. He went down with as sickening a thud as I'd ever heard. The abruptness, the violence of the moment, brought me up short. It just . . . caught me off-guard. I wasn't prepared somehow for the finality of it.

I heard the pounding of the Pok's feet as it put greater distance between us. I should have been concerned. I should have been immediately in pursuit. Poks are not renowned for their speed; even on foot, I could have overtaken it. But Stener was already forgotten. Instead my attention was focused on the guard. The other two were lying unconscious nearby, but they could well have been on one of Xenex's moons for all that it mattered at that moment.

I crept toward him. In retrospect, it's amazing how tentative I was. It wasn't as if he could be any threat to me. I had, effectively, killed him. But on some level that hadn't really registered on me. So I approached him as if he still might somehow strike at me. I drew closer, closer, until I was standing right over him. He was staring straight up, and he looked . . . confused. He didn't appear aware of where he was or how he had gotten there, and certainly he was unclear as to what had happened.

It was the first time that I actually had a chance to study him close-up. The pieces of his broken helmet had fallen away from his face, and I was able to see him clearly. I was stunned by his youth. He only looked several years older than I was. There was no belligerence in his face. He did not look . . .

. . . evil. That was it. I was expecting him to look evil. He was, after all, an agent of the enemy, a supporter of the evil oppressors. So his demeanor should have reflected that.

Except that I didn't know what evil was "supposed" to look like. The face of the enemy was not a great, monolithic thing, but rather millions upon millions of individuals, each with his own hopes and dreams and aspirations. And this face, this nameless face that was staring at the sky with a profoundly confused expression, had just had all his dreams shattered along with his helmet and his head.

I didn't know what to do. The Pok was long forgotten, Stener's getaway assured, and yet I didn't care. There were emotions tumbling through me, emotions that I had no clue how to deal with. Odd, isn't it. With all those emotions present, you would think that "triumph" would have been one of them. But I didn't feel that at all. In fact, it might well have been that I felt everything but that.

And then he said something that utterly confused me. He said . . ."Hand."

I was clueless as to what he was talking about. The word, bereft of context, meant nothing.

Then I saw that his fingers were spasming slightly. It took me a moment more to grasp fully what he wanted.

Slowly—even, I hate to admit, a bit fearfully—I reached out. Understand this: In the heat of battle, I was capable of slicing a man open, ripping his still-beating heart from his chest and holding it up into his face, and I say that with no sense of hyperbole. I actually did that, on several occasions throughout the years. I was not what anyone would call squeamish, and certainly had no trepidation over touching a dead or dying man.

But in this instance I did. My hand was actually trembling. I realized it and became angry with what I saw as my weakness. Taking a deep breath, I seized his hand firmly, still in a quandary as to why he appeared to want the gesture.

His fingers wrapped around mine and he looked into my eyes with infinite gratitude. I don't think he knew who I was. He didn't realize that I was the one who had struck the fatal blow. His mind was a million miles away. All he knew was that I was another being, another living, breathing soul. He knew that . . . and he knew, I have to believe, that he was dying.

In a voice that was barely above a hoarse whisper, he said, "Thank . . . you. . . ."

I knew that he was beyond help, and furthermore, that more of the Danteri would be back before too long. Not only that, but the unconscious soldiers would come around sooner or later. I tried to get up, to get away, to extricate my hand from his, but he gasped out, "No." He didn't seem afraid of dying. He simply didn't want to be alone.

I lifted him, then. I was surprised by how light he was. The entire business had taken a most bizarre turn, but I didn't dwell on any of that. I was operating purely on instinct, answering some moral code that I couldn't truly articulate quite yet. I ran with him, ran to an area of caves and crevices that I knew about not too far away. It was a labyrinthine area which I had known about for quite some time, and explored extensively in my youth. I knew I could hide there indefinitely, and there were underground passages as well so it wasn't as if anyone could reasonably lay siege to it.

I brought the young guard there, my mind racing with confusion. I was unable to determine any reasonable answers as to why I was doing what I was doing. I brought him to a secluded place within the caverns, and there I sat with him.

This was the enemy. I kept reminding myself of that, over and over again. He was the enemy, his people had enslaved my people. I had no reason whatsoever to feel the slightest bit of empathy for this individual. But I did. Here I had had my first taste of destruction, had taken down my first opponent . . . and I have never felt weaker. I wanted to get up, to flee the caves, to leave his rotting corpse for whatever scavenger creatures might take a fancy to it.

Instead I stayed. Perhaps I felt that leaving him behind would have been cowardice. Perhaps I needed to prove to myself that I was capable of taking it. Perhaps I was simply morbidly curious. It may have been all of those or none of those. In the final analysis . . . I just couldn't. I sat there with him, and his grip did not lessen on my hand. Every so often he would tremble, shuddering, his body convulsing slightly. He faded in and out, and never once that entire time did he comprehend that the man who had killed him was next to him.

I was looking into his eyes when he died. He had lain there, in the cool of the cavern, staring into space as if searching for some sort of answer. He said nothing. And then his head rolled slowly in my direction, his gaze fixing on me—truly fixing on me—for the first time. "You . . ." he managed to say.

I waited for the rest, or at least whatever it was he was able to manage. You destroyed me. You bastard, you took my life. You are the one who is responsible. You did this to me. Anything, everything, I was ready for it.

"Thank . . . you . . ." he told me. Then his head lolled to one side and I heard a sound that I would come to know all too well: a death rattle, his spirit leaving the meaty shell in which it had spent its mortal existence.

I stared at him for a very long time, and then I saw a large spot of wetness appear on his face. It took me a moment to fully comprehend what it was. It was a tear. It was not, however, from him. It was from me. Large, fat tears were rolling down my face, and I was so numb that I was unaware of it at first. Then they came faster and harder. My body started to tremble, great racking sobs seizing me. I couldn't believe it. I fancied myself already as a hardened warrior, determined and ready to lead his people to freedom. What sort of warrior and leader allows himself to fall apart in the face of killing an enemy? But the more I tried to pull myself together, the more the tears flowed.

I tried to stand up, tried to run, but there was no strength in my limbs. I collapsed and continued to cry, and I have no idea for how long it continued. It was probably minutes, but it felt like days.

Eventually it subsided, the sobbing tapering off. Still I lay there for some time, feeling the coolness of the stone against my face. Then I pulled myself together and dusted myself off. I picked up the body of the first man I had ever killed. He was significantly larger than I, and his body was even heavier dead than it had been alive. But my strength was rather formidable and I had no trouble hauling him out to the mouth of the cave. Prudence would have dictated that I simply leave him . . . it . . . there. After all, I was putting myself at risk weighing myself down, and if there had been any Danteri hunting parties passing by at that particular moment, I would have been at a disadvantage. The sun was already quite low in the sky, the shadows stretching like darkling fingers across the plains, as I left the corpse behind me and set off into the darkness.

I've often looked back on that day and wondered what possessed me. After all, I had known that slaying others would be necessary if I were to accomplish my goal and lead an insurrection that would result in Xenex's freedom. Why, then, did it affect me in such a way?

Perhaps I was mourning my lost innocence, or at least what passed for innocence. Never again would I be anything other than a slayer.

Perhaps the tears, in some way, were an expression of fear. In having irretrievably made that first strike, I had determined a course not only for myself, but for my planet. The Danteri would demand Xenexian blood by the ton in exchange for the assault upon their collector and the death of one of the guards. My people would not stand for it—that I would see to personally. Perhaps I was shedding tears in advance for those of my people who were destined to die in the insurrection. With a stroke of my sword, I had doomed them. They would die fighting for a greater cause, but they would die just the same, and so those deaths would be on my head.

Or perhaps it was simply because I never knew my victim's name, or anything about him. Did he have a wife back on Danter whom I had just transformed into a widow? A son who would never see his father again? He himself had parents, that was likely. How would they react upon learning that their son was dead? Would his mother still hear the cries he uttered as an infant, like a haunting, mournful song in her head, and cry until her heart broke over the loss of that child? Or perhaps he was an orphan, with no parents, and had not yet had time to marry or sire children. In that case, he would leave no one behind to mourn him or those accomplishments that he might have achieved had his life not been cut short. Here I was, planning to lead a rebellion that—if it succeeded—would definitely give me a permanent place in the annals of Xenex, and the first casualty in that course might be a young man who was so without attachment to the world that he might as well not even have lived in it.

There was no way for me to know, no way for me to ever know, and perhaps that was what caused me to cry my heart out. But once it had been cried out, I then carefully and meticulously began to build a great wall of brick around it. The slaying of the young man was the first brick, and more bricks would follow while their thickening blood provided the cement between them.

In the final analysis, it might have been all of those plus one more: the evil irony of a young man dying while thanking the one who had killed him since his delirium had prevented him from understanding who I was.

I returned home, told my older brother, D'ndai, what I had done. He blanched considerably, and then his jaw set in grim determination. At the time he had no great love for the Danteri, and was as susceptible to my exhortations as was any other man. Although I would be designated warlord within a very short time, at that time I was given the appointment of a rank we called *"r'ksha"* . . . or what you would term "captain." D'ndai had several private fliers, all of which were pressed into work as our preparation for battle against the Danteri loomed. The largest one was given to me, out of deference to the fact that my determination was setting the entire situation into motion. I also had my first crew, and ten truer and braver men never walked the surface of Xenex. "Men." What a word. More like young boys, they were. We all were, although we felt much older, of course.

Sadly . . . I was the only one who grew to become older. The rest of them died within the first year of combat.

The last of my crew was wiped out in a devastating raid on a Danteri outpost which went horribly wrong. I had had several early successes, you see, and became emboldened as a result. Consequently, I became sloppy. I trusted a tip from a source who proved to be not as reliable as I had previously thought. What I had intended as a surprise attack on a strategic outpost turned out to be a crafty trap by the Danteri. I have a "sixth sense" for danger, I always have. Just before their trap sprang shut, I sensed that we were heading into an ambush and tried to get us out of there before it was too late. In one respect, I accomplished that goal. Had I not realized when I did, we would have been slaughtered within seconds. As it was, we narrowly avoided capture, but the firefight that resulted from the nearly perfect ambush was catastrophic. My vessel limped back to the city, with my urging every last bit of speed out of its failing engines. I was hoping, praying that I would be able to save at least a few lives of the handful of men—boys—who were left to me. But by the time I made it back to the city, it was too late. The last of my crew died in my arms. Unlike the time with the first man I killed, though, this time I felt nothing. Absolutely nothing. The wall that I had built around my heart was a strong one by that point, and not easily pierced. No more tears would I, could I, shed over the deaths of others, be it at my hand or not.

That was the theory, at least. Nonetheless, the guilt weighed heavily upon me, despite D'ndai's assurances that it was not my fault, that I had no way of knowing. That was no excuse. I should have known. It was my first major setback, my first major loss to the Danteri, and part of me was angry that I had survived while the men who had been counting on me had lost their lives. My resolve was not shattered . . . but for the first time, I began to doubt myself. I had never wavered in my belief that I would triumph over the Danteri . . . until that moment.

I wandered the streets of Calhoun aimlessly that night. I had a slight limp from an injured leg, and I had not washed off the smoke and soot from battle or the crash of my vessel. My hair was wildly askew. In short, I wasn't especially pretty to look at, I can tell you. I passed the fortifications that had been erected around the city of Calhoun. The perimeter guards saluted me, nodding in approval as I passed, gave me gestures of assurance. All of it felt hollow, empty. They still had confidence in me, but I did not have it in myself.

Understand, I knew every foot, every square inch of the city. Nonetheless, after walking aimlessly for a time, I found myself in an area of town that was oddly unfamiliar to me. Furthermore, I was drawn to one particular door that had an odd sign hanging on it. In Xenexian, it read, "R'Ksha Foldes." Or, to translate into English: "the Captain's Table." I had no idea what it was referring to. I had never heard of the establishment, if such it was, and that alone was very odd since I had thought I knew every place of business in all of Calhoun.

I placed an ear against the door and heard what amounted to a faint murmur from within, but nothing I could distinguish. It sounded like voices, but I couldn't make out anything that anyone was saying. For a moment I thought of turning away, but something within me rebelled at the notion. It smacked too much of cowardice, and therefore was an intolerable option.

Taking a deep breath, I pushed open the door.

It was a very odd sight.

In many ways, it seemed no different than a standard Xenexian tavern. Weapons hung upon the wall as a convenience for drunken customers, as was always the case in Xenexian taverns. The reason, you see, is that customers who allow themselves to get too drunk to fight, but try and do so anyway, are too stupid to live and therefore duels with such individuals should be facilitated. That way they won't continue to cause mischief.

But there was something about the place that I couldn't immediately identify. A scent, perhaps, like sea air, and a breeze wafting through which was of mysterious origin considering that outside on that night there had been no breeze at all. Furthermore—and this, I assure you, was the oddest part—I couldn't help but feel that the floor was rocking ever so gently. Not a quake, most definitely, but just a very delicate swaying motion, as if I were standing on the deck of a ship of some sort.

What was most peculiar of all, however, was the astounding mixture of alien races who populated the place. At sturdy wooden tables were representatives of all manner of species, including any number that I could not identify. It's not as if Xenex has a large number of visitors. Despite the fact that Calhoun was one of the larger cities, Xenex was—and is—largely the province of Xenexians. Nevertheless, there were individuals with blue skin, green skin, red skin . . . every permutation of the spectrum, it seemed. Some with antennae, others with multiple eyes or no eyes, one with tentacles, another with a spotted shell and a perpetual scowl.

There was one man off to the side at a table by himself. Of the species I now know as "humans," he was dressed in blue, with a trim white beard. He was simply shaking his head as if in perpetual annoyance and confusion, and there was the sadness of the grave in his eyes. He kept muttering the same words over and over again: "Damned iceberg. Goddamned iceberg." I had no idea what he was talking about. I started to approach him, and then felt a hand on my shoulder.

I whirled because, of course, I had no idea who was behind me. I was conditioned to anticipate attacks at all times.

"Just leave him be, son. You'd be wasting your time anyway. Poor devil's off in his own world."

The man who had spoken, who had stopped me from going near the bearded man in blue, had somewhat unkempt white hair himself. He wore an apron, and had a ready smile that I found comforting somehow. He was not Xenexian, but in an odd and fleeting way, he reminded me of my father. "They call me Cap," he said.

"Are you the owner of this place?" I asked.

"Yes and no. In a way, we're all owners of this place. You, me," and he gestured to encompass the rest of the bar, "them. This is your first time here, but eventually you'll understand." He smiled. "Congratulations, by the way."

"For what?" For a moment I bristled. I was still angry, bitter over what happened to my men, and some part of me thought he was sarcastically alluding to that tragedy.

"For being the youngest captain ever to visit the Captain's Table. Previously the youngest we had was Alexander. He was only here once, and then on a technicality, since in truth he was a king. But he fancied himself a captain of great armies, and that was sufficient to gain him entrance in a sort of probationary status. It was just the one time, though. He tried to take over the bar." He shook his head resignedly. "Should have expected that."

"Should I . . . know this person you're speaking of?"

Cap tilted his head back and declaimed as if in the theater, " 'And Alexander wept, for he had no new worlds to conquer.' " The mention of the name drew glances from several of the other patrons, and there were what appeared to be grim smiles of acknowledgment and recollection.

I decided not to pursue it. As if sensing my thoughts, he guided me to a small table to one side. "I think it best, what with this being your first time and considering your age, that you simply observe rather than try to interact extensively. We do not, after all, want to have any problems."

"I . . . suppose not," I said. I was having difficulty understanding where I was or what was happening. Without really paying attention, I sat down at a table.

"No, not that one," Cap said quickly, and he pointed off to my left. "The one over here."

I was beginning to become annoyed. The eccentricity of the place, the odd atmosphere that was a bizarre blend of strange-yet-familiar, and my own state of mind thanks to my recent setbacks, were serving to put me on edge a bit. "This one seems fine," I told him. "I think I will stay right—"

A huge dagger slammed down into the tabletop with such force that it threatened to split the wood in half. The hilt quivered slightly.

"Captain Gloriosus," Cap said with clear warning in his voice. "You know the rules."

Slowly I glanced up, and up, at the man whose powerful hand had wielded the dagger. He was dressed in glittering chestplate armor and a metal skirt that ended at about midthigh. His legs were powerful, his arms no less so. He had a long, bristling beard so thick that it looked like wire, and a fierce scowl that showed from beneath a plumed helmet. The scabbard for his dagger was on the inside of his right calf, and from his left hip hung a massive sword.

"This pup is at my table," the one called Gloriosus said.

I did not appreciate the tone of his voice, and told him so. This seemed to amuse the one called Gloriosus, and he laughed in a booming tone that was unbearably condescending. "Cap," he bellowed, 'are we letting any upstart who wishes it to sit at the Captain's Table? Have we no standards anymore?"

"The standard is that patrons have to be captains of one sort or another," Cap told him as if addressing a small child. "He fits the criteria, Miles, as do you. As does everyone here."

The others were making no pretense of looking away anymore. About forty or so pairs of eyes took in the entire confrontation. They sat back and observed as if watching a vid or an adventure in a holosuite.

"That means," continued Cap as if unaware that this situation were anything other than the most intimate of disagreements, "that he is under the protection of the bar . . . as are you, Miles."

"A captain of the Roman legions needs no protection from a whelp," the one called Miles Gloriosus said.

I didn't like this tone, or his arrogance. More, I felt as if he had made it a point to try and shame me in front of the others who were scattered around the bar. I had no idea why the opinions of these strangers mattered, but something within me simply refused to allow myself to be treated as a laughingstock.

Captain Miles Gloriosus was continuing to boast about his own general fabulousness. I didn't bother to listen. Instead with my right hand I yanked the dagger from the table, and with the left I reached up and grabbed a fistful of his copious beard. Before he was aware of what I was doing, I yanked down as hard as I could. His head hit the table and I brought the dagger around and down, driving it squarely through the beard and into the tabletop with a resounding thud. Gloriosus was pinned, momentarily immobilized as his beard was entangled with the blade. Given time, of course, he would have managed to pull it loose, but time was not something I was inclined to afford him.

I was on my feet then. I could have used my sword, which was strapped onto my back, but instead I yanked out the Roman captain's own sword from his scabbard. He yelped in frustration and grabbed at the knife to extricate it from his beard . . . and suddenly he became very quiet, probably because he felt the edge of his own blade against the back of his neck. One movement downward and I could have severed his head.

The tavern, which had been bustling with energy only moments before, suddenly became very quiet. Every single individual was watching with stony, impassive silence. It was impossible to tell whether they approved or disapproved of my actions. Cap said nothing, but merely stood there with his arms folded, inscrutable.

I had his sword in a firm double-handed grip, and the blade did not waver so much as a centimeter. I had one of the cutting edges of the blade tucked just under the bottom of his helmet. Very quietly, very deliberately, I said, "It would appear you need some protection from the whelp after all. Wouldn't you say that's true?"

He muttered something that sounded like a curse, and I repeated, "Wouldn't you say that's true?" To underscore my point, and the delicacy of his situation, I pressed the blade down ever so slightly. A thin line of blood welled up. I couldn't see his eyes from the angle I was standing, but from the sudden tensing of his body I was quite sure he felt it.

"M'k'n'zy," Cap said warningly.

And then Miles Gloriosus growled, "Yes."

"Yes what?" I wasn't going to let him get off quite that easily.

"Yes . . . on reflection, I would say it's true . . . that I could have used . . ." He hesitated, and I applied just a hair more pressure. "Protection against the whelp!" he practically spat out as quickly as he could.

I stepped back then and he spun with a good deal of speed, forcibly tearing himself away from the table with such violence that a generous chunk of his beard was torn right from his chin. He didn't seem to notice. He was too busy focusing the fullness of his ire upon me. For a moment, just for a moment, I envisioned what it would be like to face him on a true battlefield. I had a sense of him, a feeling of the environment from which he came. I realized that the truth was that I had been rather fortunate. Had he not been so swaggeringly confident, I never would have been able to manhandle him so easily.

He extended a hand and I thought he wanted to shake mine. Then I realized that he wanted his sword back. I handed it over to him hilt first. This was a tactical gamble—some would say error—on my part. I was holding the blade as I offered the sword to him. Had he wished to do so, he could have grabbed the hilt, swung the sword around and tried to gut me like a freshly caught fish. Whether he would have succeeded or not is debatable, but he certainly could have had a good shot at killing me. Instead, however, he took his sword from me without comment and slid it into his scabbard. I was impressed by the soundlessness of it, since both the steel and scabbard were so well oiled. There was no hiss of the metal against the leather; instead it went in noiselessly, and presumably was pulled in much the same manner.

"You," he growled, "were lucky."

I couldn't disagree. I felt the same way.

"You would be well advised to stay out of my way," continued Gloriosus, "lest things not turn out quite so well for you the next time." Pulling together what was left of his pride, Gloriosus swaggered away.

My gaze swept the other captains who were in the bar. Many of them didn't seem interested in meeting my glance, but were instead suddenly very preoccupied with looking in other directions entirely. I felt very unwelcome and unwanted, and had no idea what the hell I was doing there. I started to rise from my seat, intending to head for the door, but Cap put a hand on my forearm and quietly said, "Stay. You have as much right to be here as anyone else."

"I doubt that," I said, but I sat anyway.

Cap placed a mug in front of me. I have no idea from where he pulled it, but there it was. "First drink for a first-time customer is always on the house," he said, gesturing to it. I reached for it tentatively.

My general paranoia and uncertainty made me hesitate, but then I sniffed at it and looked up curiously. "What is this called?" I asked.

"Beer."

"Bihr." I rolled the unfamiliar word around in my mouth, then took a sip of it. It was more pungent than I'd expected, but had a certain degree of kick to it. I must have been quite a sight: the scruffy barbarian, surrounded by men and women who were, for the most part, far more cultured and civilized than I could ever hope to be. Everyone was watching me, even those who were pretending to look in another direction. They probably wondered what I was doing there. So did I.

I swallowed half the beer and found the sensation somewhat relaxing. I looked at Cap, a gentle warmth beginning to develop in my gut, and I realized, "You called me by name before. How did you know my name?"

"How did I know you?" He feigned surprise that such a question could even be posed. "Why, everyone knows the name of the great M'k'n'zy. Weren't you aware of that?"

"I was not aware of any greatness," I said bitterly. "My men were depending on me, and I let them down. It was my fault."

"Yes. It was," Cap said, matter-of-factly.

I looked up at him. His comment was a stark contrast to D'ndai's words of consolation. "What should I have done, then? How could I have avoided it?"

"Oh, you couldn't have," said Cap. He had seated himself opposite me, and was holding an empty glass, which he was wiping clean with a white cloth. "There was nothing you could have done differently. You made all the correct decisions based upon the information you had available to you. Any other person here, in your position, would have done the same thing."

"But . . . you're still saying it's my fault. . . ."

"Of course it is. You're the captain. You're the leader. That makes it your responsibility. All these people," and he nodded his head in their direction, "oversee vessels or armies or crews, some of them numbering in the thousands. And whatever happens, these people here are the final authorities. Theirs is the final responsibility. Even when it's not their fault . . . it's their fault. Tell me, M'k'n'zy . . ." He leaned forward in a conspiratorial fashion. "Do you feel something filtering through the air? A sort of sensation, a distant heaviness that seems to settle around your upper torso?"

"I . . . suppose. Yes . . . yes, I think I do at that." I flexed my shoulders. "What . . . is that?"

"It's the weight of the world," Cap said with a ragged smile. "Everyone here carries it on them, and it just kind of leaks around and filters through the atmosphere of the Captain's Table. The nice thing about this place is that we all share each other's weight, and that makes it all the more bearable."

I stared at him skeptically, unsure whether he literally meant it or not. I found my gaze resting on the man in blue once more, the one with the beard who was off by himself. "What's his problem?" I asked.

"He lost his vessel," Cap told me. "Over a thousand souls perished, claimed by icy waters. As his vessel was sinking, he discovered a door on his deck that he had never noticed before. He stepped through it . . . and found himself here. He's been here ever since. Nothing for him to go back to, really."

"How long has he been here?" I asked.

"A few minutes. A few centuries." Cap pulled thoughtfully at his chin. "It's all subjective, really. Never an easy answer to that one. Somewhat like being a commander, really. The easy answers don't always present themselves readily."

A slow, eerie feeling began to creep over me. "Cap . . ." I said slowly.

"Yes?"

"Am I . . . are we . . . dead?"

He laughed loudly and boisterously at that. "No, young M'k'n'zy. We, and you, are not dead. Oh, in a sense, we're dead to the world, I suppose, in a small way. It's really the only way this bar can function, because there is so much responsibility borne by its patrons that they'd be pulled out of here by those demands if those requests could reach them. But in the standard sense, we are very much alive. The land of the living awaits just beyond the exit."

I looked in the direction he was pointing, and then I asked suspiciously, "How do I know that, if I pass through that door, I won't wind up splashing about in the icy waters that took his vessel?" I indicated the white-bearded captain.

"So many things you desire to know, young M'k'n'zy," Cap said, and if a man less charming had said it, it might have sounded patronizing. "I'm afraid that there will be some matters which you will have to take on faith. Besides, you have a destiny to fulfill, and that destiny certainly doesn't include sinking beneath the surface of the Atlantic Ocean."

"Of the what?"

"Of an ocean," Cap amended.

"And what would this destiny be?" I asked.

"How would I know that? I'm simply a bartender, M'k'n'zy. I'm not God."

"Are you certain of that?"

He didn't seem to answer at first, but merely smiled, and then I realized that the smile itself was indeed the answer. "If you need a refill," he said, "just hold up a hand and someone will attend to you directly. And M'k'n'zy . . . be aware of something. . . ."

"Yes?"

"Every single person here has had failures, setbacks, and frustrations. Every one has blamed himself, sometimes rightly and sometimes wrongly. The important thing is to keep to the hope of all the things you can do to benefit others. You can do great good, M'k'n'zy. Never forget that your men are depending upon you . . . but also never forget that you are not a god. You are not infallible. You are simply . . . a captain. Just worry about being the best captain that you can be, and let the rest sort itself out as it will."

"That's too easy, too facile an answer," I told him, but he wasn't there anymore. He'd moved away from the table, and a quick glance around the room did not reveal him.

I sat there for a time longer. A waitress would bring over another beer whenever I wanted it, although interestingly I never actually had to ask her for it. It was simply there. And when I had enough, the table space in front of me remained vacant.

I realized that Cap was right. What made me realize it was that I kept going over and over it in my mind, and I wasn't feeling any better over what had happened, but on the other hand I wasn't coming up with anything I would have, or could have, done that would have made it any better.

Eventually, I knew it was time to leave. To this day, I don't know whether the impulse came from within or without. But I was already in motion before my mind had fully adjusted to my imminent departure. I had left a random amount of Xenexian currency behind as a tip, having no clue as to how much would be appropriate. But Cap, who was behind the bar, tossed off a salute. I had never seen one before, since Xenexians tend to bow in deference to commanding officers. But I returned the gesture and from his approving smile I surmised that I had done so correctly. "M'k'n'zy," he called to me. I turned and waited expectantly. "Next time," he said, "a story."

I looked at him oddly. "A story? You'll tell a story?"

"No," he told me. "You will."

"About what?"

He shrugged. "Whatever." Then, effectively ending the conversation, he picked up another glass and whistled as he wiped it down. I was going to continue to ask him what he was talking about, but decided that it would be best simply to be on my way.

I walked out of the tavern back onto the Xenexian street. The evening had grown colder. I had no idea how much time had passed while I was in there. Drawing my cloak more tightly around myself, I started down the street . . . and then hesitated. His words about a story were still with me, and I felt myself overwhelmed with curiosity. I turned and retraced my steps so that I could ask Cap for clarification.

I couldn't find the place.

I was certain that I passed the tavern's location several times. It wasn't as if there was now a vacant area where once the tavern had been. The shops and eateries had simply closed ranks, as if they were hiding one of their own from prying eyes. On the off chance that I had headed down the wrong street, I went to the nearest intersection and circumnavigated the block. Nothing. Gone. Completely gone. It wasn't at all possible . . . but it had happened. The Captain's Table had somehow managed to make itself scarce.

I thought of ghost stories that I had heard, strange tales of visions and such that I had always half-kiddingly traded with my friends. I was convinced, though, that this night I had had an experience very much along those lines. Perhaps I had been given a preview of an afterlife set aside for warriors . . . such as your Earth's Norsemen, I would learn in later years, described their Valhalla. Or perhaps I had wandered into what could best be termed a haunted house. Perhaps some bizarre interdimensional anomaly had situated itself smack on a side street of the city of Calhoun and had allowed me into it.

Or perhaps I just wasn't getting enough sleep.

Resolving to do something about the last circumstance, at least, I went into the night without a backward glance. This was deliberate: Part of me was afraid to admit that I would not see the place again when it had so clearly been there, and the other part was concerned that the Captain's Table had somehow sprung into existence again. If the latter occurred, I would not be able to resist entering once more . . . and it might be that, given a second opportunity, I might never leave at all.

That was my first time at the Captain's Table.

This . . .

This is the second. . . .

SECOND ENCOUNTER

I WAS GOING OUT of my mind with boredom.

I read over, for what seemed the hundredth time, the dispatches from Starfleet regarding the Dominion War. When the chime sounded at the door of my ready room, I didn't even hear it the first time. That's how absorbed I was in the recounting of the various battles and skirmishes. In fact, it took the voice of my first officer, Elizabeth Paula Shelby—"Eppy," I called her, when I felt like being either affectionate or annoying—calling, "Captain!" through the door to get my attention.

I glanced up impatiently, wondered why she wasn't standing in front of me, and realized that she was still on the other side of the door waiting for permission to enter. "Come," I called.

The door slid open and Elizabeth entered.

Now there is something you should understand

about Elizabeth: I love her. Deeply. Madly. Completely. Even when we broke off our engagement, I never stopped loving her. Even when looking at her was a knife to the heart, I never stopped loving her. She is my soul mate, my better half, my significant other . . . any nickname you choose to give it, that is what she is to me. However I can never tell her that. I know myself, you see. I need to be in control of situations, and to admit to her how I feel would be to surrender a part of myself that I am not willing to give up. In order for me to love Elizabeth as truly as I wish to, I must bring myself to a state of mind where I cannot live without her. In my time, however, I have seen too much death, too much slaughter. I have lost too many loved ones, time and again. I cannot remember a time where death was not a reality rather than an abstract concept. My very first memory, in fact, is someone dying. I don't remember the details; I could not have been more than two seasons old. But I remember the blood, and the death rattle, and staring into lifeless eyes before the strong hand of my father yanked me away.

If I ever reach a point where I cannot live without Elizabeth, then I will feel as if I have attached a beacon to her back that is serving to summon the Grim Reaper. I cannot leave myself as vulnerable as that. It would be wrong. Wrong for me, wrong for the crew . . . just . . . wrong.

So I keep my silence, wrap my feelings for her within a cloak of toughness mixed with irreverence. When I argue with her, what I truly want to do is hold her tight. Every time I say her name, I imagine myself brushing my lips across hers. She doesn't know any of this, or at least I pray she does not. Otherwise she might think the less of me. For in some ways, that mind-set makes me a coward, and it would pain me if she regarded me in that manner.

"Commander," I greeted her formally with a slight nod.

"Are you all right, Captain?" she asked without preamble.

"Fine. Why do you ask?"

"Well, you got those recent war updates, and you've been stewing in here ever since."

"Stewing?" I raised an eyebrow in mild offense. "I wouldn't say 'stewing.' "

"Then how would you term it . . . sir?" she asked.

I didn't reply immediately, because to be honest, "stewing" wasn't all that far off the mark. Finally I let out an annoyed sigh. " 'Smoldering,' perhaps. I have a good deal of anger, Eppy, and no clear idea of what to do with it."

"Anger? Why?" She sat opposite me. I could tell she was concerned about my state of mind, because she allowed my use of her hated nickname to pass without comment.

"We should be there," I said, tapping my computer. On the screen there was a display of Federation space with key points in the ongoing war marked for easy reference. "The *Excalibur* is as good a starship as any of them, Eppy, and this is a damned fine crew. A little odd in places, I admit, but I'd gladly lead any of them into battle and be confident that they'd give as good a fight as any opponent is likely to get. Instead we're out here, in Thallonian space. We're . . ."

"We're pursuing our mission, as per our orders, Mac," Elizabeth reminded me.

"Our orders, our orders. To hell with our orders. *Grozit,* Commander . . . Captain Picard ignored his orders when the Borg assaulted Earth. Starfleet had him rooting around the Neutral Zone. He followed his conscience and if it weren't for him, Earth would be the sole province of the Borg by now." I pointed in the general, vague direction of Federation space.

"There are men and women I trained with in the midst of one of the most formidable wars since the Romulans first swarmed their borders, and I'm reduced to hearing about it secondhand."

"It was a different situation with Picard, Mac," Shelby replied. "He'd been assimilated into the collective at one point, and that made him suspect as far as the Fleet was concerned. But as he proved, it also made him uniquely suited to attack and defeat the Borg. That was a one-in-a-million set of circumstances."

"Our place is with the Fleet," I said firmly.

"Our place is where we're told to be," she shot back, but she didn't do so in an angry manner. I could tell that she was as torn up about the conflict as I was. For all I knew, she'd love to sit there and voice the same complaints. But it's part of Shelby's value to me that she will readily take an opposing viewpoint, if for no other reason than to make me think more carefully about whatever it is I'm saying. The fact is, she challenges me and I learn a lot from her. Not that I would admit that, of course.

"I smell Jellico behind this," I told her. At that point I rose from behind my desk and pulled my sword off the wall. It was the sword that I had taken off an enemy, back when the bastard had sliced open the right side of my face and left me with a permanent scar . . . or, at least, a scar that I had chosen to leave permanently. "He doesn't trust me any more than the rest of the Fleet trusted Picard. Perhaps I should respond the same way that Picard did." I swung the sword through the air. It made satisfying, sharp hissing sounds as it cut. Elizabeth flinched slightly; perhaps she was worried it was going to come flying out of my hand and decapitate her.

"It's more complicated than that, Mac. There's not one big battle going on where we can ride to the rescue. Besides," she continued in a less strident tone, "has it occurred to you that this might not simply be Admiral Jellico?"

"Believe me, Eppy, if anyone is capable of doing something to annoy me, it's Jellico."

"Perhaps," she admitted, "but Mac, the bottom line is: We don't know truly how the war is going. We know what Starfleet is admitting to, but it might be worse than they're letting on, and what we're hearing already isn't that great to begin with."

"Starfleet, less than candid?" I feigned horror at the very notion. "Careful, Eppy. You might cause the entirety of my world to come crashing down around me."

She didn't seem the least bit impressed by my dazzling repartee. I couldn't entirely blame her. The subject matter didn't lend itself to it; it felt clumsy and forced. Considering what she said next, I can somewhat understand why the conversation seemed labored.

"Have you considered the possibility that the Federation . . . could fall?"

It was not an easy question for her to pose. It was more than just a case of her tossing out a scenario and asking whether I had thought about it. In a way, she was voicing her own greatest nightmare.

I stared at her. The fact was, it hadn't even occurred to me. "Of course I've considered it," I lied smoothly.

"No, you haven't," she said, reminding me of the typical futility in trying to put something past her. "You're so convinced of the intrinsic 'rightness' of your 'side' that you haven't thought for a moment that the Federation might end up on the short end of the stick. If that happens, Mac, if things go badly," she said patiently, "they're going to need ships that they've held in reserve. Not only that, but those ships will need to be captained by the men with the most experience at operating on their own, without any guidance from home."

I knew precisely what she was referring to. All captains, particularly starship captains, function with a good deal of autonomy. But there are some captains . . . more than I care to think about, really . . . who are referred to as "homebodies." They check with Starfleet constantly about every move they make, wanting an official stamp on everything they do in order to avoid second-guessing or potential charges.

I was definitely not one of those types. Eppy knew that all too well. If anything, I tended to operate from the philosophy that rules were not only made for other people, but for other galaxies. If Starfleet disappeared tomorrow, I wouldn't give a single glance back.

"You're more comfortable on your own, Mac. Happier. Not only that," and she leaned forward on her elbows, "but how many captains out there actually have experience in rallying troops against oppressors. You led an entire planet in revolt before you were twenty. If you were brought in now, you'd simply be part of the fleet. You'd probably feel that the situation was cramping your style. Ahhh, but if it goes badly with the Federation, and we discover ourselves in a sort of frontier situation, who better than you to try and rebuild the society we've all come to know."

"I . . ." I let the thought trail off for a moment, and then shrugged. "I suppose you're right."

"Of course I am."

Her flat tone certainly sounded like the old Eppy. I smiled gamely at her. "Your confidence is most appreciated."

"One of us has to be confident." But then she reached across the table and took my hand. Her voice softened and she said, "Mac . . . I know you've spent your whole life refusing to settle. You look at the world around you and you say, 'How can I change it? How can I make it better? How can I improve upon it so that it better suits the needs and desires of one Mackenzie Calhoun?' "

"You make me sound like the most self-centered bastard that ever walked the galaxy."

"No," said Elizabeth ruefully. "That title belongs to the guy I dated right after I broke off with you. I was never so angry, before or since, with a man. We won't discuss him."

"I owe him a great debt, then. How many men make me look good in comparison?"

"The point is, Mac . . . that mind-set of yours has made history. You looked upon the people of Xenex, saw where the problems were, saw what had to be done, did it . . . and an entire people breathes free because of you. That's one hell of an accomplishment, and no one can ever take that away from you. But sometimes, you just have to settle for the way things are. You have to allow things to happen in their own time and way. I can give you an example, from centuries ago . . ."

"I don't need to hear this."

"Yes, you do." She settled into her chair. "It used to be that when children's feet turned sharply inward, causing them to walk oddly, orthopedists would provide all sorts of elaborate braces and heavy-duty tools. And eventually the child would walk normally. And the doctors were all quite pleased with themselves until they did a study and noticed that all the children left untreated . . . eventually, they walked normally, too. There was no cause and effect; if left alone, the problem righted itself as time passed. All they had to do was let matters develop naturally. You see what I'm saying?"

"Yes. You're saying that if I trust in the natural

order of things, then sooner or later my efforts will prove pointless and I'll be out of a job."

She sighed once more. "You're hopeless. And will you please put the sword away? I know it satisfies your notions of male posturing, but I'm always afraid it's going to fly out of your hand and give me another navel."

"That'd be a waste, considering you already have three." I replaced the sword on the wall. "I'm sorry, Commander. The fact is, I know I'm hopeless. My ex-fiancée has informed me of that, any number of times."

"Mac . . ." She regarded me with open curiosity, more so than I could recall in the past. "Speaking of ex-fiancées and such . . . do you ever wonder what would have happened if we . . . uhm . . . if we . . ."

"No," I said quickly.

"Neither do I," she was just as speedy to reply.

And we left it at that.

I wasn't able to sleep.

Despite my lengthy conversation with Elizabeth, despite the fundamental belief that we were doing what we were supposed to do, where we were supposed to do it . . . I still felt a sort of gnawing frustration. I was supposed to be doing my duty as a Starfleet officer, continuing on my mission of mercy in the former Thallonian space, Sector 221-G. And besides, Elizabeth was likely correct. The *Excalibur* was very possibly being held in reserve, minding our own business in Thallonian space while at the same time ready at a moment's notice to fight on behalf of the Federation. Perhaps it was my famous ego talking, but I was convinced that somehow, in some way, we could wind up making a difference.

But it was becoming quite clear that we weren't going to be given the opportunity. At best, we were being held in reserve. At worst—to speak in the spirit of the Borg—we were irrelevant, depending upon what angle you wished to view the matter from.

I was in my quarters, bursting with energy and having no outlet for it. I did some brisk exercises, trying to burn off some of the frustration. I imagined I had a sword in my hand, practiced stabbing and thrusting, my old instincts coming to the fore. I had removed my shirt and was moving so quickly I would have been a blur to any observers. At least, I like to think so. One does have one's mental images of how one looks.

After an interminable time, I stopped. There was a thin coat of sweat on my chest. Knowing that I wasn't going to be getting any sleep, I dried myself off with a towel, got dressed, and exited my quarters.

As I walked the hallways of the *Excalibur,* I tried to look as if I were heading somewhere definitive, or had deep thoughts on my mind. Anything except appearing simply as a restless commanding officer who didn't know what to do with himself. I nodded briskly and greeted assorted crew members, but didn't bother to engage in small talk. I wasn't feeling especially chatty.

For reasons that I didn't even fully comprehend at first, I stopped in front of the main holodeck. The controls on it indicated that it was not in use. The timing was fortuitous. Obviously I was meant to try and use the holodeck to let off some steam.

"Rigel Nine. Main marketplace, Tamaran City." I said. I was literally picking it at random. I'd been to Rigel IX once, many many years ago. Briefly stopped in at Tamaran City, had a look around, got rather drunk and consequently had little memory of the place. But I was reasonably sure that it was in the memory of the holodeck computers, since it was frequented by any number of Starfleet personnel.

Moments later the doors had opened and I was standing in a perfect replica of Tamaran City. As soon as I was in, the doors hissed shut behind me and blended seamlessly with the rest of the environment. I should have been used to it, I suppose; that was the whole purpose of the holodeck, to foster the illusion of reality if one was willing enough to accept it.

And what an illusion it was. The rather pungent smell of Tamaran City's marketplace filled my nostrils as I began to stroll along the main boulevard. Frying meats, and assorted potatoes on open grills, and every block that I walked more merchants would be running out into the streets with their wares. None of them were real, and yet they performed with such eagerness that one would have thought their very livelihood hinged on their making a sale. I politely nodded off each one of them. I didn't want anyone—even fake beings—to perceive me as an easily targeted sucker. Odd, when one thinks about it, how pervasive pride can be.

I wandered the streets, moving into the back sections, making my way through the alleys. I wasn't heading anywhere in particular; I was simply seized with an urge to amble aimlessly about. I still wasn't getting tired; not the slightest bit of fatigue was pulling at me. From the corner of my eye, I noticed a man sneaking valuables from the pocket of another—a holy man, of all things, a Tellarite. I stepped in and snagged the thief in the act. He pulled away from me and bolted into the crowd, and I was about to take off after him when I realized that it seemed rather absurd to be chasing a criminal hologram. That might be taking the compulsion for crime and punishment just a bit too far. So I allowed him to escape and started to turn away when the Tellarite's hand was on my shoulder. I turned toward him slowly. Most Tellarites were aggressive and warlike, but there was a small white-clad religious sect that was not only harmless, but generally considered wise, pious, and peaceful. Even among their own, they didn't really fit in.

"Are you troubled, my son?" asked the Tellarite.

"I'm fine. Really," I said, turning away.

"Do you know what you need?"

"I said that I would be fi—"

"You need a drink."

It was startling words to hear coming from a holodeck replication. I turned back and looked thoughtfully into his face. There seemed to be no artifice, no sense of guile. For someone who was fake, he seemed one of the most "real" individuals I had ever met.

"A drink, holy man?" I replied cautiously.

"Yes. A drink. I think that may be where you want to go," and he pointed toward the end of the street. "I have heard good things about it."

I looked where he was pointing, and couldn't even begin to believe what I was seeing. A sign hung outside. The logo was in Rigelian, but the meaning was abundantly clear:

The Captain's Table.

By that point I was nothing short of stunned, for even though my encounter with the Captain's Table had occurred decades ago, the memory of the place was as vivid as if it had happened the previous day. Was it staggering coincidence? Two places in two different star systems, both with the same name?

And what was most bizarre about the situation was that I had walked those actual streets in the past. Not holos of them, but the real items. If the holodeck was supposed to be an accurate representation of the area, why would it have manufactured a doorway to a tavern that wasn't there?

I turned back to the holy man, but there was no sign

of him. He had disappeared back into the crowd. I looked to the door and rubbed my eyes, as if doing so would somehow expunge the contradictory sight. But no, it was still right there. I felt as if it were mocking me.

"All right. Enough's enough," I said. I walked up to the door of the Captain's Table and pushed it open.

The weight of the world was still there. It hit me the moment I entered. Somehow, though, it didn't seem quite as heavy as before. Perhaps I had built up strength in my upper torso from years of carrying it myself.

There was also that faint aroma, the smell of sea air. As opposed to the first time, when it had puzzled me, this time I felt invigorated. I inhaled deeply, and my lungs fairly tingled from the sensation.

Then my rational mind took over and informed me that this simply couldn't be. It was flat-out impossible for the Captain's Table, for the real Captain's Table bar, to somehow have materialized within the holodeck. Perhaps it was some sort of elaborate prank. Perhaps it was just wishful thinking. No matter what the case, there was no way that I was going to allow it to continue. The memories of that place were too deep, too personal to me. I couldn't permit a shadow of it to exist. Since I was in the holodeck, of course, there was a simple way to put a stop to it.

"End program," I said.

Nothing happened. The patrons of the bar continued in their conversations, although one or two of them might have afforded me a curious glance. It wasn't like the last time, when the presence of the incredibly scruffy and disheveled barbarian youngster immediately captured the attention of all the patrons. I was older, more "normal"-looking. Still, in many ways I was just as confused as I was the first time I'd walked into the place. I was simply a bit more polished in my presentation.

"Computer, end program," I repeated. Still nothing happened. That was a flat-out impossibility. "Computer, end program!" When I received no response, I tapped my communicator. "Calhoun to bridge." No response.

I started to head for the door, and then a very familiar voice stopped me. "Leaving so soon, M'k'n'zy? Oh, that's right. You go by 'Mac' these days. At least, 'Mac' to your friends."

I turned, knowing ahead of time what I would see. Sure enough, there was Cap. The fact that he was exactly as I had remembered him from more than twenty years earlier was almost proof positive that I was in a holodeck re-creation. "I'd like to think," continued Cap, "that I can still count myself among your friends. That is the case, isn't it?"

"How . . . is this possible?" I asked.

He looked at me strangely as if he found it puzzling that I could even question it. "Why shouldn't it be possible? It's the most natural thing in the world. You saw a door for the Captain's Table, you walked through it, and lo and behold, you're in the Captain's Table. It's not as if you entered a door with our sign on it and found yourself in the middle of a baseball field."

"It would make equally as much sense," I said.

"Mac," and he shook his head disappointedly, "are you going to spend all your time here complaining and questioning? Or are you going to . . ." He stopped and stared. "What's wrong?"

I had totally lost focus on what Cap was saying, because I had spotted . . . *him* . . . across the bar.

He was just as I remembered him. The only difference was that he seemed a bit younger than he appeared to me when I'd first seen him. Maybe it was because I felt so much older, or maybe it was . . .

. . . maybe it was something else.

His hair was that same odd combination of gray with white at the temples. The same heavy eyebrows, the same jowly face and eyes that seemed to twinkle with merriment which gave him, in some ways, an almost elfin appearance. His Starfleet uniform was as crisp and clean as I remembered it. And his comm badge was right in place, with no drop of blood on it. He was engaged in an active discussion with several other captains of assorted races, and he didn't even glance my way. I might as well have been invisible to him.

"Kenyon," I whispered. "Captain Kenyon."

He didn't hear me, of course. I was on the opposite side of the tavern. But I was going to change that very quickly.

"Mac," Cap said. I knew that tone of voice; it was the same warning tone that he had used when I had confronted the Roman captain. In this case, it sounded even more firm and strident than it had the previous time. But I didn't care; it wasn't going to slow me down for a moment.

I started to make my way across the pub, toward Kenyon. That was when things started to happen.

It was subtle, at first, and then it became more pronounced. A waitress getting in my way, turning me around. Then a crowd of revelers moved between Kenyon and myself. When they passed, I had lost sight of Kenyon . . . and then spotted him, apparently as he had been before except it seemed as if the table had relocated somehow. I angled in that direction . . . and encountered more bar patrons, another waitress. A bus boy dropped a stack of dishes, and I reflexively glanced in the way of the crash. When I looked back,

Kenyon was somewhere else again, except there was no indication that he'd moved.

"What the hell?" I muttered.

Cap was at my elbow. "Sit down, Mac," he said firmly.

"Cap, I . . ."

"Sit . . . down."

Had someone else taken that tone of voice with me, I would have bristled, barked back, had any of a hundred reactions, all of them aggressive. But something in Cap's look and tone prompted me to sit down as meekly as a first-year cadet. More meekly, actually, come to think of it, considering that in my first year at the Academy I dislocated the jaw of a third-year student when he made some condescending remarks.

There was sympathy in his eyes, but also firmness, as he sat opposite me. "There are certain rules of the Captain's Table, Mac," he said not unkindly. "And one of the big rules is that no one here can do anything to change the timeline or fate of anyone else. That falls under the category of duty, and at the Captain's Table, one is expected to leave one's duties at the door."

"But I can't just let him sit there and not know . . . not when I can tell him . . ."

"That, Mac, is precisely what you not only can do, but have to do. No man should know his own destiny. No man can know; otherwise he just becomes a pawn of fate and no longer a man."

"That's a nice philosophy, Cap. And I'm supposed to just stand by and—"

"Yes, Mac," and this time his tone was flat and uncompromising. "Rules of the house. I'm afraid that that is exactly what you're supposed to do."

I stared forlornly across the tavern at him. Never had the cliché, "So near and yet so far" had quite as much meaning to me. "Why am I here, then?" I asked in annoyance. "I mean . . . I would have thought that the reason one comes here is to relax."

"It is."

"How can I relax? How am I supposed to do that when I see Kenyon there, right there. It's within my ability to help him, to warn him . . ."

"It wouldn't help, Mac. In fact, it would very likely hurt, in ways that you can't even begin to imagine. You can't say anything. More to the point, you won't say anything."

My temper began to flare ever so slightly. "And if I simply choose to walk out the door rather than stay here under your rules?"

"All of us have free will, Mac. You can go as you please."

"But not necessarily come back?"

He smiled thinly. "We've always been a bit of a catch-as-catch-can operation, Mac. If you're looking for a guarantee that you'd be back, well . . . no promises. But if you did continue to try and flaunt the rules of the house, well . . ." He shrugged noncommittally.

I looked down. "I've never been much for rules."

"Yes, I know that," he said. "Sometimes that has served you quite well. After all, if you stuck to the rules, your homeworld would still be under the thumb of the Danteri. And you would not be as good a captain as you are."

"You think I'm a good captain?" I asked.

"Yes. But why does it matter what I think?"

"I don't . . ." I considered the question, and then said, "I don't . . . know. But it does. Maybe it's you. Maybe it's this place."

"Maybe it's a little of both," said Cap. "We bartenders, we're surrogates. Surrogate parents, father confessors, what have you. We try not to judge."

"That a house rule, too?"

"No. Just a bit of common courtesy." Suddenly he

turned and snapped his fingers briskly once. I was confused for a moment, but then a waitress came over as if by magic and, without a word, deposited a beer in front of me.

"I take it your tastes haven't changed, even though your appearance has somewhat," he said. "The scar, in particular. Very decorative."

"Thank you," I said ruefully. "Sometimes I consider allowing someone else to lay open the other side of my face so that I'll have balance."

"Not a bad idea," Cap replied, and I couldn't entirely tell whether he was being sarcastic or not.

The glass was frosted, and the beer felt good going down. I lowered the mug and tapped it. "I take it I'm old enough that my drinks are no longer free."

"You take it correctly. There is a price attached. A story."

"A story. You mentioned that last time. You want me to tell you a story? It sounds rather juvenile."

"Not me," Cap said in amusement, as if the mere suggesting of such a thing was an absurdity. "No, I'm just the bartender."

"There's something about you, Cap, that makes me think you're not 'just' anything."

He let the remark pass. "No, the tales told here are for the customers, Mac. For your fellow captains, who love tales of adventure and derring-do."

"I don't think my do is particularly derring. Besides, I . . . don't particularly like stories. Especially stories about myself."

"I'm surprised you would feel that way, Mac. I would have thought that someone like you, a planetary hero, would be accustomed to hearing stories of his adventures bandied about."

"I am. That's part of the point." I took another sip of beer. "When I worked to liberate Xenex, I heard tales of my adventures and endeavors, spreading from town to town. Sometimes a storyteller would speak to an audience spellbound by the manner in which he wove tales of my exploits. And I would sit at the outer fringes of such gatherings and gather no notice at all, for the M'k'n'zy of Calhoun who featured in those tales was seven and a half feet tall, with eyes of blazing fire, muscles the size of mighty boulders. His preferred weapon was a sword so massive that it took either one M'k'n'zy or three normal men to wield it, and when he walked the ground trembled beneath his mighty stride and beautiful women threw themselves upon him and begged him to sire their children."

"And none of that was true?" Cap asked.

"Well . . . maybe the part about the women," I allowed.

We both laughed softly for a moment, and then I grew serious. "But I knew that these fables were just that, Cap . . . fables. They bore no resemblance to the real world. In those stories, I single-handedly slaughtered hundreds—no, thousands—of Danteri troops. My troops supposedly stood in awe of my prowess and fell to their knees in worship of me. It was all nonsense. Stories are not real life. In real life, good does not always triumph, and decent people suffer for no purpose and receive no final redemption. Stories are the antithesis of life, in that stories must have a point. I live in the real world, Cap. Sweet fictions have no relevance to me."

"Don't sell such fables short, Mac. You do them, and you, a disservice. Consider the effect such stories had on your own people. When they heard tales of the great M'k'n'zy, they drew hope from that. It sustained them, nourished their souls in their time of need. So what if there were exaggerations? Who cares if the reality did not match the fancy? What was important was that it took them out of themselves, gave them something to think about besides the difficulties of their lives. Dreams are very powerful tools, Mac. By hearing the stories of your great deeds, the Xenexians dreamed of a better life. From the dreaming came the doing. Life imitates art which imitates life in turn, and stories of your adventures are just part of that cycle."

"I suppose. . . ."

"No supposing. Take my word for it. And now, Mac, this is what you're going to do: You're going to find another captain or captains here, and you will sit him, her, or them down, and you will tell a story of your exploits. If you feel constrained to adhere to reality . . . if you must tell a story where good does not triumph, or decent people suffer . . . if that is what's required for you to maintain the moral purity of your soul, who am I to gainsay you?"

"Who are you indeed?" I asked. "That's actually something I've been wondering about. Who are you when you're not being you, Cap?"

"I am," Cap smiled, "who I am." He patted me on the shoulder as he rose. "Find a willing audience, Mac. Find it and share something of yourself. You owe it to them, to yourself . . ." He touched the mug of beer. ". . . and to your tab."

I watched him head back to his bar. I noticed for the first time that he walked with a very slight limp. I had no idea why, nor could I find it within me to ask. I had the feeling that I'd just get another roundabout, vague answer.

For a moment I considered getting up and heading out the door. But part of me was concerned that I really wouldn't be able to find the place again, no matter how hard I looked. I still wasn't entirely sure what I was doing there in the first place, or how I'd gotten to it. But it had become apparent that, when it came to questions about the Captain's Table, less was generally preferable to more.

"I still think it's a waste of time," I called after him.

He slowed long enough to say over his shoulder, "There are some things in this galaxy that are for us to think about. And there are other things that are for us to do. This is one of the latter. Understand?"

I didn't, but I said that I did.

I suppose the real truth of it is that I simply don't like to share things. I don't like to say what's going on in my mind. Call it my military upbringing, if you will. I tend to dole out information on a need-to-know basis. Otherwise I tend to keep things to myself.

But I like Cap, and I like this place. I would hate to think that I should never find my way back to it again, be it by happenstance, cosmic direction, destiny, or plain dumb luck. So for once even the mighty, rule-flaunting Mackenzie Calhoun will play by the rules. You seem like a worthy individual to tell my story to; indeed, you may be the best qualified here.

My previous post to the captaincy of the *Excalibur* was as first officer aboard the *Starship Grissom.*

Perhaps the name should have cautioned me. It was named after an Earth astronaut, Virgil "Gus" Grissom. His career in space started off impressively enough. Grissom was the second American in space, flying a suborbital vessel called the *Liberty Bell,* which was part of the Mercury program. He flew in the Gemini program after that. He was well liked and respected, and his career was on the fast track for greatness . . . just like mine seemed to be.

And then he died. He did so horribly, asphyxiating aboard a flight simulator which erupted in flames. A man like that, if he were to die in action, deserved to die in space. That's where his heart was, where his destiny was. Instead his career was cut short thanks to a terrible accident. It should not have happened that way.

That reminds me of me as well.

But I knew none of that when the assignment

aboard the *Grissom* was presented to me. I simply saw it as an opportunity, a chance to advance in the career that I was quite certain was to be mine by divine right.

I was to learn otherwise. And it all ended . . . rather badly.

Here's what happened.

THE INTERVIEW

CAPTAIN NORMAN KENYON was the epitome of the word "avuncular." (That means "uncle-like," in case you do not wish to scramble to a dictionary.)

Kenyon had been something of a lady's man in his younger days, and the ladies ostensibly loved it. In fact it was rumored—although never proven, at least to my knowledge—that there was a secret society which called itself "the Norman Conquests," and that it was something of a badge of honor to join the club. I have no idea whether meetings were held, secret handshakes were established. For all I know, the entire matter was apocryphal. I never quite mustered the nerve to ask the captain himself about it. Since Kenyon was always one of the more gentlemanly of men, I suspect that if I had, the question would likely have elicited nothing more than an enigmatic smile. And that, I daresay, is how it should be.

However, even the most rakish of men tends to settle down at one point or another. The good captain eventually married (and again, perhaps apocryphally, the Norman Conquests had a symbolic wake) and produced a daughter who was, by all accounts, quite impressive, a lively and intelligent daughter named Stephanie. I shall tell you more of her a bit later.

The marriage was quite happy, and Kenyon and his wife served together as a research team, while rising up the ranks together, and Kenyon eventually achieved the rank of captain. His wife—Marsha was her name, as I recall—served as his science officer aboard Kenyon's new command, the *U.S.S. Harriman.* However, two months into their tour of duty, the *Harriman* was caught in a crossfire between a Klingon and Romulan vessel. Casualties were light . . . but unfortunately, Marsha Kenyon was among the few. Light, I suppose, is cold comfort when it's your lover who is lying cold in the cargo bay awaiting transport back to Earth.

Norman Kenyon was devastated by the loss, of course. Starfleet offered him a leave of absence. He didn't take it. Stephanie was grown and following her own career, and to Kenyon, Earth was simply another alien world for all the meaning it had to him. Starfleet had a hearing over it, because they were concerned about his state of mind. Those who were witnesses said that Kenyon spoke on his own behalf in quiet, controlled tones that nonetheless were so moving that even hardened admirals were having trouble choking back tears. "I have lost my love," he told them. "Do not take my life from me as well."

They gave him command of the *Grissom.* From what I understand, the crew wasn't sure how to act around him at first. Obviously a captain is to be treated with respect, but the mood that can best be ascribed to the crew at that point was "tentative."

They knew that he was mourning his loss, and consequently acted in a cautious manner. They needn't have done so. Kenyon was all business at first, and after a bit of time passed, became downright pleasant. As a captain, he was absolutely unflappable. Calm, patient, easygoing . . . and yet he never came across as a pushover. He had no trouble making the tough decisions, but never did so in anything other than an unhurried manner. In no time at all he knew the name, first and last, of every single person on the ship, and greeted them by name rather than rank. If he encountered a crewman who had some sort of problem, no matter how much the crewman tried to cover it, Kenyon always knew. Some people believed he was part Betazoid, even though he was born in Kansas from two very human parents. And Kenyon would take the crewman aside, even take him to Ten-Forward, and talk the difficulty out. Sometimes he came up with some angle that the crewman hadn't considered, sometimes not, but talking to him always managed to at least make the man in question feel better.

And no matter what situation he faced with other races that he encountered, not only did he always appear in control of matters, but he met every crisis with coolness and more than a modicum of charm. He had a ready smile, and even opposing captains tended to find him rather likable. It was easy to see how he would have been capable of amassing so many female admirers that he would have acquired his own followers, but once he became captain of the *Grissom,* and a widower, he had no known involvement with any women on board ship, or even on shore leave. He was urbane, even flirtatious on rare occasions, but that was as far as it went. Even though his wife was gone, he was still loyal to her. It was sweet in a way. Bittersweet, really.

There are command officers who are respected, there are those who are admired, there are those who are simply obeyed. Kenyon was all that and more: He was beloved. By the time I came on the scene, there wasn't a man or woman on the ship who wouldn't have been willing to walk barefoot on broken glass for him. He'd been serving as captain for two and a half years by that point. Kenyon's first officer, Paullina Simons, had just gotten her own command aboard the *U.S.S. Houston.* So Kenyon was interviewing for a new first officer.

Enter one Mackenzie Calhoun.

I already had something of a reputation as a hell-raiser. However, I also had a major supporter within Starfleet. His name was Admiral Edward Jellico, and considering how matters eventually turned out between us, it was really rather ironic that it was his recommendation which jumped my name to the top of the pile.

I cooled my heels at Starbase 27 for a couple of days, waiting to rendezvous with the *Grissom.* Mostly I kept to myself. It wasn't all that difficult; the savage known as M'k'n'zy Calhoun was much nearer to the surface in those days than now. I had managed to cloak him with respectability, paint him over with a thin veneer of civilization. But I would still reflexively appraise anyone who came near me, sizing them up, dissecting them with a glance. Looking to see if they had weapons, whether they were spies, whether they appeared to be a threat. It wasn't as if I was some spring-loaded, demented nut who was prepared to leap to attack at any time. I had that much reined in, at least. It was simply reflex, looking for danger at every turn. It was instincts that had served me well and saved my life any number of times, particularly back on Xenex when the Danteri started sending in spies to infiltrate us. One of them got so close to me that I barely had time to disembowel him before he took a shot at me. Got blood on my boots. It was quite a mess.

I'm getting off track here.

The point is that what had served me so well on Xenex was somewhat off-putting to the more civilized tastes of Starfleet and associated races. People rarely said anything about it directly to me because, really, what was there to say? I never said anything threatening, never attacked, never did something untoward. Were they supposed to go to their COs and say, "That guy over there with the scar and the purple eyes is looking at me funny!"

I was an object of curiosity, but not much more than that.

So I sat around and thought for two days. My life at that point was split into two times: Before I joined Starfleet, and after. It was a very curious circumstance for me, the first Xenexian to join up. I suppose that, deep down—or perhaps not so deep down—I felt a bit of a fraud. To me, everyone else who was in Starfleet seemed born to it. They had every business being there, and I didn't. No one else had that deep, abiding violence in their heart that I did. I was a wolf in Starfleet clothing.

I also missed Elizabeth.

There was something in her that had calmed me. I was able to bury myself in her, leave behind that part of me that in some ways I would almost have preferred to forget. Ultimately that may be what caused the relationship to be doomed. I wasn't ready for it, wasn't grown-up enough. I used her to satisfy my own needs and never really knew or understood what her own needs were. Not that I would have admitted to it, of course. Xenexian pride and all that.

At the time, though, sitting there in the starbase, I didn't have the emotional distance or maturity to understand that. All I knew was that I was angry, and lonely, and sullen, and resenting the hell out of Elizabeth. I also resented myself and my limitations, but I wasn't entirely able to admit that to myself. I wanted company, female company, but by the same token I didn't want to let anyone else near me. I had left myself vulnerable with Elizabeth Shelby, and when it hadn't worked out I was determined to be nothing but alone. Not the most reasonable of goals, but—as always—the instinctive one.

So when the *Grissom* arrived, I was not in the greatest of moods. Just where one wants to be when facing an interview that could make or break one's career.

I beamed aboard the *Grissom,* and I have no doubt that there were more than a few sighs of relief on the starbase once I was gone. She was a much larger ship than any I'd served on, with easily twice the number of crewmen. More than any other vessel I'd been on, she seemed like a floating city in space. To me, it was dazzling. But I tried not to let any of that awed attitude show through, since I felt that it would be viewed as unprofessional.

I was extremely surprised by the woman who greeted me in the transporter room of the *Grissom.*

She was a tall woman, with broad shoulders and an air of infinite superiority about her. Even though she was fully clothed in uniform, of course, I could tell that her body was lean and hard. She stood with her jaw slightly outthrust, her dark blond hair tied in a severe knot. Her eyes were cobalt blue and instantly captivating.

But her most prominent feature was something totally unexpected. She had a scar. Not exactly like mine, but not totally dissimilar. It was on the left side of her face, as opposed to mine on the right. It was thinner as well. My guess was that it had been made with some sort of a sword, as mine had been, but a thinner one: a rapier, perhaps. It had long since healed over, but it was still quite visible. Like me, she could of course have had the scar removed or repaired. With modern cosmetic repair techniques, it would have been the work of minutes at most. But she had chosen to keep hers, just as I had mine. I was curious about the reasons. Indeed, I was curious about her altogether.

The moment she saw me, I could have sworn that a fleeting look of amusement played over her features, but then she immediately covered it rather deftly.

"Commander," she said crisply. Her voice had the faint hint of a German accent. "I'm Katerina Mueller, ship's XO." She stuck out a hand and I took it in a firm grip as I stepped down from the transporter pad. She was about an inch taller than I was.

"I'm surprised to see you awake, XO."

She tilted her head slightly like a curious dog. "Sir?"

"The executive officer generally runs the night shift. Unless I've completely lost track of time, we're solidly in the middle of the day shift."

"That's correct. However, with Commander . . . I'm sorry, *Captain* . . . Simons having already departed for her command, I'm performing double duty until she's been replaced."

"Sounds rather grueling."

"We learn to adapt, sir." She gestured toward the door, and I preceded her out into the hallway.

I tried not to look around too much. It would have made me feel like a tourist. But I couldn't help but steal glances here and there, and I could only hope that I wasn't coming across as an idiot to XO Mueller. "How long have you been serving with the *Grissom,* Mueller?" I asked.

"Two years, one month, twenty-three days," she replied.

I smiled slightly. "Sounds to me like you might have some Vulcan blood in you, Mueller, with answers like that."

"Merely trying to be accurate, Commander."

"Not interested in the second-in-command slot yourself?"

"I don't feel I'm quite temperamentally suited to it. I prefer the nightside, and the duties of XO. The second chair is a stepping-stone to captaincy, and at this point in my career, I'm not angling for that."

"You seem to know yourself quite well, XO."

"If I don't, sir, who will?" She paused a moment and then said, "I know it's been a rather short period of acquaintance, Commander, but do you mind if I ask you a personal question?"

"Let me guess: My scar."

"Very perceptive, Commander."

"Got it in a fight. Someone came at me and I was a hair slow in dodging."

"I would say you were a hair fast. If you hadn't been, your opponent would have split your skull, by the look of it."

"That's about accurate, yes."

"You killed him, I take it?"

I looked at her with what must have been a puzzled expression. "You sound rather sanguine about it."

"It's just common sense. If someone endeavors to bisect your cranium, seeking to open negotiations doesn't quite seem to be a proportionate response. Clearly it was kill or be killed."

I nodded approvingly. "Quite right, XO." Oddly, I found myself warming to her quickly.

"May I ask how you attended to the wound at the time? It looks rather comprehensive. Why are there no stitches?"

"I fused it together myself using a laser welder."

She stopped dead in her tracks and stared at me. "Pardon?"

"I said I fused it with a laser welder."

She nodded, pondering this, and then picked up the pace once more. "Is that a procedure you would readily recommend?"

"Only for an enemy. Hurts like hell."

"I would imagine."

We stepped into a turbolift. "Bridge," said Mueller, and the lift immediately headed us toward the nerve center of the ship. Why in God's name the bridge, arguably the most important strategic point of the vessel, is an easy target at the top of the saucer section is something I never completely understood. Why not just paint a big target on your ship and write, "Aim here for best shot at the captain"? Unfortunately, no one in Starfleet had ever consulted me on techniques of vessel design.

"So how did you get—?" I tapped the side of my face, clearly referring to her own facial laceration.

"This?" She traced the length of her wound with her index finger and seemed to smile at the memory. "Heidelberg fencing scar."

"Heidelberg? That's a school, isn't it?"

She nodded. "University in Germany. Renowned, among other things, for its fencing. It was discontinued for a time, but a push for returning to traditional values brought it back about a hundred years ago. I picked up this memento during a fencing exercise."

"Shouldn't you have been wearing a protective face mask?"

She regarded me with open curiosity. "Why?"

"So you would have been protected."

"This is a badge of honor, Commander," she told me archly. "I wear it proudly . . . as, I suspect, do you."

"What about your opponent? How did he, or she, turn out?"

Without a word, she drew her finger across her throat in a swift cutting gesture. I laughed uncertainly. She showed no signs of indicating that she was kidding, and I decided that it might be best if I didn't try to press the point.

The turbolift opened onto the bridge. A man was seated in the captain's chair with his back to us, but his hair was blond and even from the back I could see that he was much too young to be captain. The man half-turned in the seat and saw XO Mueller. Immediately he rose to make way for Mueller, and seemed only mildly curious as to my presence there. Perhaps he'd had advance notice of my arrival.

He was the first blond Asian I'd ever seen. It didn't appear to be any sort of cosmetic change, but rather his natural hair color. His hair was fairly round. He had remarkably young features; indeed, if I didn't know better, I'd have thought he hadn't even started shaving yet. But with the rank of lieutenant, obviously he had a few years on him.

Mueller waved him off. "Take back the conn, Lieutenant, I'll be a few minutes still. Commander Calhoun, this is Lieutenant Romeo Takahashi, science and ops."

When he spoke, it was with a voice that was at odds with his face (which was already fighting with his hair). He spoke slowly and in an intonation that could best be characterized as a deep Southern drawl. "Call me Hash," said the lieutenant, shaking my hand firmly. "Ev'body does."

"No, we don't," Mueller said with what appeared as faint disapproval. But it was difficult for me to tell whether she was really annoyed by him, or whether she found him amusing.

"*You* don't, XO." He looked at me with what

appeared to be a search for sympathy. "You'll find our XO, she tends to be on the formal side," Hash said.

Hash reached out and shook my hand, and I was astounded by the strength in his grip. He wasn't a particularly tall man, but he shook my hand so firmly that I thought he was going to break my fingers. "Why do they . . . or at least some people . . . call you 'Hash'?" I asked.

"Because," he replied, "aside from the obvious shortening of Takahashi, I also make the best corned-beef hash that anyone on this li'l starship has ever tasted. It's become so fundamental to so many people's diets around these parts, they're thinking of adding it to the periodic table as an element."

"Is that a fact?"

"No, it's not, Commander. This way," said Mueller, looking as if she felt enough time had been wasted on him.

"XO," Hash remonstrated her gently, "we have simply got to get you a sense of humor."

She stared at him as if he were a microbe. "Lieutenant, if it's not issued at the Academy, I live without it. Besides, the fact is that your own wit is just so devastating that, had I an actual sense of humor, I'd be too busy being convulsed with laughter and therefore unable to fulfill my duties."

"Then I suppose it's all worked out for the best," he said.

"Yes, I guess so," she agreed, and led me quickly to the captain's ready room. I caught Hash out of the corner of my eye grinning in amusement and shaking his head even as he settled back, however temporarily, into the command chair.

"Come," I heard a deep voice issue from behind the doors of the ready room. Mueller gestured that I should enter, but stood to one side. It was clear from her posture that she had no intention of going in herself.

My first impression of Kenyon was an air of unfailing pleasantness . . . but with an undercurrent of firm command. I sensed immediately that there were many layers to him, all hidden securely below the surface. I almost envied him that. Me, I was not tremendously skilled at keeping my "layers" out of sight. There was the Calhoun who was struggling to fit into Starfleet, wearing his façade of respectability like a too-tight second skin. And there was the Calhoun who was barely civilized enough to know how to fold a napkin . . . or even use it properly. He bubbled and percolated just below the surface. That pretty much summed up the extent of Mackenzie Calhoun.

"Captain Kenyon," I said, standing several feet away from him, "Commander Calhoun reporting for interview as instructed, sir." I wasn't entirely sure whether I was supposed to shake his hand or simply stand at attention and await his preference for how to conduct the interview.

I didn't have long to wait. As the doors started to hiss closed, with Mueller on the outside, Kenyon looked me up and down: my perfect posture, my eyes staring resolutely straight ahead as if I'd found something in midair incredibly fascinating. He said, "I'd invite you to sit down, Commander, presuming that you *can* bend at the waist with all that starch in your shorts."

I noticed that Mueller was smirking slightly, shaking her head, as the doors closed, blocking her from sight. I was rather glad. No . . . make that rather relieved.

I sat, feeling rather annoyed. "I can't say I particularly appreciate that assessment, Captain."

"It wasn't for you to appreciate, Commander. Just react to." He was studying what appeared to be my service record on the computer screen. "You come highly recommended by Edward Jellico. That's very rare. Jellico's a hard nut to crack."

"Yes, sir."

"And what's impressive is that you do not have exactly sterling recommendations from your commanding officers. That's also very rare. Generally everyone in Starfleet pulls together for mutual gain when it comes to climbing the ranks, which means you must have put a few noses out of joint along the way." He paused. "Not speaking up in your own defense?"

"I wasn't aware you were waiting for a reply, sir. Seemed like a fairly self-contained statement."

"Mm-hmm. So." He leaned forward, his hands folded. "You want to tell me why it is that Jellico sang your praises?"

"I . . . did him some small service. Him and his son."

"I see. Care to go into detail?"

"I don't see that it's necessary, sir."

"Just being modest?"

I shrugged. "Maybe."

"You don't seem particularly comfortable here, Calhoun."

"I'm not, sir. It's the starch in my shorts."

He guffawed at that and then quickly reined it in. "For what it's worth, you don't have to. Jellico told me all about it. Couldn't stop talking about it, actually."

"He probably exaggerated it, sir. You know these things . . . they always become bigger in the retelling."

"Something about how he'd been temporarily assigned to your previous ship for the purpose of him and his son going into a first-contact situation. The first contact went sour. The natives were not only restless, they tried to capture and/or kill both Jellico and his son. Mackenzie Calhoun, the ship's third officer and tactical officer, happened to be there, along with a security escort. In the melee, the entire security escort died in defending Jellico. It came down to Mackenzie Calhoun versus about twenty men who were trying to get to the admiral. And Calhoun, with a phaser that was tapped out, took them down barehanded despite suffering multiple abrasions, contusions, two broken ribs, and a skull fracture. Now, was any of that exaggerated?"

"Yes, sir," I said immediately.

"Which part?"

"It wasn't twenty men . . . it was fifteen. The phaser wasn't completely depleted, good for at least two more shots. And I wasn't barehanded. I managed to break apart a chair and use the legs for clubs."

"Oh, well, that's a completely different story." He rose from behind his desk and circled the room, his hands draped behind his back. "So anything that Admiral Jellico says about you should be attributed to the stress of the moment. Words like, 'heroic, bravery above and beyond, determination, stamina . . .' "

"Those could all be used to describe a long-distance runner, sir, but I don't know that I'd put one in charge of a ship," I pointed out.

"Don't you want to get ahead, Calhoun?"

"I hadn't given it much thought, sir."

"Oh, nonsense. What sort of career officer doesn't give much thought as to whether he wants to get ahead or not?"

He was behind me, but I didn't turn to face him. Instead I continued to look straight ahead. "The kind who doesn't want to worry about second-guessing himself. The kind who wants and needs to trust his instincts, without being concerned as to how it's going to look on his record or who it's going to upset so that he can't get good recommendations in the future. That kind."

I thought he nodded, although since he was behind me, I couldn't say for sure. "Previous commanders or superior officers describe you as headstrong. As insubordinate. As a maverick. As someone who thinks that the rules do not apply to him. Do you feel that the rules apply to you, Calhoun?"

"All but the stupid ones, sir."

"Indeed. And to whom do those apply?"

"Those who are too stupid to realize the stupidity of them."

"And who makes those judgments? You? Don't you have any respect for authority?"

Now I turned to face him. "I acknowledge authority. I acknowledge that those in authority have power over me. But that is not a condition that I take either lightly or for granted, no matter how much they endeavor to drill the chain of command into me. When those in authority are acting stupidly, I do not feel constrained to join them. That doesn't make for good officers. Just more stupidity. Rules and regulations are not handed down on high from the gods. They're made by people, mortal people, no more, no less. People who can't be expected to anticipate every eventuality. What some individuals perceive as immutable laws that restrict our actions, I see as guidelines that indicate what a particular body of opinion-makers believes to be the best way of completing a mission and coming home safely. But just because they believe it to be the best doesn't automatically make it so, and under no circumstance is it the only one. And if there are consequences for deviating from the limits that others have made, then I will accept those consequences. But no one, sir, with all due respect, is going to tell me how to live my life or force me to do that which I know, in my heart, to be wrong. I will be free, in thought and action."

"Have you considered the possibility, Calhoun, that you might be in the wrong field of endeavor."

"Every day since I entered the Academy, sir."

"And yet you stayed. Why?"

I laughed. It wasn't a particularly pleasant sound. More rueful than anything else. "Because, sir . . . I had nothing better to do."

"Well well," Kenyon said after a time. "I can see how you've managed to endear yourself to your superiors. You don't just take on responsibility for yourself. You don't just take the word of others. You feel it necessary to take on the entirety of The Way Things Are every time out, and let the consequences fall on you. You remake the galaxy in your image."

"I think that's overstating it, sir."

"Really? I don't."

I shrugged, seeing no reason to press the point.

"And what would you do if you were my first officer and I stepped out of line, eh? If I did something that you felt to be stupid. Or do you feel it wouldn't be your place to make that kind of judgment?"

"It would not only be my place, Captain, but my responsibility. If a j.g. down in the sickbay does something stupid, that doesn't necessarily have broad-ranging impact. If you do it, it could have dire consequences for everyone on ship."

"So you'd be second-guessing me."

"Every time, sir."

"And you wouldn't be afraid to tell me so."

"No, sir."

"In front of the entire bridge crew, if necessary?"

I didn't reply right away. The silence seemed to surprise him. "You hesitate," he said.

"Not in front of the bridge crew, no, sir."

"Really. You would curtail your right to voice objections?"

"There are limits, sir," and I smiled thinly, "even to me. It is possible to exercise one's right to judge others, and act on that judgment, without curtailing another's right to command. If I had a dispute with the way that a captain was handling matters, I would make certain that that dispute was handled in private. To openly argue with the CO could have a negative impact on the CO's ability to lead, and that would be . . . it would be inappropriate. Besides, think of the unnecessary damage to morale if I challenged the captain in front of the crew and it turned out that my concerns were groundless."

"Are you saying, Commander," and he feigned shock, "that you allow for the possibility that you might be . . . wrong?"

"It has been known to happen, sir," I allowed. "On one or two occasions."

"And if I were risking myself, and my personal safety, in a circumstance where the crew was not directly involved? Where it was just me and my conscience? If you thought I was misguided in my endeavors, would you allow me to risk myself?"

"Of course," I said promptly.

"You would?"

"You're a grown man, Captain. You have free will, you're a free man. If you felt strongly that you must risk yourself, it would be insulting of me to try and curtail that instinct. Insulting and condescending."

"So you would allow me to risk death."

"Yes, without hesitation."

He seemed most puzzled, as if he couldn't believe I was saying it. As if I'd admitted some horrible secret. "You would stand by and let me . . ."

"Stand by?" I made no effort to hide the surprise I felt. "Of course I wouldn't stand by. If you felt that facing danger was unavoidable, I would do nothing to stop you. But I would naturally feel constrained to share that danger. I could do no less."

"Why?"

"Because in making the decision to not oppose your intentions, I am taking on the responsibility to make certain that you get back to the ship in one piece. So I would have to be at your side to make sure that happened."

"Aren't you concerned that you might fail in that endeavor?"

"No."

"Some small measure of dou—"

"No," I repeated.

He shook his head in disbelief. "How can you be so positive?"

"Ask Admiral Jellico," I replied.

He laughed curtly at that. "Good point. Tell me, Calhoun: What do you feel is the single greatest responsibility that you, as a Starfleet officer, have?"

"To do the right thing," I said without hesitation.

"What about exploration? What about adherence to the Prime Directive? What about—"

"Captain," I cut him off, "I suspect you have a great many things to do. If you're going to ask me a question, get a straight answer, and then doubt and challenge my answers repeatedly, this is going to take a much longer time than I truly think you need to spend."

He sat on the edge of his desk, a foot away from me, and leaned forward. "Who decides," he said, "what is right?"

"The gods. I just do my best to interpret."

"And do you truly believe in gods, Mackenzie Calhoun? Do you?"

I smiled. "I believe in myself. That's generally been good enough."

To my surprise, he slapped his knee as if I'd just told him a fabulous joke. "You are an original, Calhoun, I'll give you that." Then, surprisingly fast, a change came over him. Very soberly, he said, "Do you know what my biggest problem is, Calhoun?"

"No, sir."

"I," he said with what seemed like great sadness, "am beloved."

"Most men would not consider that a problem, sir."

"My crew," he said, "has my best interests at heart. They are concerned about me. They watch out for me. No one ever disagrees with me, or challenges me, because I'm just so damned beloved, it could make you sick."

"I have a strong constitution, sir."

"I don't doubt it. I have to tell you, Calhoun, I never met someone who freed their entire world from planetary conquerors before they were twenty years old. Must have been somewhat difficult to find anything that challenging. You think being my first officer would begin to approach that?"

"Probably not, sir. But it'll do until something better comes along."

He stared at me . . . and then he laughed. This time it was a large, open, boisterous laugh that, to my surprise, I actually found was infectious. I started to laugh, too, which I hadn't been expecting at all. . . .

"The job's yours if you want it, son," he said. I would later find out that he tended to call people "son" a lot. Oddly, he never addressed any of the women by a similar endearment. Perhaps it was because he had a daughter, and didn't want to imply—even to himself—that anyone could possibly be a replacement for her.

"Yes, sir. Yes, I think I do."

"Good." He extended a hand and I shook it firmly.

"Welcome aboard the *Grissom*. By the way . . . how'd you get the scar?"

"This? Bar fight. Three big guys, with knives. There was an argument over a woman, things got out of hand . . ." I shrugged. "It happens."

"Seems to me you got off lucky. Why didn't you have the scar removed?"

"Well," and I touched it gingerly, "I keep it around to remind me that no woman is really worth the aggravation."

"Oh, I would disagree with that, Commander. There are some women who are worth all that and more. Didn't you ever have a woman who stole your heart?"

I thought about Shelby, about her smiling at me. About the very first time that I'd seen her even before I knew her name . . . as an image of my future, smiling at me, naked and alluring, across the years.

"No, sir. Never. I keep my heart carefully hidden just to avoid any such situations."

THE BATTLE

AS IT TURNED OUT, I was right. XO Katerina Mueller had a remarkable body.

There are some who will tell you that shipboard romances are a remarkably bad idea. This is nonsensical, of course. After all, it's not as if we can all work our shifts, then leave the ship at the end of the day and go home to someone else. The people we work with are the same people that we see in our off hours, and at any other given time of the day. So it's fairly inevitable that something will develop.

I wasn't expecting it with Mueller, though. Indeed, she would have been the last person I would have expected. Then again, calling it romance probably would have been an exaggeration. It was . . . recreational, I suppose. Letting off steam. Having a good time with each other, secure in the knowledge that neither of us needed or wanted more.

It came about in a rather unexpected fashion.

I had been serving aboard the *Grissom* for several months. Up to that point, everything had been surprisingly routine. I suspect that, to some degree, the crew didn't quite know what to make of me. My manner could be brusque, and I was not terribly skilled at suffering fools gladly. I suppose it could be rather daunting trying to deal with me, particularly at that point in my life. Certain of everything, confident in my opinions, not hesitating to tell other people that they didn't know what they were talking about . . .

Hmm.

Come to think of it, I guess I'm not all that different now. It's just that now I do it with a good deal more charm, I suppose. At least, I like to think so.

In any event, the crew seemed to be treating me with respect, and that was ultimately all that I needed or required. I was seen as something of a loner, and that was fine with me. I wasn't looking for attachments or to strike up friendships. If I sat in Ten-Forward, I did so alone. No one approached me. Really, I don't suppose I would have been upset if they had. It might have been . . .

. . . it might have been nice.

No matter. They didn't, and that was fine, too.

One day I had just gotten off shift, and I was passing by the holodeck on my way to my quarters. Normally you can't really detect any noise from within the holodeck, but my ears are fairly sharp and, besides, there was a noise coming from within that I couldn't possibly miss. It was the sound of steel on steel in quick succession. Swords. Someone was having a duel, with more than one opponent.

It was considered something of a breach of protocol to interrupt someone during a holodeck run, but as anyone who knows me can attest, I'm perfectly capable of tossing aside the rules when and where it suits my purposes. And the sound of swordplay was an irresistible lure to a barely contained savage such as myself. The door was sealed, but I tapped in the override code and it slid open obediently. I stepped in . . .

. . . and found myself on a battlefield red with blood. It was a wide field, the grass tinted with frost and crunching under my feet as I walked. I stepped over bodies and moved to the side of the dried blood that was everywhere. Ahead of me was a small, rather confined area where battle still seemed to be raging.

These were not small blades being bandied about. There were warriors with large, double-handed swords, the kind that were capable of gutting a victim from crotch to sternum with just one blow. They were dressed in furs, their faces painted blue, and they were emitting loud war cries as they battled others dressed in similar garb.

And in the midst of it all was Mueller.

She was attired similarly to the others, and she was whipping her own sword through the air with such speed that it seemed to buzz. She was quick and adept. I saw someone coming in behind her, but somehow she managed to catch the movement out of the corner of her eye and intercepted it. She had a look of burning fury in her eyes, and her clothes and face were splattered with blood . . . in all likelihood, the blood of her opponents.

Two men were coming at her from either side. She spun in place, her blade like a scythe, and her attackers went down. Her head snapped around and she saw me. She froze in place, clearly surprised to see me there. Her breath floated from her mouth in a lazy mist.

Then, from over a rise, there was another war cry. It

drew both our attention and we saw a squad of attackers heading toward her. She had several allies still alive and remaining with her, and they lined up beside her, ready to battle. But her gaze had not left me.

"Well," she said finally. "Are you just going to stand there, or are you going to grab a sword and make yourself useful?"

The enemies were charging forward, their howling filling the air. Unhurried, I picked up swords off of fallen soldiers, hefting one in either hand. I tested the weight, chose the one that was in my left hand and dropped the other to the ground. Gripping it firmly, I whipped it through the air a few times.

You have to understand, my relationship with Mueller up until that time had been perfectly formal. She had struck me as coolly efficient, slightly disdainful, and not particularly interested in doing anything except her job. Hash had been correct in that humor did not seem to be her forte. We didn't have all that much interaction, what with being on different shifts. But what we had didn't begin to hint that she was capable of such brutal, bloody means of entertaining herself.

To be honest, I found it somewhat stimulating.

The first of the attackers were getting closer, closer. Something within me couldn't wait. I shouted *"Rakaaaash!"* and, my legs pumping, charged forward and met them while they were still about twenty feet from Mueller. I only had a second to wonder whether or not Mueller had overridden the holodeck safeties and whether I was in real danger. Then I promptly stopped caring as I gutted the first of my attackers. Without slowing in my turn, I cleaved open the second one and eviscerated the third, all in a matter of seconds.

A fourth man was coming at me, and I was prepared to block him when suddenly Mueller was there, stopping the downward thrust with her own weapon. She muscled him back and thrust forward with her own blade. The opponent's blood spurted onto my boots.

"Sorry," she said, noticing the stain.

"It'll come out," I replied. And that was all the exchange we had time for as the battle was truly joined. It was a symphony of clanging blades, of grunts and cuts and a cold fury that burned in the pit of your stomach and drove you onward, ever onward. In cases like that you tend to lose track of everything except survival. You draw a mental circle around yourself, and you concentrate on only those individuals who are attempting to enter that circle. Outside it you ignore them, inside it and your blade takes their life. It's as simple as that. You lose track of time, you lose track of yourself, and you only stop when they stop coming.

And eventually . . . they stopped.

As is always the case in such instances, I didn't realize it at first. My breath was slamming hard in my chest. I had not stinted in either my defense or offense simply because my opponents were holographic. A battle was a battle, a challenge still a challenge. My uniform shirt was torn in several places from slices by opponents that had gotten a little too close. Blood streaked my face, my hair was disheveled. My heart was pounding, and I realized I wanted more. More to conquer, more physical exertion. I felt more alive than I had in ages. I had never used the holodeck for much of anything, really. I had found the entire concept to be somewhat ridiculous and pointless: shadow dances that had no meaning. I certainly wasn't feeling that way anymore. To me, it seemed like I could actually feel my blood flowing through my veins.

I looked to see if there were any more opponents, any more challenges. There was only one other individual standing nearby, and that was Mueller. The rest of her allies had been struck down, but she had survived. Standing there clutching her sword, fire in her eyes, a wolflike grin on her face, she looked like a Valkyrie, like a warrior from a bygone age. Just us two, there on the blood-soaked plain.

I could tell from the look of her that she was undergoing the same roiling of feelings that I was. It might have been that mine was more intense; after all, I was the one who had been raised in a relatively barbaric society, had engaged in battles not too dissimilar from this one where my life was genuinely at stake, had known what it was like to fight for my life, for honor. The first man that I had killed, I had cried for . . . cried as much for myself as for him. I was long past those days. Now I felt nothing but triumph, and a euphoric exaltation.

She saw it in my eyes, and it attracted her, inflamed her, I was sure of it. She took a step toward me, another. And then she swung her sword around, the blade whistling straight at me. I intercepted the swing and the swords crashed together. Her blade slid down the length of mine, bringing us hilt to hilt, body to body, my chest pressed against her. Our breath was racing, our hearts beating together.

I said the only thing that seemed appropriate:

"My quarters, your quarters, or right here?"

"Right here," she said without a second's worth of thought.

The swords dropped down onto the ice-layered ground, and a moment later, so did we.

We never said a word.

And thus began one of the somewhat odder relationships I ever had, because we never did say a word. Whenever we encountered each other after that in uniform, we were all business. No one could have told that we were anything other than coworkers.

But every so often, as if we had a bond on some level, we would just . . . know. I would show up at her quarters, unsummoned and unbidden, or she would turn up at my door. And we would . . . well . . . we would.

Without a word. Never was a word exchanged. As if to say anything would serve to break the spell.

Absolutely no one knew. Well . . .

. . . one.

There was one evening where we lay in my bed, basking in the afterglow. The perspiration on both our bodies was slowly drying. We'd had a particularly successful outing, and we were enjoying the time after . . . although, once more, in silence.

I felt as if I should say something, but I had no idea what. I couldn't say whether she felt the same way, but the moment simply seemed to require some sort of intercourse of the social kind. Just as I started to open my mouth, though, a chime came from the door.

"Yes?" I called.

"Commander?" came a familiar drawl. "Got something for you."

"Not now, Hash," I replied. "Could you come back later?"

"Got to strike on these things while the iron's hot, y'know, sir. It's just a li'l ol' thing. But I'd surely like to give it to you in person."

Kat Mueller looked at me with a certain degree of controlled franticness. The last thing we needed was Takahashi waltzing in with the two of us curled in bed together. "Really, Hash, later would be a better time. That's something of an order."

"There's no time like the present, sir."

"Is there any cliché he doesn't know?" Kat hissed

in my ear. It was the first time that any words had been exchanged between us while we were unclothed. It certainly wouldn't have been the first words I would have wanted to hear.

"Hash, I'm going to be a while. . . ."

"S'okay, sir. I'll just wait out here. Got nothin' better to do, really."

I could have argued it, could have gotten forceful. He was a subordinate, after all. But the bottom line was, he was basically a nice guy, I liked him, and obviously he was trying to do something thoughtful, although heaven only knew what. I could continue to debate it, or I could endeavor to resolve it. "All right, hold on a moment," I said. Kat's eyes opened wider, and I whispered to her, "Do you think it's preferable that he stand outside for who knows how long and keeps calling through the door? Very subtle, that."

"Then what—?"

I pointed to the bathroom. "Wait in the head until he's gone."

She stared at me with unconcealed annoyance and then rolled off the bed. She gathered up her clothing as quickly as she could and made for the bathroom. As the door slid shut I thought she might have tossed me an obscene gesture, but I couldn't be sure. In retrospect, it was probably better that way.

I had gotten out of bed and pulled on a robe. I belted it tightly around my waist, went to the door, and said, "Okay, come."

Hash was standing there in the doorway. He was holding a large bowl with the aid of a couple of thick mitts. "Hot off the stove," he said proudly.

"Let me guess: hash," I said.

He nodded eagerly. "I keep promising to make you some of my specialty, but you never seem to have yourself around when it's being made. Thought you might wanna help your taste buds sing." He paused. "Y'all have taste buds on Xenex, right?"

"Last I checked. So . . . why don't you come back later and I can—"

"Eat it while it's hot. Got a fork right there in the top. Dig in." He walked in and placed it on a table, then stepped back and stood there with folded arms.

"You mean . . . right now?"

"It's your first time, Commander. Got to see how you react to your first time."

I was trying to be polite, to hold my temper, but it wasn't easy. "If I do, will you go away?"

He laughed as if I'd been joking.

Realizing that there was only one way to end it—well, two ways, but only one of them wouldn't get me court-martialed—I took a forkful of the proffered hash and ate it. Then I blinked in surprise. "This is good."

He grinned.

"I mean it . . . this is really good. No, this is great." I wasn't exaggerating. It was corned-beef hash and it was absolutely delicious.

Romeo backed away, bobbing his bizarrely blond head, and he said, "Enjoy it, sir."

"Do you want to stay to—?"

The moment the words were out of my mouth, I couldn't believe I'd said them. I'd completely forgotten that Kat was stranded in the bathroom. A prolonged stay wasn't going to endear me to her.

Fortunately enough, Romeo said suavely, "Oh nooo . . . no, I don't think that'd be wise. You enjoy the rest all by your lonesome . . . you and your lady friend."

Suddenly it seemed as if the temperature in the room had dropped twenty degrees. "Lady . . . friend?" I managed to get out.

"Well, yeah. The one you got hiding in the bathroom."

"How do . . . I mean, what makes you think that . . . ?" I asked in what had to be one of the clumsiest attempts at a save ever made.

He inclined his chin in the direction of the bed. "That yours?"

I glanced in the direction he was indicating. A bra was entangled in the sheets.

"Yes," I said tonelessly. "Yes. It is."

"Mm-hmm. Commander . . . I want to assure you that I am, despite all appearances to the contrary, a genuine Southern gentleman. Discretion is my middle name."

I thought, *And here I thought your middle name was "Lousy Timing,"* but I didn't say it.

He grinned once more and headed toward the door. He paused in the doorway and called over his shoulder, "Sayonara, y'all," and then exited whistling.

The door to the bathroom opened and a rather steamed Kat Mueller stood there. She was wearing her uniform. Her breasts did not appear to be sagging. "You know . . . I was never wild about Takahashi before. He's entirely too cheerful for my taste. But I never actively disliked him before."

I held up the bra. "Here," I said, not having anything else particularly clever to say.

"Thanks. I hear it's yours."

I tossed it to her.

"Mac . . . this is absurd." It was the first time she had ever addressed me as "Mac." When we were on duty she used my rank, and when we were intimate no words were exchanged. She turned her back to me, removed her uniform top and finished getting dressed. "We can't continue this way."

"We can't?"

"No. We can't. I'm afraid it's over."

I stared at her levelly as she turned around. "All right."

"We'll just be coworkers."

"That would probably be best."

"Probably, yes."

And that was that. She left.

She was back three days later, you understand . . . but it seemed like a very long three days.

THE ASSIGNMENT

CAPTAIN KENYON STRODE onto the bridge and looked in a particularly good mood. "Mr. Gold," he called to the man at conn. "Set course for Starbase Nine, warp factor four."

"Aye, sir. On our way." Mick Gold, Lieutenant j.g., was a conn officer with what could delicately be called a sense of self-aggrandizement. Since he piloted the ship, he had a rather impressive ego, and oftentimes wasn't afraid to display it. The thing was, he was extremely skilled at what he did, and also had an amazing instinct—possibly better than any targeting computers—when it came to a firefight. So to a certain extent, Gold's self-importance was merited. Still, Gold never waited for the captain to actually order the ship to embark on her new heading. He would simply announce, "On our way."

When this was pointed out to him by a somewhat

irked Commander Paullina Simons, Gold calmly pointed out that standing on ceremony was silly. If the captain didn't want them to go to a particular place at a particular speed, then why in the world would he issue the order in the first place? Simons reported the exchange to Kenyon, who shrugged it off and said, "Well, when you get right down to it, he's right. If I know where we want to go, what's wrong with just going there?" Which left Gold to continue as he had been with the captain's tacit endorsement.

"Mr. Calhoun," said Kenyon, "conference lounge in ten minutes. You, Mr. Takahashi, Dr. Villers, and Mr. Cray." He turned and headed back out, still carrying himself in a very cheerful manner.

Dr. Villers was a Starfleet veteran. She was heavyset with gray hair, and had the bedside manner of a Romulan interrogator. She was also the most physically imposing woman I'd ever met. She wasn't tall, but she was wide: "Built like a Tenarian *vass.*" She worked out in the gymnasium every day, lifting weights and wiping the floor with karate partners. Part of me was almost perverse enough to mentally match her against Kat and wonder who would come out on top. I had the feeling it might be Doc Villers.

Cray was something else again.

Cray was an Andorian, the head of security. When he spoke, which was not often, it was just above a whisper so that you had to strain to hear him. I had witnessed him in combat situations—we had stumbled upon some Orion raiders while on a mineral survey—and he was easily one of the most vicious fighters I'd ever seen in action. He carried a phaser, but I'd never actually seen him use it. He seemed to prefer hand-to-hand, and he was frighteningly good at it. And he did not like me, not one bit. I make no bones about it, I may not have been the most popular first officer who ever sat in the second chair. There were those who simply didn't like my style. Who felt that I walked with too much swagger, or felt that I didn't act with sufficient deference to the captain (an opinion, I cannot emphasize enough, that the captain did not share). And there were crewmen who, as I told you earlier, felt disconcerted by what they saw in my eyes and felt constrained to look away. As always, Starfleet and I did not remain the smoothest of fits, and that caused occasional bumping of heads.

With Cray, though, it was different. Cray had no desire to remain in the security track. To be specific, he'd had his eye on the second chair. He was technically next in line after the first officer; the day I'd arrived, Hash had been at the conn because Cray was temporarily off the bridge attending to other duties. Cray had felt that the promotion was virtually guaranteed once Commander Simons had gotten her captaincy and Mueller had made no effort to step in for consideration. He had not expected Kenyon to seek a new first officer from outside of the personnel on the *Grissom,* and was convinced that the only reason I was there was because I'd had Jellico pushing for me. He might well have been right.

Much of Cray's state of mind I was able to garner from a few conversations with various crewmen. Cray, you see, hadn't been particularly reticent when it came to his feelings about me, especially once he'd gotten a few slugs of synthehol into him. Once I became aware of his feelings of annoyance, I tried to sit down with him in Ten-Forward to work things out.

I've told you how others didn't like what they saw in my eyes. I can assure you that, when I looked into Cray's eyes, I wasn't ecstatic with what I saw there, either. Our talk did not go particularly well, nor did I endeavor to pursue it in the future.

Not that he presented a danger to me, you understand. There was no reason to think that he would perform his duty in any way other than to the best of his abilities as a Starfleet officer. Nor did I think that he would expose me to danger, or that he wouldn't watch my back if we found ourselves in a sticky situation. On the other hand, I was reasonably certain that he would be among the first to laugh loudly if I made a muddle of things. It can be very disconcerting if you're aware that someone is waiting for you to screw things up. It can make you tense, make you second-guess yourself.

Not me, of course. Cray's attitude was his and he was welcome to it. I shut out my concerns with relative facility.

As per the captain's orders, we had assembled in the conference lounge at the appointed time. The captain's exceptionally good mood persisted, and within minutes he explained to us why.

We had been assigned to escort a diplomatic team to oversee peace talks between two races on two worlds in the Anzibar system. The world of Anzibar II, populated by a race called the Carvargna, was a temperate, even tropical world. The Carvargna were—perhaps not coincidentally—a relatively benign people who far preferred peace to bloodshed.

For millennia, the Carvargna was the only sentient race in the Anzibar system. Then an ark ship arrived in their system, carrying an entire race of people known as the Dufaux, themselves refugees from a system whose sun had aged out and rendered their world uninhabitable. The Carvargna extended their hospitality to the Dufaux, their reasoning being that on their world there was room for all. The Dufaux settled there, and turned out to be an extremely prolific race. They didn't breed quite as quickly as tribbles, but they were certainly not lacking in their birthing capabilities. Over the decades, not only did their populace increase exponentially, but so did their desire for land. They were also far more warlike and savage than the Carvargna, and when the Carvargna resources began to reach the stress point, the Dufaux simply resolved to obliterate the Carvargna. Obviously, the Carvargna—peace-loving as they were—nonetheless did not go quietly into that good night. The warfare became intense and bloody, and the Dufaux wound up being driven off the world of Anzibar II. Anzibar III was uninhabitable, so they wound up on Anzibar IV. It was not, however, remotely as hospitable a world as the one they'd left. Years had passed, but resentments had not cooled. The two worlds continued to snipe at each other, every so often launching missile attacks or sending in raiding parties. It was not a good situation.

The Carvargna had tired of the assaults and battles over the years. They had approached the Federation and asked that it take a hand in the matter. The Federation had long desired to bring in Anzibar II and the Carvargna, and this seemed like the ideal opportunity. Consequently, it had assigned a diplomatic team to go to the Anzibar system and endeavor to heal the wounds between the neighboring worlds.

It was the identity of the diplomatic team that apparently had Kenyon in such a good mood: Byron Kenyon, the captain's brother . . . and his attaché, Stephanie . . . Captain Kenyon's daughter.

"Wait until you have the pleasure of meeting her," Kenyon said to us. "Some of you who might remember her beloved mother, or might have met Stephie when she was a little . . . I guarantee you, you're in for a treat." He beamed at the memory. "She is the image of her mother, let me tell you. She has her mother's spunk, her vivaciousness. She's quite a young woman, my Stephie."

"I remember her very well, Norm," said Villers. Of everyone on board, Doc Villers was the only one who addressed the captain by his first name, no matter what the situation. "Although she couldn't have been more than ten last time I saw her. It was great seeing her with you. She seemed to idolize you. I always thought that she'd follow you into the Fleet."

"Yes. Yes, that's what I thought, too." For just a moment, there seemed to be extreme sadness in his face, and then with effort he forced it off. "So." He rose and clapped his hands briskly, which was his general signal for the end of the meeting. "Once we pick them up from the starbase, we bring them to the Anzibar system and stay on station for as long as they need us. Any questions?"

"Security," Cray said in that whispery tone of his. It was a word, a statement, and a question all rolled into one.

"Of course we'll want them to have a full security escort," Kenyon replied. "I'll want you to head up the squad, Cray."

"Honored."

"Permission to go planetside with them, sir, particularly if it's Anzibar Four which is potentially the more hostile," I said.

"Actually, I was planning to go down myself, Calhoun," said the captain.

"That, sir, is not an appropriate course of action," I replied.

"Oh? And why would that be?"

"Because," I told him evenly, "you would be going into a situation where you could not be counted upon to act in a dispassionate or reasonable manner. The fact that both your brother and daughter are involved may cloud or dull your judgment. It would be inappropriate of you to accompany them. You need someone with emotional distance."

"Are you saying," Kenyon asked, "that I am incapable of acting in a professional manner where my daughter or brother are concerned?"

"I have nothing upon which to make that judgment," I said. "However, sir, if it's all the same to you, I'd prefer not to find out. I think none of us would."

There were nods of agreement from all around the table, which I found surprisingly heartening. At first Kenyon seemed inclined to protest, but then he saw the prevailing sentiment and simply shrugged. "If that's how you all feel . . . then I must certainly acknowledge your concerns and act accordingly. Very well, Calhoun. You will accompany my daughter and brother planetside. And bring them back to me in one piece."

"We will," Cray said before I could get a word out. And he looked at me out the side of his eyes in a manner that indicated I would be wise to leave the particulars of this mission to him. It was rapidly beginning to develop into a situation that was making me exceedingly uncomfortable.

THE DAUGHTER

SHE WAS A STUNNER.

I had to admit that the captain had not exaggerated his daughter's attributes in any way. The moment she materialized on the transporter pad, where Captain Kenyon and I awaited the arrival of her and her uncle, I was captivated by her. If she indeed resembled her mother, then Kenyon had been one of the luckiest bastards in the galaxy.

She was slim and small-waisted, but she had an open face that seemed to appreciate the world it was looking at. Her hair was brown and straight and amazingly long, hanging to just below her hips, and braided down either side. When she smiled, which seemed her natural state of expression, she had dimples in either slightly chubby cheek. Her eyes were green, like a cat's, and she had a long slender neck around which she wore a simple choker. She was dressed in a pale blue dress that clung in the right places but opened out into a large, flowing skirt. When she moved, it almost seemed as if she were floating along the floor rather than treading upon it.

With her was Kenyon's brother, Byron, and if I had not known that they were brothers, I still would have figured it out immediately. Byron, even though he was the younger of the two, was nevertheless the larger of them. He had to be at least fifty pounds heavier, his hair was thinning at the top, and he had a thick mustache. Nonetheless, his general look and deportment made the familial link exceptionally clear. He and the captain embraced as Byron stepped down from the pad.

Stephanie was staring at me.

She seemed immediately captivated by me, and to be honest, she herself wasn't exactly difficult on these old purple eyes of mine. "Stephie," her father said, several times, before he managed to pull her attention away from me. It seemed to me that he was definitely aware of the interest she had displayed in me, but he chose not to comment on it. Instead he hugged her so tightly I thought he would break her in half, and then he gestured toward me and said, "May I present my first officer, Mackenzie Calhoun."

"You're Xenexian, aren't you," she asked.

I made no attempt to hide my surprise. "Why . . . yes. . . ."

She nodded as if she had needed to confirm this for herself. "Yes, the general coloring of the skin and cranial shape implied that. The purple eyes, of course, were a strong indicator. They're of a shade that one virtually never sees on Earth, but they are not uncommon in Xenex—relatively speaking—occurring in about thirty-eight percent of the populace."

"That much?" I let out a low whistle.

"Which would mean your name isn't really 'Mackenzie Calhoun.'"

Rather than shake her hand, I bowed slightly in a manner that encompassed both her and her uncle. "I am M'k'n'zy, of the city of Calhoun. I changed it, or at least unofficially modified it, once I got to the Academy. I got a little tired of hearing the properly accented way of pronouncing it mangled all the time."

"You mean they had trouble saying 'M'k'n'zy'?"

I made no effort to hide my surprise. Her accent had been damned near perfect, her pronunciation of the guttural and hesitant syllables unassailable. I'd never heard any lips other than Xenexian capable of saying it so accurately. If everyone on Earth had said it that perfectly, I'd never have changed it. Hell, she said it better than Elizabeth, and we were almost married, for pity's sake.

"It's hard to believe, I know," I allowed. "But call me 'Mac,' please."

"All right, Mac." If it was possible, her dimples seemed to sink in even more deeply.

Kenyon tapped his combadge. "Kenyon to conn. Gold . . . they're aboard. Set course for the Anzibar system."

"On our way," came back Gold's voice, not waiting as usual for the captain's go-ahead. Sometimes I wondered if Kenyon had an official rule book somewhere of just how far, and no farther, he could be pushed.

"It's good to see you, Byron," the captain said, an arm draped around his sibling. He slapped his brother's stomach. "You've put on weight."

"Not at all," replied Byron. "It's just that somewhere, someone else has lost it, and it came through space and leaped onto me. Fat, like matter, cannot be destroyed, but merely transferred to another host body. I'm doing you a favor, Norm. If I lose it," and he slapped his belly, "it'll probably all wind up leaping onto you."

"The sacrifices you make for me," said the captain.

I felt almost envious, seeing the two of them together that way. My own brother and I had never had that sort of easy, give-and-take relationship. There had always been an undercurrent of tension between us, even when we were allies against the Danteri. And in later years, my brother had made himself over into little more than a Danteri stooge, accommodating them wherever he could and selling out the greater concerns of our people in return for personal profit. Seeing Norman and Byron Kenyon interacting in that way—the teasing, the joy at seeing each other, the obvious affection they held for one another—it got to me a bit.

Naturally, though, I kept my true feelings buried. It was no problem, really; I'd had a lot of practice on that score.

We showed them to their respective quarters. I was certain that it was my imagination, but Stephanie appeared unable to take her eyes off me. I bowed slightly, formally, when the captain and I brought her to her quarters, and then as I turned to leave, she said, "Dad? Do you think I might get a tour of the ship?"

"Of course, honey." He gestured that she should precede him, thereby indicating that he himself would conduct the tour.

"Oh, Daddy, I wouldn't think of taking up your time," she told him. "If you'd want to assign . . . someone else?" She looked straight at me.

Credit the captain: Nothing slips past him. Of course, it's not as if Stephanie was being exactly subtle. "Commander." Kenyon turned to me, looking very formal. "Would you be so kind as to escort my daughter around the ship? Show her the points of interest?"

"I would be honored, sir."

"And, of course, I can trust you to be a perfect gentleman?" he added gravely.

"Of course, sir."

And that was when I heard Stephanie mutter, "Damn," under her breath.

Well, Stephanie turned out to be quite a woman, let me tell you. And no, before you start getting ahead of me and conjuring up scenarios in your own mind, I will tell you in advance: No. Nothing happened.

Not that it was for lack of trying.

Stephanie was easily one of the most charming, intelligent, sophisticated, and downright fun women that I have ever encountered. From the first tour that I gave her of the *Grissom,* to the time we spent dining together, to the late hours we spent debating everything from Federation politics to obscure strategies of ancient generals, Stephanie Kenyon proved to be nothing short of amazing.

"I feel guilty," I said to her at one point. "I think I'm monopolizing your time. You should be spending it with your father."

It was the first time that I actually saw her hesitate to say what was on her mind. "That . . . might not be wise," she said finally.

"Why not?" We were alone in one of the forward observation lounges. "Don't tell me you two don't get along with each other. I can't believe that."

"I just . . ." She paused. "I'd rather not discuss it."

"All right," I said readily. I was perfectly comfortable not discussing it. I genuinely liked Captain Kenyon, and felt a bit voyeuristic. I realized that I didn't want some sort of inside glimpse into his personal life. I was perfectly happy to keep that aspect of his life at a distance.

Naturally Stephanie took my being perfectly comfortable with not hearing her discuss it as an invitation to discuss it.

Women. Xenexian, Terran . . . they're all the same. Well . . . maybe not Vulcans, but otherwise, all the same.

"I just think that . . . well . . . my father is disappointed in me."

"Disappointed? How can you think that?" I was genuinely astounded. "He thinks the world of you. He talks about how proud he is of you. . . ."

"He also talks about how he wishes I'd gone into Starfleet, doesn't he. He's disappointed that I didn't."

I thought of the obvious sadness in his eyes when his daughter's career path had been casually brought up in the conference lounge. He had obviously endeavored to push it away, but it was there just the same. "No," I said quickly. "I didn't get that impression at all."

She smiled sadly. "Mac, you're a terrible liar."

"Actually," I protested, "I'm generally pretty good at it. I'm just not especially good at it with you."

She stared out at the stars that hurtled past us, and she seemed very sad. "My dad's had so much hurt in his life . . . I hate the thought of adding to it. I hate not being what he wanted me to be. But I couldn't . . . it was ego, that's all."

"Ego?"

"I didn't want to spend my life being Norman Kenyon's daughter. If I'd gone into Starfleet, that's exactly what I would have been. I would have had my life, my career, defined by my relationship to him. It's not that I don't love him; I do. It's not that I'm not proud of him; I am. But I wanted to do, and be, something that was separate from him."

"So you chose the diplomatic corps."

"It seemed a worthwhile direction in which to go. Besides," and she laughed, "I couldn't help but have the burned-in desire to meet and experience other races. That much, my father managed to make such a part of me that to deprive myself of those opportunities would have been like cutting off an arm. Living your own life is one thing, but one shouldn't have to be mutilated . . . oh. Oh God. I'm sorry."

"What?" I didn't try to cover the fact that I was puzzled. "Sorry about what?"

"Oh God, now I'm making an even bigger idiot of myself. I'm sorry, it's just . . . well, I was talking about mutilation, and you with that . . ." She touched the side of her face.

"Oh! The scar." I waved off her concern. "Don't worry about it."

"May I ask, uhm . . . how did you . . . ?"

"Jealous husband," I told her. "My fault. I didn't know she was married. Shouldn't have taken her word for it. One moment we're rolling around in the sheets, the next thing I know, I'm hearing bellowing from this man the size of a small asteroid heading toward me, waving an axe with a blade twice the size of my head. All things considered, I was damned lucky. *Grozit,* he could have taken my head off."

"Good lord."

Inwardly, I smiled. At least I wasn't a hopeless liar when it came to the daughter of Captain Norman Kenyon.

That was when she kissed me.

It was long and sensuous, and she gave freely of herself. And when our lips parted, she looked up at me with . . . I don't know what. Longing. Interest. Perhaps just a touch of boredom that she was trying to kill.

"I'll . . . walk you back to your quarters," I told her.

"Would you stay awhile?"

"I have duties to perform."

"Can they wait?"

"Probably. But they won't."

There was surprise on her face. I turned her to face me, taking her shoulders in my hands. "Stephanie . . . I think you're terrific. But . . . your father is my captain. I wouldn't feel comfortable."

"I'm a grown woman," she said. "Dad knows that. Do you think he doesn't know I find you very attractive? He respects my freedom."

"Good. But, you see . . . I respect *him.* I would not feel . . . right. Even if any involvement would be with his approval, even if he sent flowers and a balloon assortment. I would feel . . . not . . . right. And to be honest . . . I think you should be spending more time with him than with me. All right?"

She laughed softly, low in her throat. "I won't say I'm not disappointed."

"I won't say it either. But it's how I feel. And I know I can count on you to respect that."

"True enough. But I'm telling you, Calhoun," and she smiled in a very saucy manner, "sooner or later, you're going to regret it. Regrets are terrible things to have, because you know what? Life's just too damned short."

That was the last I saw of her that day, except for the very end of my shift. As I was about to go off duty, Stephanie showed up on the bridge, kissed her father on the top of the head, and together the two of them left the bridge to go to dinner. She cast a very quick glance in my direction, winking just before the turbo-lift doors closed.

When I returned to my quarters, Kat was there. She was fully dressed, sitting on the edge of my bed. "I hear you're quite the couple," she said without preamble.

"Oh, we're going to talk," I said with feigned surprise.

"Well? Are you?"

"If you're referring to Stephanie Kenyon and myself . . . I think she's terrific. A wonderful woman. Then again, considering her pedigree, it's not surprising."

"We're not discussing a dog, Calhoun."

"What happened to 'Mac'? I thought you were calling me 'Mac.' "

She stood. Although she was only an inch taller, at that point she seemed about two heads higher than me. "Are you involved with her?"

"What does it matter to you?"

Her expression hardened. I had the oddest feeling that there was about to be a lightning storm in my quarters. "It matters."

"Why?" I started to raise my voice, feeling a bit exasperated. "Why does it matter? Do we have a relationship, you and I? What the hell *do* we have? We have a . . . a mutual outlet for pent-up emotion, that's what we have. Are we supposed to build on that?"

"I'm not concerned about building. I'm concerned about the kind of man you are."

"I'm not following you."

"I'm curious to know," and she took a step closer, seeming to loom over me, "whether you're the type of man who would endeavor to solidify his position using whatever means necessary. Because that would drastically reshape my opinion of you."

It took a moment for it to sink in . . . and then I started to laugh. "Are you . . ." I was laughing so hard that I had to clutch my stomach because it hurt. "Are you . . . are you implying that I'm trying to . . . to sleep my way to the top?"

"Stop laughing."

I leaned against the bulkhead and waited until I was able to compose myself. "If you must know . . . if you really must . . . if Stephanie Kenyon were anyone else, I would most definitely be involved with her. But because she is who she is, I have made clear to her that friends are what we are, and friends are what we will remain. So it's the opposite of what you're suggesting. All right?"

Mueller seemed mollified at that. "You're being honest with me?"

"If you have to ask me that, then we really have nothing else to talk about."

"All right. Well . . . good. All right."

"So this was all because you were concerned with my integrity. Not because of any personal involvement that you and I might have, or feelings you might have for me."

"I don't have feelings for you, Mac," said Mueller. "We have what we have, and that's all. I don't want or need anything beyond that. I thought you didn't either."

I eyed her curiously. "Then why do you care about what sort of man I am? If it's purely about physical needs, then why should any aspect of my personality factor into it? Endurance, breath control . . . that should be all you're concerned about."

"I will be concerned about what I choose to be concerned about."

"Really. And what about me?" We circled each other in my quarters. "Should I be concerned about the fact that I'm involved with a woman who wants nothing beyond physical gratification? Why is that? Why is that all you care about?"

"It's not all I care about. But it's all I want."

"Why? Why are you this way?"

For a moment, there was a flicker of sadness in her eyes. "We are what we are, Mac. We are what circumstances make us."

There was a long silence between us . . . and, I had a feeling, something else between us as well. "Kat . . ."

"I have to go," she said.

She walked toward the door, and stopped short of it. She stood ramrod straight, her back to me. She didn't move from the spot.

"Kat . . . ?"

Her straight, squared-off shoulders were shaking ever so slightly. "I have to go . . . and I don't want to."

I took her by the arm, turned her around to face me. Her face was absolutely dry. All of her crying was on the inside.

I held her close to me, and one thing led to another . . .

. . . and once again, we didn't speak. But this time, it wasn't because we had nothing to say. It was because we didn't need to.

THE DUFAUX

ANOTHER MEETING had been called in the conference lounge, with the Anzibar system only hours away. The mood on the part of Stephanie Kenyon seemed fairly grim, as it did for the captain as well. It was immediately made clear to Doc Villers, Cray, Hash, and me just what the problem was. Byron wasn't there, which had me somewhat apprehensive. But Stephanie didn't seem inclined to wait.

"There's been a development," said Stephanie. She glanced at her father, but the captain simply nodded as if to indicate that she should continue. "We've been in touch with the Dufaux. Understand that it was the Carvargna who requested, and pushed for, the intervention of the Federation. The Dufaux were resistant to it . . . very much so. However, they finally agreed to it . . . albeit somewhat reluctantly. A recent missile barrage by the Carvargna helped to change their minds, I think."

"So what's the problem?" asked Hash.

"The problem is," the captain now stepped in, "that there's been an overthrow in the leadership of the Dufaux. Apparently, to some extremists, the fact that they were willing to talk at all was seen as a sign of weakness. There are new leaders in place, and they seem disinclined to meet with any UFP representatives."

"So we meet with the Carvargna only," said Hash.

"Pointless," whispered Cray.

Stephanie nodded. "I must agree with Mr. Cray. We're trying to put together a negotiation here. There has to be a meeting of minds, and that can't be one-sided."

"Where's Byron?" I asked.

"He's engaged in private communication with the Dufaux," the captain said. He didn't seem especially enthused about it. "I was there for the first few minutes of it. I can tell you, people, that I am not speaking with simple fraternal pride when I say that my brother is one of the best negotiators in the business. He's pulled off some miracles in his career. I'd say he's saved more lives through words and dogged pursuit of the peace process than everyone in this room combined, with all our starships, our weapons, and our strength. But these Dufaux . . . they sounded completely resistant. He said he'd be coming in here to give us an update, but I think you're going to see a very frustrated diplomat coming through that door."

"The captain's right," said Stephanie, being politic and avoiding a possibly cloying sentence such as, "Dad's right." "I've watched Byron in action. I know what he's capable of achieving, and this one seems to be a roadblock . . ."

The doors hissed open and Byron Kenyon practically marched into the room. His arms were swinging in leisurely fashion, and he was beaming. "So! What did I miss!" he said cheerfully.

"You missed the vote on your attitude for when you come in here," Villers told him. "I'm afraid you'll have to go out and come back in in a much worse mood."

"Byron, what happened?" asked a clearly surprised Kenyon.

Byron draped himself over one of the chairs. "I managed to make them see the light."

"You mean," said Stephanie, leaning forward, her elbows on the table, "that you got them to agree to meet with the Carvargna?"

"We must walk before we can run and, in this case, crawl before we can walk, Stephanie," Byron counseled her, sounding at his most sage. "I managed to convince the Dufaux leadership—headed up by an individual named Kradius—that they are presenting no risk to their current status by agreeing to meet with us. That no one ever died simply from talking about something."

"I can think of any number of martyrs who would disagree with you," I said. Now . . . I've always had a knack for sensing danger. Call it battle experience, call it reading signs, call it a psionic ability if you must, but I've had it before and I was having it at that moment. "This doesn't smell right."

"It'll be fine, Commander," Byron said calmly. "Oh, I know, they were resistant at first. But I've managed to work them past that. I have done this before, you know."

"Yes, and I've seen people die before who thought they were dealing with those who could be trusted," I said.

"Commander," and Byron was starting to sound

just a bit angry, "I know that you are merely trying to express your concern, but to be blunt, you are coming across as rather condescending."

"That was not my intention, sir. But I would be doing you a disservice if I didn't speak up. If the Dufaux are genuinely interested in the peace process, let's hold the discussion up here on the *Grissom.* We bring up some of their people . . . this 'Kradius' you spoke of . . ."

"I suggested that," Byron said. "Unfortunately, Kradius wouldn't go for that. Remember, these are a suspicious and warlike people. They are convinced that whoever they send up might be used for hostages."

"Oh, that's absurd," Captain Kenyon spoke up. "The Federation doesn't operate that way."

"Captain," Byron told him, "we are outsiders to them, and they couldn't give a damn how we do and do not operate. They are judging us by their standards, not ours. Now I have . . . we," and he glanced at Stephanie, "have a job to do, and I regret that it will not be able to be done here. The Dufaux have requested a private audience, with Stephanie and me, on Anzibar Four. It took me hours to bring them to that point. I'm not about to turn around and risk tossing all that aside due to paranoia."

"Very well," Kenyon said with a sigh. Clearly he wasn't happy about it, but he had his orders as well and he knew it. He turned to Cray and said, "Prepare a security team, standard armament, to accompany—"

"Just us," said Byron. "Just Stephanie and myself."

There was dead silence for a long moment.

For Cray, one-word sentences were his more common oral stylings. When he got up above two, you knew that something serious was in the offing. "You're joking, of course," said Cray, this time speaking just above a whisper.

"No, I'm not joking."

"I won't permit it," Captain Kenyon immediately said.

"I beg your pardon?" Byron was staring at his brother. "Captain . . . this is not within your province."

"You're on my ship," Kenyon shot back. "My concern is for your safety and welfare."

"We are not part of your crew, Captain," replied Byron. "You are not responsible for baby-sitting us, holding our hands, or changing our diapers. I am perfectly capable of assessing a situation and dealing with it accordingly. And if you think that you are in a position to do so, then I strongly advise you to think again."

"This is madness," said Kenyon. "I won't allow—"

"Captain," Byron said with what appeared to be infinite patience. "Your powers aboard this ship are vast; I understand that. But they are not infinite, and I think that if you review regulations, you'll find that when it comes to a diplomatic mission, I have the right to refuse any action on the part of the captain which I think could be injurious to the successful completion of the mission."

The captain started to reply, but I immediately jumped in. "To hell with regulations," I said. "I've done some reading on the Dufaux. My people would be classified by some experts as savages, and I'm telling you right now, even we would be appalled by some of their activities. Brutalities, capricious cruelties . . ."

"Commander," began Byron.

But I wasn't letting him get a word in. "My people kill to defend themselves and to achieve freedom.

These people kill to display their strength . . . or for fun."

"I'm familiar with the reports and surveys you've read, Commander, and I'm telling you they are outdated. The Dufaux, as they stand now, are not eager to continue the conflict."

"So say the people who killed their predecessors because they sought to achieve peace."

"Once someone is in power, Commander," Byron replied, "they tend to view things a bit differently. I believe that to be the case here."

"And you're willing to stake your life on that?" the captain asked. "Yours . . . and hers?"

And Stephanie suddenly spoke up, and she sounded far angrier than I would have imagined. "Don't you do it, Captain. Don't you dare. Don't you dare act in any way other than with the concept that I am a professional diplomatic aide, out to do my job. Our relationship doesn't enter into it, and if you act like it does, I will never forgive you for that."

It was as if a thunderclap had erupted in the room. No one quite knew what to say; the outburst had seemed to come from nowhere. Except I knew exactly where it came from: from deep in the heart of a young woman who was determined to make her own way in the galaxy, and would not do anything that required her, in any way, to live in her father's shadow.

It was Byron who broke the silence. "I have a job to do, Captain," he said. "I must be allowed to do it to the best of my ability, as must my aide. Not only do the regs back me on this, but you yourself know it to be true. You cannot allow your personal feelings to—"

For the first time, I actually heard the unflappable, the always patient, the perpetually cheerful Captain Norman Kenyon sound genuinely angry. "Do not," he said with a voice that could cut castrodinium, "presume to tell me my mind, sir. You overstep yourself. Is that clear?"

"Captain—" began Byron.

"Is that clear!"

Byron opened his mouth, clearly intending to say something else, but then closed it again and simply nodded.

Kenyon weighed the situation for a time, and then he turned to Doc Villers. "I want you to implant subcutaneous transponders on them, on the back of their forearms."

"Oh, for God's sake," said an annoyed Byron.

"What?" Stephanie looked momentarily puzzled. I was surprised; I had started to think that there wasn't anything she didn't know. "What are—"

"They're wafer-thin tracking devices," Villers explained. "They're inserted just under the surface of the skin. Not as sophisticated as a comm badge or communicator because you can't talk on them. "

"However," Hash said, "not only can we lock on to them, but you can send a simple pulse as a way of letting us know you're all right. Since the captain wants them implanted here," and he indicated the back of his arm, just under his uniform shirt sleeve, "all you have to do is press on them. It'll feel like you're pressing on bone. It'll send a brief signal burst to the ship on our tracking frequency."

"You'll do it every hour, on the hour," Kenyon told them. "That way, we know everything is all right. If you signal at any other time, or don't signal at all, we beam you up immediately on the assumption that there's trouble."

"You're already operating on an assumption, Captain," said Byron. "You're assuming that we'll be unable to fend for ourselves."

"Absolutely," Kenyon said readily. "If I go down to a planet on an away-team expedition, I bring security people, weapons, and comm badges. I don't go down in my underwear and socks and figure that I'll be able to fend for myself. I don't see why I should treat you any differently."

"Captain, I can handle the situation, and your condescension is—"

"Entirely my prerogative," said Kenyon. "Perhaps I can't stop you from going down. But there's nothing in the regs that says I can't unobtrusively keep track of you, and so help me, Byron, if you give me grief on this, then you are acting in blatant disregard to my authority. That is a violation of regs, and you can spend the next two weeks cooling your heels in lockup for it. Are we clear on this?"

Byron growled something unintelligible, and then he just shrugged. "Yes . . . sir," he added, almost as an afterthought.

"Good. You will accompany Dr. Villers to sickbay. Hash, coordinate with the doc to make sure of the transponder frequency and run a couple of tests on them. Cray . . . assemble a security squad and keep them on alert, just in case."

The captain hadn't given me any specific orders, and then I saw by the look in his eyes that he wanted me to stay put. I did so as the others left, and moments later it was just the two of us in the room.

"You think I'm making a mistake, don't you," he said.

"I don't know, sir."

"You said it yourself. To hell with regulations."

"I have that luxury," I said. "I'm only the second-in-command. I only have to answer to you if I go outside the regs, and I'm reasonably sure that I'd get a fair hearing and—at worst—a slap on the wrist from you, as long as the outcome of my actions was one you approved of. You have other considerations."

"Yes. I do. Do you know what the hell of it is, Calhoun?"

"I can think of several, but I'd be interested in yours."

"That to a degree, Stephanie was right. If it weren't my daughter and brother involved, I wouldn't have hesitated to let them deal with the situation as they saw fit. As it was, I second-guessed them."

"You say that now, sir. You don't know that for sure. If you're asking my opinion, my guess is that you'd have reacted in the exact same manner no matter who was involved. You care too much about people to just let them recklessly risk their lives."

"And if you were in charge, Calhoun? What would you have done?"

"Probably the same thing you're doing."

In years to come, I would think about that meeting between Kenyon and me, the conversation we had as to what I would do and not do. Years down the line, I would face a similar situation shortly after I became a captain. A group of refugees whom the *Excalibur* had saved would accept the offer of asylum from a world about which I had suspicions. My instinct would be to keep them aboard the ship. Shelby, my first officer, would stridently inform me that I could not act against the wishes of the refugees. And I would end up yielding to her insistence. Against my better judgment, I would allow the people to go planetside. Almost immediately upon doing so, they would become pawns in a game with the planetary government as the government would endeavor to blackmail me into providing it with Starfleet weaponry and technology. A few people would die in that encounter, and I would end up counting myself lucky since it could have been a lot more people than just a few.

If I were writing the Starfleet regulations, they would boil down to exactly two: Rule 1—The captain is always right. Rule 2—When in doubt, see Rule 1.

Kenyon leaned back in his chair and stared up at

the ceiling. "I hope I'm doing the right thing, Calhoun. I hope I am."

"You're doing the only thing you can do, sir," I said in what was meant to be a consoling tone.

He smiled at me. "Thank you, Calhoun. I needed to hear that."

And with those words . . . with what I had said to him, and his reply, which I had allowed to pass . . . I damned myself.

Because that wasn't what I wanted to say at all. But, damn me, for a moment I allowed weakness within myself. He had already made his decision, and I didn't want to make him feel worse. So I kept my silence.

They say that silence is golden.

They don't know what the hell they're talking about.

THE MESSAGE

PLANETS ALWAYS LOOK SO peaceful.

We sat in orbit around Anzibar IV, having beamed down Byron and Stephanie Kenyon. It continues to be amazing to me: I've been to planets where the various populations are waging wars with the intention being complete genocide. Where border skirmishes reign, where hatred and terror hold sway . . . and the planets continue in their path, unknowing, unheeding, and uncaring. Sometimes I wish I could take every warring race and haul them high above their world. I would make them look down at the sphere beneath us and say, "See? See what you have beneath your feet? What are you fighting over? Why are you bothering?"

On the other hand, if someone had endeavored to yank young M'k'n'zy off his homeworld of Xenex and given him a stern talking to about the joys of peace,

M'k'n'zy would very likely have handed his head to him.

From the moment that the Kenyons had been beamed to the planet's surface, the bridge had settled into an extraordinarily quiet routine. Usually there was some chatter, some spirited back-and-forth, even casual conversation. Not this time. Captain Kenyon remained in his command chair as if bolted into it. His posture didn't change for ages. Crewmen approached him from time to time for exceedingly routine matters, such as fuel-consumption reports. He dealt with each and every call for his attention with brisk efficiency, but nothing more than that. His attention never wavered from the planet that turned on the screen.

At one point, though, in a very low voice, he said, "Commander . . ."

I turned to face him.

"They're going to be all right, aren't they."

I wasn't sure if it was a question or not. Trying to sound reasonable, I said, "I think so, sir. It's not as if your brother is a novice at this sort of thing. If his judgment was that he could handle the situation, I would be inclined—much as you were—to permit him to do so."

He nodded, but said nothing.

The first transmission from the planet's surface had gone without incident. Precisely on the hour, both Stephanie and Byron had quietly been able to push in on the top of their respective forearms. Takahashi got a beep on his ops board and, moments later, a second one. "Both accounted for, sir," he said and smiled in that broad, odd way he had. "Don't you worry about a thing."

Again Kenyon nodded but said nothing.

In one way, this drove home for me just how lonely a captain's life could be. It was the captain's job to make assignments, to treat everyone equally, to deal with crewpeople as crewpeople first and individuals second. If a captain formed truly strong attachments to anyone—and heaven forbid any of them should be romantic attachments—it made it exceedingly difficult for him to do his job. What if a particular member of the crew was the best suited to deal with some hazardous situation, but the captain was reluctant to send him or her because of personal feelings? Sending a less-qualified individual could endanger an entire mission. The captain owed it both to himself and to his crew to remain as neutral and uninvolved as possible.

And yes, yes, I know, before you say anything . . . when I became captain of the *Excalibur,* I appointed my former fiancée as my first officer. People search for purity of character, for perfection of consistency. Life doesn't happen that way. We set an ideal and just because we don't always manage to stick to it doesn't mean that the ideal is any less devoutly to be sought. I had a teacher back at the Academy, specializing in strategies, who would put forward one theory of warfare and then mention another that would seem to fly in the face of what he had taught earlier. What he was trying to put across to us was that rules of war are not immutable, and one has to be able to adapt quickly or one will run into trouble. On those occasions when he would give us conflicting information, he would always quote an Earthman called Walt Whitman, who apparently said: "Do I contradict myself? Very well then I contradict myself, (I am large, I contain multitudes.)" To be honest, I was never entirely sure what that meant.

The second hour went by, and the third and fourth, and each time there was a comforting signal that let us know the two of them were safe. I found myself falling into a rather exhausting rhythm: As we would come up on the appointed time, I would feel my pulse racing, my body getting tense. We would come upon the hour, and occasionally a minute or two or three after the appointed time, at which point I would feel a cold sweat beginning to bead on my forehead. I would see Stephanie's laughing face in my mind's eye, the dimples, the long hair. I would hear the coy teasing of her voice, and the tempting way in which she had spoken.

I was regretting it already. I knew that I had done the right thing by not getting involved with her. But, damn, it would have been fun. Not wise, but fun. Still, even though I wasn't sure exactly where we stood with each other or what we meant to each other, there was still Katerina Mueller to consider. . . .

"Am I early?"

I looked up in surprise and realized that—for I don't know how long—I had completely lost track of the time. As if she had sensed my thoughts and materialized in response, Mueller was standing at the turbolift door. She was looking around in surprise to see that the day shift was still in place, with nobody apparently making any preparations to leave.

Slowly Captain Kenyon became aware that no one was moving. As if trying to reorient himself to the moment, he looked around and saw that Mueller was standing there with a mildly puzzled expression on her face. "Nightside already, XO?" he asked.

"This is generally when it's done, sir." She cocked her head in concern. "Anything I should know about?"

"If it's all the same to you, XO . . . I think I'll stay here a bit longer."

"She's your boat, sir. Stay as long as you like." She glanced around at the rest of the crew. No one said anything, but it became clear that no one else was budging. She looked to me and said, "One big happy family, is that it?"

"Seems that way."

She tapped her comm badge. "XO Mueller to night-shift bridge crew: All bridge crew hands, at ease until further notice. It would appear that the sun isn't setting quite yet. XO out." She turned to Takahashi. "Ops . . ."

"Yes, sir." For once, even Romeo's somewhat loose attitude was firmed up, as if he considered anything other than full attention at that point to be in somewhat bad taste.

"I've got the nightside squared away. Would you be so kind as to adjust the auto wake-up calls for everyone on the graveyard shift as well. Let them sleep in until we know what time we'll need them."

"Aye, sir." Hash set about doing as he was instructed . . . but then he stopped. He turned in his chair to face the captain. "Sir."

"It's running late, isn't it," Kenyon said. He spoke with absolutely amazing control. If I were in that situation, I doubt I could have maintained such equanimity. "The signal."

"Yes, sir, it is."

"How late?"

"Four minutes, sir. Going on five."

"Could be in the middle of a fairly heated debate, sir," I pointed out. But I was already starting to get an extraordinary sinking feeling.

Kenyon was up out of his chair. "Mr. Cray, would you be so kind as to raise—what was their leader's name? Kradius. Get me Kradius immediately."

The moments that passed as Cray endeavored to do so seemed endless.

"Five minutes," Hash said.

"Nothing," Cray said.

"Nothing?" His voice sounded hard although his face remained impassive. "They're ignoring us?"

"Yes."

"Five minutes, twenty seconds overdue."

"Bridge to transporter room," Kenyon said without another moment's hesitation. "Lock on to transponder signal and beam them the hell out of there, now! *Now!* Bridge to sickbay. Villers, get down to the transporter room. Bring two emergency setups, just in case. Bridge out. Mr. Calhoun, you have the conn."

"Captain, with all due respect, I suggest you stay here. I'll go."

He spun and looked at me with astonishment. "Why?"

He didn't have to ask, and I didn't really have to reply. We both knew why. We both knew that, just in case something really, truly horrific had happened, the captain would not be in a position of coming unraveled in front of any of his crew.

The unspoken exchange hung there, and then he turned to Mueller and said, "XO, the conn is yours. Calhoun, with me." He headed into the turbolift and I quickly followed.

The moment the door shut behind us, he rounded on me with as much anger as I'd ever heard. "Don't you ever do that again."

"Sir?"

"Condescend to me. Imply that there's something I can't handle."

"I never said there was something you couldn't handle, sir," I told him. "But there are some things you shouldn't *have* to handle."

Before he could respond, his comm badge beeped. "Transporter room to captain."

He tapped it in acknowledgment. "Kenyon here. Go ahead."

"Sir, we've locked on to the transponders. Beaming them up now."

"Is Villers there?" asked Kenyon. Now that he was speaking to someone other than me, his voice was its calm, unflappable, normal tone.

"She's right here. She's . . ."

The transporter chief stopped talking . . . but the comm line remained open.

"Transporter room, go ahead. What's happening?" said Kenyon with growing urgency.

"Oh my God," came the startled gasp from the other end.

"Transporter room, report! Have you got them?"

But the transporter room made no reply. Instead there were shouts, alarmed voices, and above them all the sound of Doc Villers shouting orders. The words "Get them to sickbay!" came loud and clear over the comm channel.

Kenyon took no time to demand further updates. Instead he cut the link and snapped at the turbolift controls, "Destination override. Sickbay." The lift immediately reversed course and sent us to the sickbay. During the trip, no words were exchanged. We both stood there in apprehensive silence. Both of us alone with our concerns and prayers, and both of us having the sinking feeling that we knew what we were going to find when we got there.

The turbolift doors opened and we charged down the corridor. I was in the lead, practically shoving crewmen out of the way if they didn't scatter fast enough. Kenyon was right behind me, and actually doing a fair job of keeping up. We darted into sickbay, and Villers was waiting for us . . . waiting for us just inside the door, and blocking the way.

"Captain . . ." she started to say.

"Where is she? And he. Where are they? Are they all right?" There was no panic in his voice, no sound of desperation. His tone of voice was that of a superior officer demanding information of a subordinate. How he managed to keep himself together considering what was going through his head, I haven't the faintest idea.

And then, Doc Villers—her face a dispassionate mask—said the two words one never wants to hear in that kind of situation.

"I'm sorry."

Kenyon froze where he was. I put a hand on his shoulder, but it was numb. I doubt he felt it at all. Instead he said quietly, "I want to see them."

"No. You don't," said Villers.

"Show me."

"Captain, nothing will be served by—"

Kenyon didn't hesitate. "Doctor, you're relieved of duty. Dr. Ross, show me my daughter and brother, if you please."

Doc Villers looked as if she'd been slapped across the face. But then the chunky woman simply stepped aside and turned to Dr. Ross, a tall, narrow-faced, and somewhat stunned-looking assistant. She nodded to him and Ross said, "Uhm . . . this way, Captain."

Kenyon seemed to have forgotten that I was there altogether. Consequently, I followed him without a word as Ross led him to the back section of sickbay. There, on two med tables, were the bodies of Stephanie Kenyon and Byron Kenyon.

At least, what was left of them was there.

In my time on Xenex I had seen brutality in all its forms. This was not the worst I had ever seen, but it definitely ranked high up there. I didn't have any medical training, but there were electronic representations of their bodies up on the monitors, giving a fuller picture of their internal structure, and even I could see what had been done to them.

Quite simply, they had been beaten to death. They

had died brutally and horribly, their skulls crushed in, their bones shattered. There were rope burns on their wrists. They'd probably been stunned by blows to the head, and when they came to, their wrists being bound made it impossible to activate their transponders. There was blood everywhere, my God, it was everywhere. Their faces didn't look like faces, but rather like crimson masks. Stephanie's long hair was thick and matted with blood. Her mouth was hanging open and most of her teeth had been knocked out, as had Byron's. Their clothes were shredded, huge gashes laid open their thighs, the . . .

. . . I'm sorry. I need a drink. Excuse me.

You know . . . you'd think with everything I've seen, everything I've done . . . describing that wouldn't get to me. You'd think that, wouldn't you. You'd think enough time would have passed, that I could be more dispassionate. That I . . .

I think, for everyone, there comes a moment where they come face-to-face with their belief system. Something happens that is so ghastly, so calamitous, that you look not only deep into your soul, but to the being or beings who put that soul there in the first place. And you wonder if they're there, or if they're listening, or if they care about anyone and anything at all.

I think . . . I think that's when I lost my faith. Right then, right there. Oh, I have moments, I admit . . . moments now when I still pray out of habit. When I toss out a random request for help in a pinch. But in my day-to-day existence, in my endeavors to cope with each passing day, I have lost the conviction that there is some greater being watching over us. People don't usually have instant epiphanies, not really. What you usually have is a very small revelation, a tiny peek behind the fabric of our reality to see the gnawing, monstrous evil that hides behind it all. The darkness from which forlorn voices cry out in hopelessness and misery. It leers at you and knows with grim satisfaction that it can bide its time because, sooner or later, it gets you in the end. So it can afford not to worry.

Kenyon stood there, looking at the remains of his daughter and brother for a time. I kept waiting for him to scream, to rant, to moan, to cry . . . anything. To display some sort of reaction. But there was nothing, nothing at all. Instead he simply walked over to his daughter, took the blanket that was at the far end of the med table, and pulled it up and over her head to cover her. Then he went to his brother and did the same for him. As he did that, everyone in sickbay had lined up behind him, just watching. No one knew what to say. What could anyone say? "I'm sorry, Captain"? Something like that? How could any expression of sympathy even begin to approach the depth of agony that he had to be feeling at that moment?

His comm badge beeped and he tapped it. "Bridge to captain." It was Mueller's voice.

"This is the captain." I couldn't believe it. His voice sounded almost chatty.

"Sir . . . we received a reply, finally, to our hail to the Dufaux. It's from Kradius."

"Really. And what does he have to say?" He might have been discussing the technical aspects of tracing a warp signature for all the emotion that he was displaying.

"All it says is: Let that be a lesson to you."

"I see. Mr. Takahashi . . ."

Hash's voice cut in. "Aye, sir?"

"Hash . . . kindly arrange for the storage of two corpses. We'll need to make a convenient rendezvous for a cargo ship heading back toward earth. XO, if you wouldn't mind contacting the Kenyon family burial site. Inform them that we'll be having two new clients for them. Thank you."

"What? Capt—"

"That will be all. Kenyon out."

It was obvious to all of us that he was in shock. In comparison to what he was giving off, Vulcans were screaming mental cases. He rested one hand on the sheets which now covered his daughter and brother. "Go in peace" was all he said.

Then he turned and walked away from them with that same, confident gait he always employed. "Captain . . ." I said.

He blinked in apparent surprise. He *had* forgotten. He'd forgotten I was there. "Yes, Calhoun?"

"You . . ." Everyone was waiting for me to say something, and I didn't have a clue where to start. Then I noticed something as I looked down. "Sir . . . you have blood on your hand."

I indicated his right hand with a small nod. He held up the hand and looked at the crimson-tinged fingers in surprise. "I'll be. Must've happened when I pulled the blankets up over them."

"And on your comm badge too, sir," I said. "Must have happened when you replied to the hail, sir."

"Really." He looked down at the comm badge with only the vaguest interest. Then he removed it from his uniform jacket and flipped it to me. I caught it reflexively. "You can have it."

"Sir, it's yours . . ."

He wasn't listening. Instead he walked out of the

sickbay without another word, walking at a slow saunter and appearing for all the world like a man who was simply ambling down a peaceful street of a small town, perhaps heading down to the local eatery to chat it up with the other townsfolk. He gave no indication at all of a man who had completely cracked.

That, of course, is what made him so dangerous.

THE BLAME

I WALKED STRAIGHT INTO Kenyon's quarters and told him that he should relieve me of my position.

He was sitting in a chair in the middle of his quarters, just sitting there as if it were a command chair. He didn't move from his spot, but instead simply fixed a gaze on me like an owl in a Starfleet uniform. "Why would I want to do that?" he asked. Again, he didn't sound surprised or stunned or anything. He sounded crushingly, frighteningly normal.

"Because I fell into the trap that I should not have fallen into, sir," I told him flatly. "You needed me to be honest with you. You needed me to tell you everything that was going through my mind. The fact of the matter is that I wanted to tell you not to allow them to go down. I wanted to fight you on it every step of the way. You needed to hear me say that, and I . . .

I let you down. I was reluctant to contradict you because of . . ." I hesitated.

"Because of her," he finished. "You didn't want to risk embarrassing me in front of my daughter."

"More or less, sir. You . . . you gave me the opportunity to tell you what I really thought. You did so repeatedly. I should have ignored the dynamics of the interpersonal relations I was witnessing and gone with my instincts . . ."

"And your instincts said that the regs should have been ignored."

"Yes, sir. That's right sir."

"Don't worry about it, Calhoun." His voice sounded faint and distant.

"Don't worry about it?" I was pacing the room. "Captain . . . I was supposed to watch out for your best interests. And I fell into the same trap that everyone else here does. I went too easy on you. I didn't present enough of a challenge. I let you down, and her and him down, and now they're dead because of it."

"What are you looking for, Calhoun? Absolution?" He gestured in the air several times as if he were tossing holy water on me. "I give you absolution, my son. Go. Go and sin no more."

"Captain, I . . ."

"Calhoun, it's not your fault." His tone had changed, become more confident, even conversational. "The captain is the final decision maker on the ship. If I'd been of a mind to violate regs, or second-guess my brother and daughter, I would have done so without your endorsement. By the same token, if—and this happened to be the case—I hadn't been convinced that ignoring both the regs and their wishes was the proper way to proceed, not a hundred Mackenzie Calhouns could have convinced me otherwise. Calhoun, it's . . . Calhoun, look at me."

I was mortified. I felt an actual stinging in my eyes. I hadn't cried in years, not since the death of my first victim, and I was not about to start bawling at that point. I managed to pull myself together and turned to face my captain.

"Calhoun . . . what these people did, these Dufaux . . . they did this. Their leader, Kradius, did this. We, you and I, did not do these . . . these terrible things. We can chastise ourselves all we want for not foreseeing it, or not managing to get Byron and Stephanie to foresee it. But the bottom line is that, as much as we care to blame ourselves for not preventing it . . . that doesn't automatically mean that we caused it. Let us keep the blame placed where it properly should be: with Kradius and his people. And if the blame is to be placed anywhere besides there, then it should be upon me. Mine was the decision, mine was the responsibility, and yours was simply one voice in the crowd. Whether you feel you should have been tougher with me or not is truly beside the point. The same thing would likely have happened."

I stared at him for a long time. His face remained impassive, except for the hints of a small smile at the edges of his mouth. "How can you be so calm?" I asked. "With all respect, sir, how can you seem so . . . so unaffected."

"My reactions aren't really for public consumption, Calhoun," he said easily. "Whatever's going through my head, I prefer to keep it in there. Do I feel grief? Of course. But beating my breast in the presence of my officers is hardly going to be of any use to anyone, is it. We still have a job to do. We still have a peace to negotiate."

"A peace?" I couldn't quite believe it. "A peace? Between the Carvargna and the Dufaux?"

"That was our assignment, I do believe."

"Captain . . . you can't be serious. The Dufaux are—"

"Oh, I have no intention of meeting with the Dufaux," he said. "I'll be meeting directly with the Carvargna myself."

I began to get that same feeling of danger that I had earlier. "Yourself, sir?"

"I am the ranking officer, last I checked," he said in that same eerily calm tone. "Why? Don't you trust me, Calhoun?"

I had the sense that I was treading in an extremely dangerous area. Choosing my words as delicately as I could, I said, "It's . . . not a matter of trust, sir. You've had a terrible shock, a traumatic loss. Perhaps . . . this isn't the time to pursue a matter that could just as easily wait."

"Wait?" He raised a curious eyebrow.

"They were at war before we got here, and they'll be at war after we leave."

"You were talking to me about responsibility, Calhoun. Taking responsibility for lost lives. If people die because we delayed trying to rectify the situation, then aren't those lives on our heads? At least to some degree?"

"Captain . . ."

"Mac," he said gently, "I'm fine. Truly. I'm fine. Perhaps . . . well, perhaps I'm still in shock in many respects."

"That thought had occurred to me, sir."

"Well, you may be right. And that's fine. The human psyche lets us deal with things in our own way and in its own time. I'm willing to let that develop naturally. In the meantime, I have a job to do, and I'll be damned if I let this setback stop me from doing it."

The word rocked me. *Setback?* Saying that he was simply in shock was turning into something of an understatement. I didn't think he was dealing with any aspect of it.

"The best thing that I can do," he continued, unaware of what was going through my mind, "is complete Byron and Stephanie's work. They always—both of them—they always were concerned first and foremost with the grand scheme of things. I can . . ." He smiled. "You'll say I'm foolish . . . but I can hear their voices in my head."

"Haunting you, sir?" It was not a concept that I lightly dismissed. On Xenex not only did we believe in visions, but connections with those who were lost to us were not uncommon.

"Nothing quite that exotic," he said. "I hear them as one would hear the advice of someone who is dear to you. And they are telling me that the last thing they'd want me to do is allow this, their last mission, to go unfulfilled. Now, I know what you're thinking, Calhoun, and you needn't worry. I will be consulting directly with Starfleet on this matter. This is a situation of some delicacy, and I wouldn't want to do anything that could make matters worse. Any actions I take, no matter what, will be done with the full approval and backing of Starfleet command."

"Any 'actions,' sir? Actions . . . such as what?"

He smiled once more. "Trust me," he said.

That should have been the moment. Right there. Even as I tell it to you now, I see it with such blinding clarity that I cannot believe, in retrospect, that I didn't do something right then and there. But what could I have done? Tried to relieve him of command? Simply because he was saying he was going to get the job done? How insane would that have been?

Besides, my overall imperative at that point was to protect him, to be the best first officer possible and support him in whatever decisions he was to make.

Within me, though, my blood was boiling, and it wasn't simply out of concern for completing a peace initiative. I was appalled to the core over what had been done to them. And more . . . even during our brief time together, I had felt a connection with Stephanie that perhaps even went beyond what Elizabeth and I had had. I fully admit, I may be adding to it at this point with the intervention of years. I may be looking back at what was the most brief of encounters, which might have led to absolutely nothing, and imbuing it with a richness and texture that wasn't really there. But, as are all mortals, I am limited to telling stories by how I remember them. It's difficult, impossible even, to separate hindsight and wishful thinking from whatever the reality of the situation was. To the best of my recollection . . . the loss of Stephanie, in particular, and the brutal way in which she died, inflamed a desire for revenge in me such as I had not felt in years. But I could not let that flame touch the captain. He had greater duties to which he had to attend. He had to stand for something more. He had to be shielded from the hurt and pain and anger. I had to help him . . . but had no idea how to go about it.

And he seemed

So

Calm.

It was frightening in a way. Even before anything happened, before any of the subsequent events occurred, I felt cold, burning fear in the pit of my stomach. Not for myself, but on the captain's behalf. It was a fear that I spoke of to Mueller. It was one of those rare instances where we were together, relatively alone, and fully dressed. We were in Ten-Forward, huddled close in at a table. The *Grissom* was on its way to Anzibar II—not a terribly long voyage at that point, mere hours at most—with the captain busily arranging for a meeting with that world's leaders. Indeed, the only thing that was delaying us was the captain, who was, good as his word, taking the time to consult with Starfleet before taking any actions. He was also handling all contact with the Carvargna himself. Said it was his preference.

No one was paying any particular attention to Kat and me. Everyone on the ship was shaken up by the turn of events, and the captain's welfare was on everyone's mind. I spoke in a low tone, saying to Kat, "Something's going to go wrong. I can feel it."

"You're not implying that the captain can't handle the situation, are you?"

"I'm not implying anything. I'm just stating concerns, that's all. You've served with him far longer than I have . . ."

"Yes. I have. And let me tell you this, Commander," and she leaned forward so that our faces were only inches away from each other, "I trust the man implicitly. He is the most thorough professional I have ever known. If he says he can handle the situation . . . if he says he's on top of things . . . then I say he can handle it. I say you shouldn't worry."

Kat Mueller's words were exactly what I wanted to hear.

Unfortunately, that worried me even more.

As it turned out, later on we would both be changing our tunes.

THE MEETING

CAPTAIN KENYON had his first meeting with the Carvargna leadership . . . and I did not attend. No one did, except the captain himself, and Lieutenant Cray, who went along as security backup. And even Cray told me that, at the actual meeting, he wasn't present. Kenyon had kept the meeting behind closed doors with the Carvargna. I felt all of the worry, all of the concern, flaring once more. Unfortunately, there was little I could do about it.

Actually, there was one thing.

I sought out Dr. Villers while the captain was on the planet's surface. I found her sitting quietly in her office, off duty, but with half a bottle of synthehol situated on her desk. One did not have to be a master detective to figure out where the rest of the bottle's contents had gone.

"Doctor? Doc?"

She looked up at me, bleary-eyed. "Yeah?" Her voice was slurred.

"I need to talk to you about something kind of important."

Immediately she sat up, the intoxicating effects of synthehol falling away from her. That was, of course, one of the joys of synthehol. It was also, to my mind, one of the drawbacks.

"What can I do for you, Commander?"

Taking a seat, I said, "I need your input about . . . competency."

"Don't be concerned, Commander," she said calmly. "I admit, your socialization skills are somewhat lacking, but I hardly think you'd qualify as incompetent."

"I wasn't referring to me. I was referring to . . . to the captain."

She stared at me for a moment and then growled, "That isn't funny, Commander."

"I wasn't joking, Doctor. I am becoming . . . concerned about the captain."

"And I am becoming concerned about you, Commander, as of this moment. Captain Kenyon is a great man . . ."

"And he's had a great loss," I pointed out. "I just wanted your medical opinion—"

"Medical opinion." She picked up the bottle and tossed back another deep swallow. I was reluctantly impressed by her imbibing skills. "In order to form a medical opinion, I would have to give him a medical examination. On what grounds do you suggest I do so?"

"You don't need grounds. You're the CMO, and all crewmen must submit to exams upon your request. That includes the captain."

"That is a very broad-ranging power I have, Commander. Since power tends to corrupt, it is not one I exercise lightly. And when the captain is involved, I do not exercise at all unless I feel it's unavoidable. Just because the captain isn't mourning on a fast enough schedule for you doesn't mean that it's going to make me the least bit concerned."

"It doesn't have anything to do with me, Doctor. . . ."

"Are you sure about that?"

I eyed her suspiciously. "May I ask what that is supposed to mean?"

"It means no more and no less than what you take it to mean."

I felt myself starting to get angry, and I pushed it as far down as I could. "That's a bit too vague an answer to satisfy me, I'm afraid. You're implying something, and I'd like to know what that is."

"All right," said Villers. She pushed the bottle aside and sized me up. "I've worked with Captain Kenyon for a damned long time. He's the best officer, and the best man I've ever known with the possible exception of my third husband, and even that's iffy. The fact is, I already had a long talk with him earlier today. He feels the loss, he mourns it in his own way. But he is preparing to carry on in the professional manner to which I have become accustomed. You, on the other hand . . ."

"Yes? Don't hesitate, pray continue."

"You, Commander, are what I would term a 'loose cannon.' Your service record is impressive in its accomplishments, and you have your curious supporters. There are some who even compare you to James Kirk in terms of your command style. But these days are not those, Commander. I dislike cowboys. Cowboys get people injured or killed. That means more work for me. Not that I'm lazy, you understand, but a day where no one comes through my door is a day that I consider a good one. Your record is shot through with foolish chances that need not have been taken, and wouldn't have been if you'd attended to the regs. The fact that things 'turned out' for you is irrelevant to me. They might not have. I don't like your command technique, and to be blunt—"

"Oh, you've been tactful until now?"

"—to be blunt, I don't like you. And I don't like what you're doing now: trying to take advantage of the captain's loss to clear the way for yourself."

I felt my throat constricting in fury. The scar on my face burned, which indicated to me that it was turning darker red. That's what usually happened when I got angry. "Is that your interpretation?"

"It's *an* interpretation. It's certainly the one I'm drawing. If that is not the case . . ."

"It is not."

"Then you may want to reconsider your actions so that you don't suggest to others that you're simply an opportunist who will do anything to get ahead."

"If that were the case, *Doctor,* then hasn't it occurred to you that—rather than being a 'cowboy' and a 'loose cannon'—I'd be doing everything I could to toe the line of regulations so that I could get ahead? I wouldn't act upon my conscience, or depend upon 'curious supporters.' I'd be trying to build as wide a base of support as possible instead of taking the actions that I felt necessary."

"Well," and she smiled in a very unpleasant way, "perhaps you're simply an inept opportunist."

"And perhaps you," I replied, "are so blinded by loyalty that you're refusing to see a bad situation developing right in front of your eyes."

"At least," she said, "some of us *have* loyalty."

There are certain comments that could best be referred to as "conversation enders." That was definitely one of them.

I'm sorry. That went a bit further afield than I was expecting it to. What was I talking about?

Ah yes. The meeting.

The captain, immediately upon his return, called for a meeting to be held in the conference lounge. I was, as it turned out, the last one to arrive. Already present were the captain himself, of course, Romeo Takahashi, Cray, Doc Villers, Katerina Mueller, and Rachel McLauren. McLauren was the chief engineer. She was easily the most diminutive engineer I'd ever seen. Word around the engine room was that that was one of her special skills. She was so narrow that she could worm her way into virtually anywhere with no problem at all. Some folks kiddingly referred to her as the "pocket-sized engineer." I couldn't say whether they ever mentioned that nickname around her, and I can only guess as to what her reaction would have been if she'd heard it. She had a shaved head and thick red eyebrows. When she was studying a situation, her deep blue eyes seemed capable of plunging to the depths of any problem and discerning not only the difficulty, but the solution, in a matter of seconds.

"Thank you all for coming," Kenyon said briskly, and he nodded toward Kat. "Particularly you, XO."

"Not a problem, sir," said Mueller. With no hint of irony, she endeavored to cover a yawn with the back of her hand. "No problem at all."

"I know this is off-duty hours for you, Mueller. Ordinarily I would just have the computer deliver a précise when you come on duty, but the extraordinary nature of the situation requires, I think, extraordinary measures."

No one really salutes in Starfleet. This didn't stop Katerina from tossing off a tongue-in-cheek semi-salute. It came across more like a waggling of fingers in greeting than a stiff salute. Kenyon didn't seem to notice, or if he did notice, he didn't mind

"However," Kenyon continued, "I wanted all key officers on this at the same time."

"On what, sir?" asked Hash. "Did the meeting with the Carvargna go well?"

"Better than well. Better than great." He folded his hands neatly and said, "The leaders of the Carvargna want to cooperate with us in whatever way possible. I've spent a good deal of time with them. They're considerate, they're thoughtful. Their emphasis is on love and poetry. How can anyone find fault with that?"

"I don't think anyone is out to find fault, sir," said Mueller. "I think, though, we'd all like to see what the point of this is."

"The point is, they fight only because they have to," said Kenyon. "They are worthy individuals and deserve to have their population safe from the ravages of the Dufaux. We are, after all, familiar with the sorts of atrocities that they're capable of perpetrating."

"The plan?" Cray asked softly, cutting as always to the heart of the situation.

"Ah yes, the plan. After lengthy discussions with all concerned . . . it has been decided that we are going to assist the Carvargna with improving and updating the weaponry of their vessels."

Rachel McLauren blinked as if in surprise. "I'm sorry. What?" There was a brief exchange of glances around the table as if everyone wanted to make sure that everyone else was understanding the matter in the same way.

"The Dufaux have more advanced weaponry than do the Carvargna." The captain seemed happy to elaborate. "The supposition is that they stole it from other races. Ultimately, the hows and whys aren't all that important. We are going to help the Carvargna win this war and stabilize the entire area of space."

Now understand—then as now—Starfleet regulations have no greater challenger than me. I'll complain about them when I feel like it, ignore them when I have to. But even I was caught flat-footed by the bald-faced assertion of the comment.

"Sir, with all respect . . ." I looked around the table and saw mostly puzzled expressions. "Sir, can we *do* that?"

"We most certainly can . . . and with the UFP's blessing, I might add. Look, people, considering the circumstances, I know it's going to sound odd when I say: It's nothing personal here."

"Odd" was something of an understatement. I was spiraling way beyond baffled at that point.

"What I'm saying," continued Kenyon, "is that whether the victims had been . . . who they were . . . or total strangers, that wouldn't change the outcome of the response to the Dufaux's actions." His voice became hard, an undercurrent of anger audible. "They took two legitimate, authorized representatives of the Federation and they slaughtered them. Animals butchered for food die in more humane fashion than those two people did. They went down at the invitation of the Dufaux, and their lifeless bodies were sent back as a clear warning. A clear warning necessitates a clear response. The Dufaux have spit in the face of the Federation, and they will be brought to task for it. Now . . . do any of you have a problem with that?"

"No, sir," said Cray. Naturally he was the first to respond, but Villers promptly voiced her support as well.

McLauren was already working up the logistics.

"I'll just have to be careful not to give them too much too fast," she mused. "Last thing we need to do is jack up their weaponry to the point where they blow themselves up."

Kenyon turned to Hash expectantly. "Takahashi?"

"I'll prepare ship's services to provide any help it can," he said evenly.

"XO?"

"I'll coordinate with night and graveyard, Captain," she told him. "If you feel that round-the-clock is mandated, we'll be able to provide it."

"Good." There was a silence then. For me it seemed that it was a fairly long one.

Kenyon was waiting for my response. Waiting for me to chime in, either with a protest or a show of support.

I thought of how I had said to him that I would never contradict him in front of others. That support for the position of captain, and his long-term authority, was mandatory. I also thought of how my silence, my tacit agreement in his allowing Stephanie and Byron to go to the planet's surface, had set all of this into motion and cost two people their lives. If I spoke up now, lodged a protest, tried to block him . . . either way, in some aspect or another, I was risking doing the wrong thing. My choices were between one bad decision and another.

But I didn't know for sure that silence, that support, was automatically bad. After all, he had Starfleet backing on this.

I thought about Kirk.

Having been compared to him, I had felt it wise to study up on him, even beyond the required reading. There had been a time when Kirk faced a situation that was not dissimilar from what I was encountering now. A planet where two factions were at war with one another . . . and Kirk had discovered that the Klingons—our enemies at the time—were supplying one side with advanced weaponry. Well . . . relatively advanced. Flintlocks and such. So Kirk supplied the other side for the purpose of evening the score. Matters escalated and eventually Kirk, soured by the experience and feeling like a warmonger, pulled out. After he left, the tribe that he'd been backing was wiped out by the Klingon-supplied side. Ironically, with no one to fight . . . but with the advanced weaponry in their hands . . . the "victors" wound up turning upon each other, embarking in a power struggle that wound up wiping out every last one of them. Every so often, I still think about the Klingons walking among the corpses that resulted from their handiwork. Were they pleased? I wonder. Were they saddened? Did they care one way or the other? I would have liked to ask them.

But this situation . . . this one was entirely different. Kirk at least rationalized that he was simply giving a proportionate response to outsiders who had already interfered with the planet's development and business. Thus he was able to justify his actions. Here, in Anzibar space . . . we were the outsiders. We were the ones who were interfering. We were the Klingons . . . the enemy.

If we mixed in . . .

Then I saw Stephanie's bloodied corpse in my mind's eye. I saw Captain Kenyon, looking at me expectantly. I saw Byron that last time I'd seen him alive, insisting that a peace initiative was worth the risk. People always speak boldly of risks when, in their hearts, they believe that they're going to come out of a situation hale and hardy. I've faced death far too many times to have a limited sense of my own mortality, but there are many others who do have such a lack of perspective. Byron was one of them. And the Dufaux made sure that it cost him and Stephanie the ultimate price.

Even before my mind had fully wrapped itself around the problem and come to a reasonable conclusion, I heard my mouth say, "Whatever help I can provide, Captain . . . it's yours."

From the corner of my eye, I saw Doc Villers nodding with a small smile on her face. Perhaps she thought that I was just a cowardly little weasel who didn't mind going around behind the captain's back, but when put to the test face-to-face, I promptly sided with my commander. Perhaps she thought I had simply come around and she had "talked sense" into me. To be honest, I didn't care overmuch what she thought.

Instead my instincts led me to glance at Cray. I wasn't sure why yet . . . but I had the feeling that he might present the biggest problem.

Cray wasn't looking at me at all. That, in and of itself, was strange. After all, the captain had just addressed me directly, and I had spoken in reply. The instinct for anyone at the table would have been to be looking my way. But Cray was staring straight ahead, almost as if he were making a point of ignoring me. That, to my mind, did not bode well at all.

"What you can provide, Mr. Calhoun," said the captain, leaning forward eagerly, "is your expertise. I've been treading the spaceways a good few decades now. Lord knows I've been involved in my share of skirmishes. But I've never coordinated a war before. You have. For those of you who might be unaware," he said (and I might have been crazy, but it sounded to me as if he were speaking with a modicum of personal pride, as if he were a proud father), "the commander here, while still in his tender teen years, led an entire world to freedom as warlord of the Xenexians."

That was when Cray spoke. Always in that quiet, almost sibilant voice, he asked with what sounded like gentle mocking, "Should we bow?"

Kenyon didn't respond directly. Instead he continued speaking to me. "The Carvargna, as I've noted, tend to be a more peaceful race. They could use work on strategy, on coordinating attacks with limited resources. It's not as if we're going to be heading in there, leading an attack with the *Grissom*'s phasers blasting. . . ."

"We're not?" I tried not to sound surprised.

"No, Mr. Calhoun, we're not," he assured me. "We're simply here to help, not storm. Teach them. Guide them. Fill them in about basic strategy, about coordinated attacks, about air versus ground assault. You're certainly suited for it."

"As am I," said Cray. At that point, Cray was indeed looking at me. Somehow the unblinking stare I was getting from him was hardly mollifying.

"No slight intended, Mr. Cray," said the captain. "But I feel it would be best if Mr. Calhoun handled this. If he's up for it, that is. Are you . . . Calhoun?"

The challenge was unmistakable. This wasn't simply an assignment. He wanted to make damned sure that I was on his side. That I wasn't going to countermand him, or doubt him. He needed to know that he had my support going in. I'm not entirely sure why it was so important to him. Perhaps it was a normal, human instinct for him to have. All of us want approval in some form or another, even if it's from those we would consider to be our subordinates.

"Absolutely, sir," I said firmly. "Just tell me where and when, and I'll be there."

"Good!" He slapped the table and it shuddered slightly. "I knew I could count on you. On all of you.

And together," and he spoke more loudly, more boldly than I'd ever heard him, "we're going to show the Dufaux that there are some fundamentals of decency that are not tampered with, some lines that are not crossed. We're going to show them what the Federation stands for . . . and that to spit in the face of that is to pay a terrible price."

As for me, I couldn't help but wonder what sort of price we were all going to pay.

It's just that . . .

There's something you have to understand.

There are aspects of myself that I don't like. Aspects that I've tried to grow beyond.

As much as I draw upon the strength of my "barbaric" upbringing, part of me is almost . . . almost ashamed of it. That's always been a conflict that I've carried around within me. Wanting to move beyond what I've been . . . but finding it impossible to leave behind because I need it, depend on it.

I've seen the face of anger, the face of hatred, the face of revenge. I've seen it reflected in the eyes of men I was about to kill as they looked in fear upon me. I saw it reflected in the water of a stream, when I went to dry my face after sobbing over my father's execution. I've seen it mirrored in the faces of men who fought by my side, seeking to avenge themselves against their oppressors.

I didn't want to see it in Norman Kenyon. I liked and respected him too much for that. He deserved better than to be . . .

. . . to be me.

Then again, I've noticed that life tends not to cooperate with those things that are the most important to us. And ultimately . . . we cannot save those who do not want to be saved.

But if we are to go down, the least we can do is go down in flames. We all owe ourselves that, at least.

I'm sorry. I'm getting off topic and I was . . . distracted . . . a bit . . .

THE QUESTIONS

MICK GOLD, the officer at conn, was the first one to come to me.

Gold fancied himself a bit more of a maverick than he actually was. He tended to walk with such a pronounced swagger that Villers had taken one look at him and prescribed an ointment for his upper thighs on the assumption that he was having a serious chafing problem.

It had been several days since the captain had instituted what he had come to refer to as "the Initiative." We'd been working with the Carvargna to the best of both our and their ability. I had been somewhat underwhelmed by their military "leaders." They had been given the rank and the responsibility, but there was very little that they actually understood about the strategies and techniques of warfare. I walked them through some of the basics, gave them what I considered some required reading—everything ranging from the annals of Garth of Izar to Julius Caesar's *De Bello Gallico.* I will credit them that what they lacked in firsthand knowledge they more than made up for in pure enthusiasm. They wanted to learn. And it wasn't simply for the sake of trying to save their own skins (skins which were, I should add, a rather startling shade of green) but also, it seemed to me, out of interest in knowledge for its own sake.

Other than me, McLauren had the heaviest burden. The ship's weaponry that the Carvargna possessed was on par with simple disruptors. It was not even in the same league as the phase-generated pulsers the Dufaux possessed. The pulsers, in turn, were no match for our phasers, but the captain's instruction was not to arm the Carvargna with firepower beyond that which the Dufaux had at their disposal. "We want to insure that the Carvargna will be safe and capable," Kenyon had told us. "We don't need to arm them so heavily that they're tempted to abuse the armament and go elsewhere to display their new strength." In short, we didn't want to risk turning them into that which we were trying to combat.

I was stepping into a turbolift, on the way to my quarters, when Lieutenant Gold ran up calling, "Hold the lift!" I did so and he stepped in beside me. As the lift started to move, he turned to me and said, "Have you seen them?"

"Them?" I wasn't quite sure what he was talking about, and it was evident from the confusion on my face. "Them . . . who?"

"'Them' the orders from Starfleet."

For a moment I was still clueless, and then I understood. "You mean the orders that instruct us to aid the Carvargna."

He nodded. "Yup. Them."

"No, I haven't. Nor do I need to. The captain has said they exist and it's my duty to carry them out."

"It's your duty not to let something be pulled on you, sir." I have to admit, that's one of the things I liked about Gold. He never mucked around with such disclaimer phrases as "with all due respect."

"Do you have reason to believe that the captain is falsifying orders? Because, Mr. Gold, that is a very serious charge."

He looked at me for a long moment, and then said quietly—uncharacteristically quietly, in fact—"No. No, I have no reason."

"I see."

"I'm just the suspicious type."

"I see," I said again. "That being the case, you might want to consider rethinking your current career path and seek instead a career in security. That is certainly the environment for someone who is of a suspicious nature."

"Security is the environment for someone who obeys blindly and follows the captain right or wrong."

" 'Right or wrong'?"

"Look . . ." Gold shifted uncomfortably from one foot to the other. "I love a fight as much as the next guy. But I generally like to know what I'm fighting for. I feel badly about what happened to the captain's kid and his brother. Everybody does. And I don't even object to the idea of kicking in the teeth of the bastards what did it. But I just want to make sure that everything's on the up and up, that a proper course is being steered. It's just my nature, y'know?"

I couldn't blame him for being concerned. After all, I'd had a not dissimilar discussion with Doc Villers . . . and had been roundly shot down for my troubles. Now I found myself in the odd position of defending the captain from the very sentiments that I had been voicing not all that long ago. But there was no way that I was going to convey any doubts that I had—particularly when, as of this point, they were still unfounded—to a subordinate. It just wasn't right.

"I will take your concern under advisement."

"So you're not going to check."

"For the first officer to contact Starfleet directly," I said, "would be a circumvention of procedure." Something within me recoiled, horrified, at the rote sound to my words. I was actually falling back on regs to excuse behavior. What the hell was I coming to? Nonetheless, I continued, "Verifying orders, as if the captain's word were being doubted, would set off bells all through Starfleet. They'd want to know why anyone was questioning the captain's orders, what there was about the captain's conduct that warranted that type of concern. And if I don't have any easy answers for those questions, then I would not only be wasting the time of all concerned, but I would be unfairly undermining the captain with Starfleet."

"So you're not going to check," said Gold as if I had not spoken at all.

"Under. Advisement," I said.

The lift doors opened not a moment too soon. Gold stepped through them, turned, and tossed off a mock salute. The doors hissed shut, closing me back in and leaving me to wonder just who and what it was that I had become. Was I being concerned over how Kenyon would be seen? Or, as the prospect of my own command began to loom before me, was I suddenly turning into a conservative, line-toe drone who valued the Proper Order of Things above all else?

It was not a situation that I wanted to dwell upon.

Nor was there anyone with whom I could discuss the matter. After all, the core of the problem involved support for the actions of the captain. If I chose to try and converse with someone about the situation, I was then, by definition, undermining Kenyon . . . which is what I was trying to avoid doing.

Mueller also floated a question to me in a much more cautious fashion. I had just returned from one of my sessions with the Carvargna. Kat and I had just had some . . . recreation . . . and she turned over, her head lying on my shoulder, and she fingered my chest hair. "Are you sure about this?" she asked. Her voice was a low whisper, as if she was concerned that someone might overhear us.

"This? Yes . . . I'm, uh . . . I'm sure this is chest hair, if that's what you mean."

"I mean are you sure about the captain. About what we're doing."

I wanted to lie to her, tell her that the captain had my full confidence. That not for a moment did I doubt the rightness of our actions. Instead I replied honestly: "No."

She made a thoughtful noise in the bottom of her throat and then, without moving away from me, she said, "I'm not sure, either."

Considering the unswerving support she'd voiced earlier, perhaps that's why she would not go into detail, even though I gently coaxed her.

I should have coaxed her less gently.

THE TIME BETWEEN

NOW, FOR STORYTELLING PURPOSES, it would probably be ideal if nothing else happened at this point in my narrative. However, life has an odd habit of not working out in ways that best suit the needs of storytellers.

"Communiqué from Starfleet, sir," Lieutenant Cray reported after we had spent nearly two weeks instructing and teaching the Carvargna the fine art of war, and working to equip them in such a way that they would be more easily able to deal with their opponents.

I watched the captain's expression carefully to see how he would react to this news. He didn't bat an eye, but instead said simply, "I'll take it in my ready room, Lieutenant." He disappeared into there for some minutes.

I was waiting for him to come out and announce

that our instructions were to blow up the Dufaux. Had that happened, well . . . it would have been easy, then. It would have been so easy. But you know, the funny thing about the road to ruin is that you rarely stride down it. It's taken in small, delicate steps, and you don't realize how completely doomed you are until you're much too far along.

Kenyon emerged from the ready room. I tensed, as if I were preparing to take a shot to the head. Without saying a word, he settled into his command chair. "Cray," he said. He spoke more loudly than usual, as if he were calling across a large room rather than addressing someone who was positioned directly behind him.

"Yes, sir."

"Please get Barhba on screen for me."

Barhba was the Carvargna head counsel who had been mainly responsible for coordinating the *Grissom*'s efforts. In less than a minute after Kenyon had made the request, Barhba appeared on the screen. In some ways, he reminded me of Kenyon himself. Green skin, a head of hair that was similarly green, but lighter in color. Hash had said at one point that the Carvargna had reminded him of a broccoli stalk, only a bit more personable. Fortunately he had not said it within the earshot of Barhba, although for all I know, the Carvargna might have agreed.

"Honored Kenyon," Barhba said. "News?"

"Unfortunate, I'm afraid, my friend," Kenyon replied. "We have other assignments to which we must attend."

"Not unexpected." Barhba smiled with his green teeth, which was, quite frankly, a bit unsightly. Natural, but unsightly. "There are others who would benefit from your help. It is a large galaxy, after all. We appreciate the aid that you have given us thus far."

"I only regret," Kenyon said, "that our efforts were not able to lead to the peace that you so richly deserve."

"Perhaps not. But you have prepared us for the alternative, as undesirable as that may be. At the very least, the Dufaux would be wise if they did not attack us anytime soon. They know of the help you have given us, and would be most foolish to challenge us again."

"If they do . . . don't let them get away with anything."

"We will not. And my warmest regards to you, Honored Calhoun, as well."

I rose and bowed slightly, as was the custom of theirs that I had observed. "You have learned well the ways of war," I said. "Let us hope that you do not have to use any of them."

"That is always to be desired," said Barhba diplomatically.

And that, as far as I knew, was that.

The *Grissom* promptly set course for the Neutral Zone. According to Starfleet, there had been talk of a Romulan buildup at one of the outlying borders, and we had been asked to investigate it.

And we did. It turned out to be not the Romulans, but instead an Orion pirate fortification that was the beginnings of a possible alliance with the Romulans. The Orion pirate ring was smashed by our efforts, and of course the Romulans denied any knowledge of the Orions' becoming their allies.

We then headed for rendezvous with the transport that would be picking up the bodies of Stephanie and Byron. At the point where the transfer was made, a memorial service was to be held. Most of the crew attended. Only a handful of them had actually met either of the decea—

Had met Stephanie or Byron. Most of them attended out of respect for the captain and his grief. For a brief time, the captain contemplated taking a leave of absence to return to Earth and see their bodies back there, but decided against it.

I know I should say "home" instead of "Earth," since most people refer to it that way. Then again, I'm not from Earth. Oddly . . . I've discovered that I've stopped referring to Xenex as home. In many ways I . . . don't feel as if I have one.

I should feel sad about that, I suppose.

Hmm.

Ah well.

At the memorial service, Kenyon was the picture of calm. That alone was enough to ring a few warning bells in my head, but I said nothing. He was unfailingly polite and supportive, accepted all condolences with unfailing equanimity. Once during all of that, he glanced my way and—for some odd reason—winked at me. It was as if he was saying, Don't worry about me, I'm going to be fine. There's no problems on this end.

Understand, I wanted nothing more than for that to be the case. You see, well . . .

Hell, how do I put this.

In many ways . . . Kenyon reminded me of my father.

I know, I didn't say this earlier. I was afraid . . .

. . . well, I was afraid it would sound trite to you. Or you might feel sorry for me. "Poor Calhoun, spending his entire life looking for a father substitute." That's not it at all. It's just there was some physical resemblance, although not tremendous, but some. And in the way he carried himself, in his infinite patience, in . . . well, in any number of ways.

You'll think it's foolish.

Well . . . the hell with you. It's my story. And I'm telling you, that's how I felt. If that's not profound enough or deep enough for you, then that's your problem, not mine.

What I'm simply trying to convey to you is that . . . I've seen people change.

I saw my father as the oppression of the Danteri wore down on him. I saw him become angry, more bitter, more defiant. I saw those attitudes drive him, consume him, until the final confrontation that saw him beaten to death in the public square.

So I was alert to it, looking for signs of it in the captain as well.

The thing is, when you look for something, more often than not you find it.

After the memorial service, we embarked on assignment after assignment. Much of it was routine, a couple of them had an element of danger. As for the captain . . . he was . . .

. . . he was different.

It was in small ways, at first, subtle ways. Nothing that anyone would really notice or pay attention to if they weren't looking for it. I was. He seemed shorter-tempered to me than before. Angrier. He stopped greeting people by name as he made his way down corridors. Previously one of the more sociable of men, he tended to keep more to himself.

I sensed problems.

I'm not a telepath, or a Betazoid. I spoke to the ship's counselor at one point, a decent enough fellow named Nugent who had several degrees in counseling and was, by all reports, a very good listener. Like Dr. Villers, Nugent had also taken time to speak with the captain, and he likewise came away from the meetings positive that—although Kenyon was understandably grieving over the loss of his daughter and brother—he was coping with it.

I wanted to believe it. I wanted to believe it more than I can possibly express. I wanted it so much that in large measure I forced myself to believe it. Certainly the captain seemed testier, more easily angered, but so what? The professionals believed that everything was going to be okay.

And who was I to judge? I am the first to admit that I don't always have the healthiest outlook upon the world. There is a layer of anger that boils within me just below the surface that is always there. It colors everything that I do, everything that I perceive. We all come into any given situation carrying our own experiences, which help to shape our viewpoints, and my experiences were certainly more traumatic than most.

The savage M'k'n'zy of Calhoun, the one who never doubted himself, the one who was confident in his convictions, was coming squarely up against Mackenzie Calhoun, trained by Starfleet to accept the rules, obey his superior officers, shut up and do the job. It was easily one of the most uncertain times of my life. I was completely torn inside . . . and the problem is that it's only now, with the distance and cool assessment that only the passage of time can provide, that I fully understand what my problem was. At the time, all I knew was that my instincts, upon which I had always depended, were in turmoil.

I let things progress.

My curious nonrelationship with Kat Mueller continued, neither advancing nor regressing. It just . . . was. In some ways, there was as much passion in our time together as there would have been in running a few brisk miles. In sex between two genuine lovers, the lovers complete a need within each other. We were fulfilling a need within ourselves. Not the same thing at all . . . but it was satisfactory, it was good exercise, no one was being hurt by it, and neither of us wanted or needed more. At least, that's what we told ourselves, although every so often the image of Stephanie

Kenyon would float to me unbidden. Once I even accidentally cried out her name, but Kat didn't hear me. At least, I like to think she didn't.

I tried to approach the captain on a social basis. Not that I suggested we date or something like that. But I spoke of going for drinks in Ten-Forward, or engaging in some sort of absurd holoadventure in the holodeck. Each time, though, I was politely but firmly rebuffed. "I have work," he would say, or "I have other things on my mind right now, Calhoun," or even more simply, "Another time, perhaps."

And so time passed.

Then it all fell apart.

THE RETURN TO ANZIBAR

"INCOMING MESSAGE from Starfleet, sir."

"In the ready room, Mr. Cray," said Kenyon.

It was no different than any other time . . . and yet, for some reason, it felt different to me. I found myself looking around at the others on the bridge to see whether, for whatever reason, they were reacting to it in the same manner. It was as if I had seen a ghost and was trying to determine, without making too big a fuss over the matter, whether others had seen it as well. But there was no reaction. No one seemed to think anything of it, and I began to wonder why I was reacting to it the way that I had. It was as if I was looking for trouble.

This time, when Kenyon emerged from the ready room, he seemed different, more energized than I had seen him in ages. He cast a quick glance at Cray, and then said, "Calhoun, conference lounge, five minutes.

Mr. Cray, Mr. Takahashi, Mr. Gold, you too." He walked out without another word.

That Cray and Hash were being summoned to a meeting was more or less standard operating procedure. But Gold did nothing to hide the momentary surprise. What, he clearly wondered, could require the presence of the conn operator?

I looked to Cray. "Any idea what that was about, Lieutenant?" I asked.

He simply shook his head. No reason he should know. Most communiqués from Starfleet were strictly between the captain and headquarters.

Five minutes later, we had assembled in the conference lounge. Also present were Kat and Villers, Kat—as usually was the case in these circumstances—rubbing the sleep out of her eyes. Fortunately enough, Mueller had become accustomed to being roused from sleep at odd hours. She had developed the ability not only to come to full wakefulness at a moment's notice, but also to nod off just as quickly. I'd seen her do it. She'd tilt her head back, close her eyes, and be asleep just like that. Most impressive, really.

"Mr. Gold," said the captain, "you are to set us a course for the Anzibar system."

Gold looked as if he thought he hadn't quite heard the captain properly. "Anzibar, sir? Weren't we . . . weren't we just there?"

"Yes. And Starfleet has ordered that we return."

"Why, sir?" asked Mueller. She looked puzzled.

Kenyon, in a surprisingly sharp tone, said, "Are you questioning orders, XO?"

It took a bit more than a jarring attitude from the captain to throw Katerina Mueller off stride. "No, sir," she replied, utterly composed. "Merely curious as to the circumstances that engendered them."

"Yes. Of course. We . . . have been asked to check back with the Carvargna. The Dufaux have apparently been making serious noises about a new, even more concentrated strike against the Carvargna. Starfleet simply wants us to make our presence known. To let the Dufaux know that we're . . ."

"That we're what, sir?" I asked when no immediate completion to the sentence seemed forthcoming.

He looked at me as if his mind had been light-years away, and he forcibly pulled himself back to the conversation at hand. "That we're there. That we're watching. That we're aware of the types of people that they are, and that we're not prepared simply to abandon more innocent lives to them."

"Captain . . . what are you saying?" Mueller asked slowly. "Are you saying that we're going to . . . attack . . . ?"

"Attack? No! No, of course not!" Kenyon laughed. It was a jarring laugh in that it was eerily evocative of the genuine, full-bodied laugh he'd once possessed . . . except there was something missing from it. Mirth, perhaps, or a genuine sense of joy. "We do what we're ordered to, XO, and nothing beyond that. Come now . . . I'd think you'd know better than that."

"Yes, sir. I do," said Kat. The message was clear . . . at least to me. She knew better. She was wondering whether he did.

"Mr. Gold," Kenyon said as if the matter were settled, "I'll want you to stay on full alert once we're in Anzibar space. You too, Mr. Cray."

"Yellow alert, sir?"

"I don't think it's necessary to put the entire ship on yellow alert, Lieutenant. I just want you and Mr. Gold to keep a particularly close eye on sensors, and on lookout for anything that is the least bit unusual. The Dufaux are a crafty and deceitful race, and we should not take anything for granted. I don't think they'd hesitate to attack us in any way they could, if we give them half a chance to do so. Half a chance is twice as much as I want to provide them. Understood?"

Cray and Gold both nodded, although Gold looked more than a little puzzled. I wasn't entirely surprised. It wasn't as if Gold wasn't always keeping a weather eye out for any possible threat. Same with Cray, although he was far too stoic to allow any of his thought process to make itself evident. Cray maintained his usual careful deadpan.

We returned to our respective stations and Kenyon said, "Mr. Gold, set course for the Anzibar system. Warp factor five.

"Aye, sir." After a moment's work, he said, "Course laid in, sir. Warp on line."

And then . . . silence.

Kenyon sat there for a time, and then he realized that we weren't on our way toward Anzibar. It took him a moment to grasp why that would be. "Why, Mr. Gold," he said in exaggerated surprise. "Why don't you have us under way already?"

"I . . . thought you would want to order it yourself, sir."

Gold's voice was carefully neutral. It was impossible to read what was going through his mind. Kenyon's eyebrows knit for a moment as he tried to see if Gold was somehow being difficult or insubordinate, or for that matter simply a smartass. But Gold's face was impassive, and besides, what could Kenyon possibly accuse him of? Daring to follow protocol?

"Very well. Punch it, Mr. Gold."
"On our way, sir."
The *Grissom,* in response, leaped into warp space and headed out for her last mission under the command of Captain Norman Kenyon.

THE ATTACK FLEET

"OH . . . MY GOD . . ."

It was Hash who whispered it in amazement, and since the reserved Southerner was usually somewhat unflappable (the most drastic a response he ever made was usually a prolonged "Wellllll"), it had to be a fairly impressive sight to get that kind of reaction out of him.

It was indeed.

All around the world of Anzibar II, there were ships. This was not simply a scattered assortment. This was a fleet. For a moment I was pleased to see that, as I had taught them, they were flying in protective formations. But that pride was short-lived as the enormity of what I was seeing hit me. They were clearly prepared to go to war. And something about the timing of the whole thing was hitting me very badly.

I looked to Kenyon to see his reaction. He seemed as startled as any of us. "Mr. Cray," he said, "raise—"

"Head counsel Barhba calling," Cray interrupted.

"Great minds," murmured Kenyon. "On screen."

Barhba appeared moments later on the screen. He looked slightly different than he had last time I'd seen him. Before, he'd been dressing in muted colors. Now he was wearing something bolder, brighter. He seemed—although I might have been imagining it—more challenging.

"Honored Kenyon," he said. "It is good to see you once more."

"We need to talk, Barhba. We need to do so now."

"For you, Honored Kenyon? Anything. I would be happy to bring you and any associates over to my flagship."

Flagship. Yes, yes I could see from his surroundings: He wasn't on the planet's surface anymore. He was in one of the ships. I had the oddest feeling it was the biggest one.

"Captain," I said quickly, "perhaps it would be best if I—"

"We will be right over there to talk, Honored Barhba," Kenyon said. He was already on his feet. "Takahashi, get the coordinates for beaming over. Cray, with me. Calhoun, you have the conn."

I spoke with more urgency than before. "Captain, if I could have a moment before you—"

He faced me and anger practically radiated off him. "Calhoun, we may not *have* a moment. I'm going to go over there and find out what's going on. I need a battle-experienced veteran at the conn, because for all we know, the Dufaux are going to attack at any moment. Now do you have any problems with that?"

"No, sir," I said tightly.

Without another word, Kenyon and Cray walked off the bridge.

There was a long silence then, and I realized that every eye on the bridge was upon me.

I had said I would support the captain. I had promised him.

To hell with the Dufaux. They'd killed Stephanie. There was no reason, I figured, that I should give them a moment's more thought.

"Attend to your stations, people," I said. I moved over and stood next to the command chair, but didn't sit. "Stay frosty. We have no clear idea what's happening yet . . . which means anything can happen." After a moment's more thought, I added, "Hash . . . take us to yellow alert."

"Yellow alert, aye."

Ensign Barbosa had stepped in at tactical. "Go to weapons hot, sir?"

I considered it. "No. I want people on station, but let's not run the full gamut yet. Not until the captain returns . . . and hopefully tells us what's happening."

We stayed that way for half an hour. The time seemed to crawl past. The yellow-alert klaxon had been sounding, but after about five minutes of that unbelievably irritating noise, I ordered status maintained but the alarm shut down. I'm not entirely certain what sort of signal I would install on a ship to indicate a yellow alert, but it would definitely be something other than the headache-inducing wailing we presently have.

After what seemed an interminable wait, Captain Kenyon and Lieutenant Cray returned. Once again we all met in the conference lounge . . . and this time, I was stunned by what Kenyon told us.

"They're launching an attack on Anzibar Four," Kenyon informed us.

"They are? And Starfleet picks now to send us here?" noted Mueller. "How's that for a stroke of luck."

"Yes, I know," agreed Kenyon. He was speaking in such a carefully neutral tone that it was impossible to get any sort of impression as to how he felt about the development. Before any of us could react to that tidbit of information, though, he then added the bombshell follow-up: "And we are going to be part of the attack fleet."

Mueller was first on her feet. *"What?!"*

"Sit down, XO."

"Captain, you can't be serious!"

"Mueller," I spoke up. She looked to me and with a flicker of my eyes I indicated that she should take her seat.

"We're not actually going to participate in the attack . . ." continued Kenyon.

"Captain, come on!" It was now Gold who was speaking. "If we're converging on the Dufaux and the shooting starts, are we supposed to just let stray shots ricochet off our shields? It's ridicu—"

Kenyon slammed a fist down on the table with such explosive force that we all jumped. None of us had ever seen him display that level of anger. *"I am not accustomed to being interrupted repeatedly during a briefing, is that clear!"*

No one said anything. There were nods of several heads, and I felt—rightly or wrongly—that everyone was looking to me. "Clear, sir," I said, speaking on behalf of all of us.

"Good." Kenyon didn't seem especially mollified. "The Dufaux have made repeated attempts at warfare during the time that we've been gone. The Carvargna have resisted their repeated incursions, mostly thanks to the aid that we gave them. But the leadership has come to the realization, as difficult a conclusion as it may be to reach, that the Dufaux are never going to stop coming. That they will continue to attack and attack, to wear down the armaments and energy of the Carvargna.

"And so the Carvargna have assembled a fighting force. A force composed not only of their own vessels, but other ships from nearby systems. They've formed alliances as a means of mutual protection, for they are certain that—should the Dufaux eventually triumph and obliterate the Carvargna—nothing will stop them from spreading their campaign of war to other worlds. They have chosen to end it here and now. It is, frankly, a decision that I can respect and support." He paused and surveyed us around the table. It was almost as if he was daring us to say something, to try and find some flaw in what he was saying. We were all mute. It seemed the wisest course.

"I have emphasized to High Counsel Barhba that we cannot actually join in the battle. We will not violate the Prime Directive. But I'll . . ." He hesitated. There seemed to be just the slightest crack in the veneer of toughness that he had created for himself. "I'll tell you something, people, and this is the brutally honest truth: I want to be there. I want the Dufaux to see this vessel, a symbol of everything that they turned away from, coming right down their throat surrounded by an army of vessels arrayed against them. An army composed of people who have said, 'No more. Enough. Enough mindless warfare. Enough callous disregard for life. We have decided to put an end to you and your kind.' This . . ." He waved a hand in the general direction of the fleet outside. "This is one of the most glorious days in the history of the Carvargna. Until now they have been largely victims. But they have refused to allow that to continue. Instead they have risen up with the confidence, weaponry, and guidance that we gave them and they are going to rid themselves of a pernicious threat once and for all. And people, I intend to be there for every minute of it. Every glorious minute. Is it petty of me? Perhaps. Vindictive? If you say so. But these people, these Dufaux . . . they are evil. Evil in its purest form, violence at its essence. I want . . ." His voice choked slightly. It was the first time he'd shown any vulnerability since the death of those whom he had loved so dearly. "I want to see them brought down. We're being offered a front-row seat for it, and I, for one, intend to occupy it. Now . . . do any of you have any problems with that?"

There was a long moment of silence.

"Permission to speak freely, sir?" said Mueller.

"Absolutely."

"I think it's sick."

Kenyon blanched. Villers's mouth thinned to the point of invisibility. Gold and Hash looked as if they'd been gut-punched, although it was difficult for me to tell whose side they were on. Cray was his usual deadpan.

Mueller was up and moving. "We're supposed to stand for something, Captain. This crew, this ship . . . we're supposed to stand for something bigger than death and carnage. War is, at best, a necessary evil, but evil nevertheless. If we are to be any different than the Dufaux, then we should not be rejoicing in their downfall. We should be mourning for lives and wasted opportunities. Not in a 'front-row seat,' rejoicing over the fall of a foe like star-going ghouls. We should not—must not—do this thing. Faced with possible annihilation, the Dufaux might be willing to talk . . ."

"No more talk." It was Cray who had spoken.

"The time for talk is long past," agreed Villers. "If it could have been settled by now, it would have been. I'm with the captain on this. You, XO, weren't the one who had to pick up the pieces of Stephanie and Byron Kenyon—sorry, Captain."

"It's all right," said Kenyon.

"I, uhm . . ." Hash said slowly, his drawl becoming even more pronounced, "I . . . well, the XO, what she's sayin' and all . . ."

"Spit it out, Romeo," Kenyon said impatiently.

"Look . . . me and the XO, we never seen eye to eye all that much, but I gotta say, she's making a piece of sense here. Captain, if you and the Carvargna, perhaps y'all could . . ."

"Could what? With the Dufaux seeing a sizable opposition coming their way, they'd have nothing to gain by fighting. They'll want to negotiate a peace, which they'll toss aside the moment that the alliance has been disbanded. In fact, the next time they attack, they'll come at the Carvargna harder than ever because they won't want to take a chance that another attack force might be mounted. Certainly you must see that."

"We're going to be pulled into a fight," Gold spoke up, shaking his head. "We can talk about not violating the PD all we want, but let's not kid each other. We're going to be smack in the middle of it."

"Not up to the challenge?" asked Kenyon.

"It's not a matter of that, sir," Gold said, bristling. "It's not a question of whether we *can,* but whether we *should!*"

"My God." Kenyon looked around the table, making no attempt to hide his disbelief. "An innocent man and woman died because the Dufaux cannot be trusted! The peace-loving residents of the Anzibar system have allied themselves to say, 'Never again.' We have to bear witness to that achievement! Anything else would be an insult to all they've achieved! We owe it to them! And to . . . to *them!"* None of us had to ask for clarification as to who the second "them" was. Suddenly he turned to me. "Calhoun . . . your thoughts on the matter?"

All eyes turned to me.

I never felt more alone in my entire life. It wasn't as if a vote were being taken: ultimately the captain would do as he saw fit. But my opinion was going to carry weight. If there was anyone who might be able to dissuade the captain from this course of action, it would be me.

And, of course, there was the other, more dreaded aspect. Namely, if there was anyone who was in a position to challenge the captain's authority in this matter, it was also me. It was the first officer's responsibility to take action if the captain was not making competent decisions.

My instinct . . .

My instinct was to go with what Mueller and the others had said. Everything about this smelled wrong. I had a feeling that we were heading into nothing but disaster, and it was within my ability to put a stop to it, quickly and cleanly. At least . . . I thought it was.

But I looked at the captain, and I realized for the first time that his eyes were very much like Stephanie's. I could almost sense her looking out at me from within him.

I've told you that, to Xenexians, ghosts and shades of the past are very real considerations. That remained the case with me, particularly at that moment. I felt as if the ghost of Stephanie had moved into the room and was just watching me, judging me.

They were murderers, the Dufaux were. Murderers and oppressors. Any number of arguments could be made for why they weren't worth shedding a tear over. . . .

But should the *Grissom* be there? Should it be on the scene? Kenyon had more or less said it himself. This was no longer about a mission of peace. This was a mission of war . . . more, it was a mission of vengeance. Blood lust and an urge to see a hated race suffer close-up were the motivators that were driving Kenyon now. It wasn't worthy of him, it wasn't worthy of the *Grissom*.

When I led Xenex to victory over the Danteri, I had always felt . . . outside of myself to some degree. As if I were being impelled by the dictates of a history already written: I was merely a player in the grand scheme of things, my presence preordained, my victory assured. I felt as if I were part of something that was greater than myself, greater than any individual. One of the main reasons that I had joined Starfleet was to be in an environment where that state of mind would be perpetuated. Starfleet, the UFP, these were bigger than any one person. To pilot the *Grissom* into a war zone purely as a means of witnessing personal revenge . . . it was . . . it was petty. It was the desires of one person overwhelming what Starfleet was all about.

But who was I to make those judgments? I was not the one who had lost his family . . . well, not recently at any rate. It had never been more clear than now that the loss had been eating away at Kenyon. He needed this, needed to see it, to be a part of it. Otherwise he would never have closure. It needed to be finished for him so that he could move on with his anger, move on with his life.

And ultimately . . . what was the harm? Really, when it came down to it . . . what was the harm? Starfleet had ordered us out here. There was no intrinsic reason that we shouldn't be witnessing firsthand the end of the hostilities in the Anzibar system. Stephanie would see it through the eyes of her father, I was positive of that. See it and smile in relief that it was over, and that those who had killed her and her uncle had paid the price.

All of this went through my mind within a second or two. There was a barely perceptible hesitation before I said, "I'm with you, Captain."

Kat looked at me as if she'd been slapped. "What? You can't be serious. . . ."

"I just don't see the conflict here," I lied. I saw the conflict perfectly well, but was choosing to try and finesse my way around it. "The Prime Directive is not at issue. We aren't instigating this battle; the Dufaux have started it, and the Carvargna have finished it. We will simply observe. It's no different than if we were watching a star die."

"You're right," Kat Mueller said. Her chin was raised high and she seemed very cold, very distant. I had the sneaking suspicion that sex wasn't in our future anytime soon. "It isn't different. Because a dying star can become a black hole . . . and we're being sucked deep into something dark and unpleasant, and there's not going to be any way out of it. You mark my words."

Looking back on it, I still don't know which to be more impressed by: that Katerina was the first person I'd ever met who used the phrase "mark my words" in normal speech . . . or that Katerina was absolutely, one hundred percent right.

The meeting broke up shortly thereafter, the growing tide of resentment and protest by the junior officers having been unexpectedly quelled by me. "Thank you, Calhoun," the captain said, clearly grateful. "I thought it was going to start getting ugly in there."

"Do me a favor, Captain: Don't let it get ugly out here."

He patted me on the shoulder. "Just leave everything to me," he said confidently.

I felt the hair on the back of my neck stand on end. My hair was brighter than I was.

I ran into Mueller on the turbolift. Katerina wouldn't even look at me. "Kat . . ." I started to say.

"I think," she said thoughtfully and with just an edge of disgust in her voice, "it would be preferable for the moment if you simply addressed me as 'Mueller' or 'XO.' "

"Kat, it's going to be fine. Don't you think that, if I didn't believe that, I would have stood up to the captain?"

She was only supposed to be an inch taller than me, but it felt as if she was looming over me. Impressive how she did that. "So you admit you backed down from him."

"No . . . well . . . I suppose, but . . . no, I didn't. You're twisting it, Kat."

"What's twisted is this situation, Commander, and I'm frankly shocked and disappointed that you can't see that."

"I'm not refusing to see anything. I just don't happen to agree with your sentiment in this matter. This is important to the captain. Didn't you ever have anything important to you?"

"Yes. I did. And it died several years ago," she said. "Under rather ugly circumstances, too. But I didn't risk an entire Starfleet vessel to make up for it."

"You're exaggerating."

She looked up and said, "Turbolift, override. Halt." Immediately the lift car came to a halt.

"Am I? Where am I exaggerating? He's risking the saucer section, but not the warp drive? He's risking the lives of the crewmen, but only the boring ones? Where and how have I exaggerated?"

"Don't lecture me, *Kat.* It wasn't all that long ago you told me you trusted him completely."

She sighed. "Don't remind me." She looked me in the eyes. "Deep down, you know what to do. But you're being kindhearted. In others, that would be a laudable ambition. But it doesn't fit you well, Mac. Do you know why?"

"Why." I didn't really want to know, but I had a feeling she wasn't going to let the question go.

"Because you're not a nice guy, Calhoun. That's why. You're not a nice guy, and every time you try to be a nice guy, it gets you into trouble. Well, the captain doesn't need a nice guy riding herd on him. He needs a son of a bitch. He needs a bastard to sit him down and say, This isn't our fight. We're a starship, a Federation starship, and we do not hover over a field of battle like filthy vultures, displaying our appreciation for the rapidly growing stack of bodies. That's what you should have said, that's what he needed to hear from you. From his first officer. The warrior that I encountered in the holodeck wouldn't have been afraid to hurl himself against his commanding officer for the good of the ship and the Fleet." She paused and, to my surprise, regarded me with curiosity. "That reminds me . . . I never got around to asking you. In the holodeck, you shouted something. *'Rakash,'* I think it was. What was that?"

I was almost relieved that the subject had switched away, however momentarily, from my shortcomings as a first officer. "A Xenexian war cry. It means, 'To the hilt.' When faced with an opponent, the concept is that you won't back down until your knife blade is buried in the body of your enemy up to the hilt."

"Charming." She nodded a moment, and then we simply stood there for a time.

"Are you . . . planning to send us on our way anytime soon?" I asked.

"Oh! Uhm . . . turbolift. Resume." The lift promptly started up again.

"So are . . . we okay?" I asked. "You and I?"

"Us. No . . . no, Mac. I think we're light-years away from okay. Because the bottom line is that I know you agree with me. You know that vengeance diminishes us all. . . ."

And for a moment, my temper flared. I stepped in close to her and suddenly she didn't seem taller than me anymore. In a low snarl I said, "I never managed to find the man who beat my father to death, or the man who ordered it done. If I were captain of a vessel, and the opportunity presented itself, I would cross the galaxy from one side to the other just to have a shot at crushing their windpipes with my bare hands and feeling the slowing and stopping of their pulse against my palm. You speak of necessary evil? One of those necessities is that if innocents must suffer, the guilty must suffer more. And the warrior that you so respect can empathize completely with what the captain is going through."

The door hissed open behind us. Without taking her eyes from me, Kat said evenly, "Then I guess the captain and you are well matched at that. A far better match than you or I could ever be."

The door closed and I was so angry that it took me a few moments to realize I'd gotten off on the wrong deck. I was on the deck where my quarters were situated. I'd meant to go up to the bridge.

I stood there, stewing. And as occasionally happens

at such times, my mind started wandering in different directions. I thought about what Mueller had said, even though I didn't want to . . . and then, more to the point, I thought of something very specific she had said. But it wasn't during our turbolift ride. It was something earlier, almost a passing remark back in the conference lounge. . . .

THE LIE

AND STARFLEET PICKS NOW *to send us here? How's that for a stroke of luck.*

Kat's offhand comment had thrust itself into my consciousness. It was beginning to bother me greatly the more I thought about it.

Here was an entire battle fleet ready to strike at Anzibar IV, and we showed up just in time to be there for the kill. It seemed . . . too coincidental. Too convenient. Of course, it was possible that somehow Starfleet had been aware of the buildup, had known the timing of it when they sent us in. If that was the case, then Kenyon simply hadn't been completely forthcoming, or perhaps he didn't even know. Perhaps it was just damned good timing, luck of the draw.

But perhaps it wasn't. Perhaps it was something else, something even more sinister.

I went to my quarters, convinced that I was being paranoid. As I entered, my combadge beeped at me. It was the captain, demanding to know where the hell I was. "A . . . momentary illness, sir," I told him. "I'm just taking some quick medication for it. I'll be there in a few minutes."

"See that you are, Commander." The captain sounded slightly mollified, but not overjoyed.

"Computer," I said as soon as I got to my quarters.

"Working," came the crisp reply.

"Access communications log, reference Starfleet communiqués."

"Starfleet communiqués communications log is confidential under security seal," the computer informed me.

"Security seal override, by authority of Calhoun, Mackenzie, first officer, security clearance zero-zero-one-zero-one."

"Processing." There was a pause of only a second and then the computer said, "Override accepted."

I couldn't get into specifics of messages addressed to the captain. Those were under direct seal of the captain himself and inaccessible to anyone with the exception of a board of inquiry composed of the top three officers below the captain. But I didn't need to get into what the message said . . . at least, not yet. One potential crisis at a time. "Read out of time for all Starfleet communiqués received within the last forty-eight hours."

"Working." And again, after the briefest of pauses, the computer informed me, "No Starfleet communiqués received within last forty-eight hours."

The sentences, damning, hung there for a moment. "None at all?" I said.

"Affirmative."

"Check again."

I have no idea why I said it, but I did. Naturally, it

made no difference to the computer. It simply repeated, "No Starfleet communiqués received within last forty-eight hours."

Cray had been the one who claimed that a communication had come in.

He'd lied.

There was going to be hell to pay, and I had every intention of collecting that debt. But first the captain had to be notified . . . and then, *grozit* . . . this would be straightened out once and for all.

THE CONFRONTATION

I WALKED ONTO THE BRIDGE and looked straight at Cray. He didn't even bother to glance at me. I didn't think he was aware that I knew what he had done; I was reasonably sure that his own security board would not have informed him that I had been researching his comm log. I glanced at the screen and saw, as I suspected, that we were already under way. The attack fleet surrounded us as we made our way toward Anzibar IV. Obviously it was not going to take us a long time to get there. That meant I had to speak to the captain quickly, because if Cray had faked the message from Starfleet, then who knew what else he had lied about. Perhaps he was a spy, I thought. At the very least, he was a traitor. It was a good thing that Andorians weren't telepathic, or I would certainly have been giving him a mental earful right about then.

Kenyon looked at me with clear concern. "Are you quite all right, Calhoun?"

"We need to speak privately, sir. Now."

"Calhoun, it will have to wai—"

"It can't wait, sir."

"What the hell is wrong with you?"

"Sir. Privately. Now."

There was something in my voice that got through to him, that let him know that this wasn't simply some casual conversation we were about to have. "Mr. Cray, you have the conn," he said. This was obviously not a choice that thrilled me overmuch, but I didn't want to say anything just yet. It would be okay; the situation could stay as it was another few minutes and it wouldn't be especially problematic. At least, that's what I was hoping.

Kenyon didn't look any too pleased as he walked into his ready room with me trailing directly behind him. He didn't even bother to go around his desk. Instead he turned to face me as soon as the doors were closed. "This had better be good, Calhoun."

"Good? By no stretch of the imagination, sir." I took a deep breath and launched into it. "Lieutenant Cray has been giving you false information."

He raised an eyebrow. "Really?" His voice didn't go up at the end of the word. It wasn't a question so much as an interested statement.

"We have received no communications from Starfleet command within the last forty-eight hours. So any claims to the contrary—including the orders that we received to come here—are false. Mr. Cray lied about any transmissions from HQ."

"And you know this how?"

"Ran a check from my own computer station, sir."

"Used the security block override protocol, did you."

"Yes, sir." I nodded.

He didn't seem particularly upset. Indeed, he seemed almost amused by it. He leaned back and stroked his chin thoughtfully. "And what do you recommend we do. About it, I mean. About Mr. Cray."

"I'll inform a security squad that they should come up here and place Mr. Cray under arrest. I also recommend that we tender our regrets to high counsel Barhba and depart this system immediately. We don't know for certain what Cray might have cooked up, but for all we know this is some sort of ambush. I simply need your authorization to have him taken into custody."

Kenyon pursed his lips and said nothing.

And something began to dawn on me.

It came to me very slowly. Indeed, it's rather embarrassing to admit to it now. To look back on it after all this time, it seems fairly self-evident. But at that point I was far more "in the moment," carried away by the current of events. But in Kenyon's attitude, in his demeanor, something began to click for me. I couldn't quite believe it. I certainly didn't want to. But there were particular conclusions which were slowly starting to seem inevitable to me, whether I wanted to arrive at them or not.

Taking a chance that maybe, just maybe, I was fortunate enough to be completely off the mark, I said, "Sir . . . I see you're preoccupied. That is very understandable. I'll attend to Mr. Cray's arrest myself, then."

"I . . ."

I waited for the rest of the sentence.

"I . . . wouldn't," he finished ruefully.

I nodded. All was becoming clear to me. "Cray . . . didn't fool you about anything, did he."

He shook his head. Amazingly, he almost looked proud of me that I had figured it out.

"He wasn't betraying you," I continued. "He was providing you with an alibi. You needed witnesses to see that the message had come in from the Fleet."

"That's right."

"Because you wanted to come back here. You knew this was going to be happening ahead of time."

He nodded. "Barhba and I worked out a timetable."

"Grozit . . . and the previous message? The one that said we were supposed to help them?"

"We received a message from Starfleet, yes." He shrugged, clearly seeing no reason to hide the truth anymore. "It indicated that we were to stay on station here for a short time more, yes. But for the purpose of trying to reestablish peace talks. Can you imagine?" He shook his head in clear amazement. "Peace talks . . . with those animals . . ."

"So you took it upon yourself to arm and educate their enemies instead."

"They're animals," he said again. I might as well not have been in the room.

"You took it," I said again, underscoring the severity of the situation, "upon yourself . . . to arm and educate—"

"THEY'RE ANIMALS!"

It was fortunate that the ready room was soundproof so that they couldn't hear that one outside, because people would have come running in with phasers drawn in consternation.

The anger, the misery that previously had only been hinted at in the earlier meeting was nothing compared to what I saw in Kenyon's face now. Blind, savage fury had completely taken hold of him. His body was quaking, and there were tears pouring down his face, his mouth contracting in a rictus of a scream that wouldn't come out.

"They killed my brother . . . they killed my baby . . . those animals, they'll pay," and he kicked over a chair, *"they'll pay, those bastards, I'm going to make them pay!"*

It would have been the exact perfect time for me to keep my cool. The angrier he got, the more reserved I should have become.

When you punch someone, it's never a good idea to make a fist and hit them on the chin. Bone on bone. Always a bad tactic. Good way to hurt yourself.

Meeting anger with anger is nearly as bad. Unfortunately, that's exactly what I did.

"You lied to me!" I shot back. "I supported you, I trusted you, and you lied to me! You and Cray! You brought Cray in as an ally to cover for you, and all of it so that you could pursue your witch-hunt against the Dufaux! How dare you!"

"How dare *I?* This is no witch-hunt, Calhoun! This isn't a search for evil where none exists, where innocent people are hurt because of superstitious nonsense! These monstrous animals don't deserve to live! And I'm going to see them wiped out!"

"To the last man, woman, and child? Every innocent will die. . . ."

"There are no innocents! The men are slaughterers, the women aid in producing more of the men, and the children will grow up to be butchers in their turn!" His voice was rising to a fever pitch and I knew then, beyond any dispute, that if he wasn't already clinically insane, then he was hurtling there fast with no brake in sight. "It's a mercy killing, Calhoun! I'm showing mercy for the entire sector!"

"You're crazy," I told him. "You've completely snapped . . . your loss, everything that's happened since . . ."

His face was purpling with rage, the veins distending on his forehead, and he was trembling with uncontained fury. "They killed my little girl. They do not deserve to live, *and I will not suffer them to live, and even if I have to tear out their living hearts with my bare hands, I will see to it that they don't!"*

"You lied to me!" I said again. "You used me, you set me up to support you out of concern and kindness and wanting to see justice done, and then I find out that it was all a lie! You scheming son of a bitch!"

"How *dare* you!" he thundered. *"How dare y—"*

He hit the desk again, and the entire ship shook.

For one insane moment I actually thought that he himself had caused it, even as I tumbled to the floor. Kenyon had been leaning against his desk and stumbled against a bulkhead, but as a result he wasn't thrown to his feet. He lurched out of the ready room, me following him in a rather undignified fashion, hauling myself forward on my hands and knees and staggering upright as I went.

The red-alert klaxon was screaming as Kenyon shouted, "Status report!"

"Dufaux battle fleet attacking, sir!" Gold called.

The screen was alive with ships. Whereas the Carvargna and their allies were in relatively large, not-terribly-maneuverable vessels with lots of firepower, the Dufaux were in smaller, faster-moving vessels. Like hornets they descended upon the fleet, buzzing about and firing with their pulsers.

In previous circumstances, the Carvargna fleet would have been more hard-pressed to stave them off. But the shield improvements had made them nearly invulnerable as far as the Dufaux ships were concerned, and the armament they were carrying was targeting and picking off the Dufaux ships. However, many were slipping through and still causing damage. Credit the Dufaux: They certainly knew how to fly.

"They're firing on us," Gold called. "Apparently

they're unaware that we're just the cheering section." If there was one thing that Gold wasn't particularly skilled at, it was subtlety.

"Get us out of here!" I called. "Retreat to a safe distance. . . ."

"Belay that!" Kenyon shouted over me as two more Dufaux vessels took potshots at us. Our shields were rattled but they held.

"Incoming message from the flagship, sir," Lieutenant Cray called. He was addressing Kenyon, but he was looking straight at me. He had to know. He had to. "They've taken several heavy hits. Hit to the engine room. Pulsers off line. Barhba is asking for our assistance."

Kenyon didn't even hesitate. "We're not about to stand by and watch good people die at the hands of barbarians. Target the Dufaux vessels near the flagship, Mr. Cray. Fire on my order."

"Belay that."

It was I who had spoken, and what was impressive was just how quiet a bridge can become even when there's a red-alert klaxon blaring.

Kenyon stared at me as if from another universe. There were no hints of the tears that had been streaming down his face. Amazingly, he looked more composed than I'd ever seen him.

"Mr. Gold, plot us a course to a safe distance," I continued. "Captain Kenyon, I regret that I must relieve you of command. If you stand down now . . ."

"If I stand down now . . . you'll what?" he asked quietly. "Not have me arrested? You seem to forget, Commander, who's in charge here. Mr. Cray . . ."

"No . . ." I said.

"Fire at will."

"No!"

The *Grissom*'s phasers lashed out in the direction of the flagship. Our weaponry, more powerful than the

Dufaux's, more powerful even than what we had given to the Carvargna, made short work of the Dufaux vessels that they struck. Two were sliced completely in half, another was blasted into space dust.

"Again," Kenyon said.

"No!" I lunged toward Cray, in order to shove him back and away from the tactical station.

It was exactly what the Andorian was waiting for. I never even saw his hands move, he was that fast. All I knew was that suddenly what felt like a ten-pound weight slammed against the side of my head. It was his fist. It whipped my head around and I felt a muscle pull in my neck even as light exploded behind my eyes. Then his other hand smashed my upper lip, and I tasted my own blood between my teeth. I stumbled back, hit the floor and lay there for a moment, the world spinning around me even as I heard the ship's phasers blast out again. More Dufaux died at our hands.

The rest of the bridge crew was stunned, unable to believe what they were seeing. At the time part of me was angry that they weren't springing to my defense. In retrospect, I can see the problem. They didn't know what I knew. They didn't know that Kenyon had lost it. They didn't know that he was pursuing a vendetta, as justified as that need for revenge might seem. They didn't realize that, after decades of service, he was throwing it all away because the voices in his head had cried for vengeance so loudly that they had drowned out everything else, including reason and sanity.

Gold was trying to watch the front screen, his instruments and me. Hash's mouth was moving but I couldn't hear his voice, which meant either I'd gone deaf or he was whispering. Considering the ringing in my head, which was aggravated by the red-alert klaxon, it might have been a little bit of both.

"Security team to the bridge," Cray was saying.

I'm not entirely sure where I drew the strength from at that moment. But suddenly I was on my feet, and I gripped the railing, swung my legs up, and vaulted over the railing with the intention of slamming my feet into Cray's face. Cray was too quick. He ducked under the sweep of my legs, came up before I'd completely cleared him, and threw me into the wall behind him with such force that I was positive that he'd just broken my face. Certainly it was numb down the entire left side.

From below, Kenyon called, "I regret you've forced me to take these actions, Mr. Calhoun. You were a good officer. I'm sorry it's come to this."

I propped myself up on one elbow and looked at him through an eye that was already swelling shut. And the weird thing was . . . I could see it in his face. He *was* genuinely sorry that it had come to this. Although his face was set and determined, in his eyes was more misery than I had ever seen in any sentient being in my life. It was as if a decent and moral man was trapped inside of the individual who inhabited the name and body of Norman Kenyon. Trapped and unable to find a means of communicating *Help me . . . I'm still here . . . I still exist . . . I'm still alive . . . help me, please . . .*

Had I not been spitting up my own blood at that point, I might actually have felt really sorry for him.

No one ever accused me of knowing when to quit. I started to pull myself to standing once more. This time Cray didn't even have to exert himself (although truthfully, I don't know if he'd been working up much of a sweat up to that point). The Andorian reached out with one foot and brought it down on the back of my head.

Fight him! It was the savage within me, shouting in my mind. *Fight him! Get him! Kill him! Rip him to shreds, the blue-skinned antennaed bastard! Don't let him do this to you!*

But I had no room to maneuver, no weapon in my hand, and he had been far too efficient in his physical dismantling of me. At that point my entire goal was simply to try and get away, to regroup.

I heard the turbolift hiss open. Several security men entered.

"Commander Calhoun has attempted mutiny," Kenyon said. "Take him and toss him in the brig."

I tried to say something—anything—but I couldn't even stand up. Hands were beginning to reach toward me . . .

. . . and then I disappeared.

THE REPRIEVE

THERE MAY HAVE BEEN times in my life where I was more confused than I was at that moment, but none leap readily to mind.

One moment I was on the carpeted floor of the bridge . . . and the next thing I knew, I was on the platform of the transporter room. My senses were so confused that the floor itself wasn't my first tip-off of my location. Rather, it was the fading hum of the transporter beams.

I raised my head slowly in confusion and looked up. My head was throbbing and I couldn't see beyond my immediate field of vision . . . that is, I could see straight ahead, but everything to the side was just a fuzzy gray area. "What's . . . ?"

The face of Katerina Mueller filled my entire vision. "Mac . . ." she called to me. Her normally stern face was filled with such worry that for a moment I was concerned that I was dying. I didn't think anything else could get that sort of reaction from her. "Mac . . . can you hear me? Say something. . . ."

"You look . . . really lovely from this angle . . ." I told her. "Did they build a tunnel in here?"

"Don't stand up until you feel you're ready to." Then, to my surprise, she pulled off my combadge, tossed it on the floor, and slammed her heel down on it. I heard the badge shatter under her foot. She turned back to me and saw the obvious surprise on my face. "You know why I did that, of course."

"Well . . . if I'm remembering the custom correctly . . . according to Jewish law, we're now married."

"Very funny."

"I wasn't trying to be funny," I said.

"You succeeded beyond your wildest hopes." As I lay there tending to the wound left by the thrust of her rapier wit, she turned to the woman, Lieutenant Melissa Shemin, at the transporter. "Now . . . you didn't see this, Melly," she said flatly. "We weren't here. In fact . . . now would be a good time for you to go on your break."

Lieutenant Shemin shook her head and smiled in an amused way. When she spoke, it was with a faint British accent. "You realize, Katerina, if this were anyone but you . . ."

"I know, I know."

Shemin looked at me and then winked, much to my surprise, before heading out the door. By that point the world was beginning to lose some of the haze that had pervaded it. "What was that all about?"

"She would have flunked out of the Academy if I hadn't helped her out."

"All right," I said once the ship had stopped spinning. "Tell me what happened."

I was seated on the floor, rubbing the throbbing that remained in my temples. Katerina slid down the wall until she was seated next to me. "You can thank Hash," she told me.

"I thought you never called him that."

"I do from now on. Through the ops board, he told me what was happening. I got to the transporter room while you were having the crap kicked out of you and beamed you here."

"Maybe they'll think I was beamed out of the ship completely."

She gave me a pitying look. "Perhaps you were hit in the head harder than I thought. We're on red alert, remember? Battle situation? Combat? People shooting at us?"

I thudded the back of my head lightly against the wall. "Of course. Our shields are up. No one could possibly beam me out. Which means that they'll know I'm somewhere in the ship and . . ."

We stared at each other. Her unflappable demeanor, her somewhat superior attitude, slipped for a moment as she realized the immediate problem.

"Shit!" we said at the same time.

We were on our feet in an instant. She pointed at the wall. "That grating . . . pull it out. Fast."

"That's just a storage bin! It doesn't go anywhere!"

"I know that." Her hands were flying over the controls. The transporter beams were humming into existence. I didn't understand what she was doing, but I obediently yanked open the storage bin. There would be enough room for the two of us if we squeezed in tightly enough. The transporter beams faded out. Mueller barely waited for them to disappear and then she crammed her way into the storage bin. She clambered over an array of boots and other equipment. "Hurry!" she said. "I hear them coming!"

I heard them as well. We had perhaps a few seconds at best. I pulled the bin covering closed and prayed that it was tight enough.

We could hear, but not see, the noise from within the transporter room. From my rough guess, there were at least four security men stomping around in there. "Check activity," came a voice that I recognized immediately as security man Meyer. "Once we finish here, we check the other transporter rooms."

"Should we be searching the rooms themselves, sir?"

"As if Calhoun and whoever bailed him out would be stupid enough to stay around chatting in the transporter room," Meyer said.

I had a feeling that Katerina was rather pleased at that moment that it was dark in the storage bay. That way she didn't have to look at my pitying expression.

"What the hell is going on in here?" It was Shemin's voice. She'd come back in.

"Where were you, Lieutenant?" Meyer did not sound particularly in a forgiving mood.

"Checking the section 28-A flow regulators. They sounded a bit off. It happens even to the best of us."

"We're on red alert. You abandoned your post during a red alert."

"Great idea, Meyer. I should stay at my post and let the flow regulators break down, on the off chance that someone shatters the laws of starship physics and beams something through our shielding. I took three minutes that may have saved our lives. You don't like it, go tell Starfleet to build the ship differently."

"Transporter activity less than a minute ago, sir," one of the security men said.

"What? That's impossible." Shemin came across as utterly shocked. She might have missed her calling; she was a damned fine actress.

"See what happens during your absences, Lieutenant?" Meyer scolded her. "Destination?"

"Utility shaft, deck thirteen, section four."

"Beam them back, Shemin."

"Beam who back?"

"Commander Calhoun!"

I heard her operating the transporter controls for a moment, and then she said, "I'm trying to get a transporter fix on his comm link. I'm not getting anything. Perhaps it . . . wait! Look there, on the floor. Someone crushed a combadge. Bet it was him. Without his combadge, I'll never be able to sort his pattern out from everyone around him . . . particularly if he makes his way down to engineering from there. With all the neutrino fluctuations from the engines, I can't possibly get a lock on him. This equipment wasn't really designed for—"

"Okay, okay! We get the message. Let's go. Shemin . . . you're on report."

"I'm devastated."

We heard the receding footsteps of the security team as they ran out the door, with Meyer already informing Cray, via comm, of our presumed whereabouts. We waited until they were safely gone, and then kicked open the storage bay. Shemin jumped at the noise, then she gaped at us. "What are you doing here?"

"Don't mind us," I said. "We were stupid enough to stay around chatting in the transporter room."

"Give me a break, will you?" demanded Mueller. "I'm nightside, okay? I just woke up. I haven't had any coffee yet. You're damned lucky I even remember your name."

"Well I just got kicked in the head!"

"Shhhh!!!" hissed Shemin. "Excuse me! But I don't need to be found out as an accessory to attempted mutiny! I don't know about you, but I can think of better things to do than spend the next ten years in the Starfleet lockup! So will the two of you please shut up! Or hasn't it occurred to you they might have left someone nearby to guard against your return, and if you raise your voices too loud, he's going to come in here with phaser blasting?"

It hadn't occurred to us, actually.

"All right. Tell me what happened," Mueller said.

I told her, in as quick and concise statements as I could manage. She listened carefully, never interrupting, and finally shook her head in slow amazement. "Incredible. We have to get word to Starfleet. This situation cannot continue."

"The problem is—"

At that moment, we heard the captain's voice throughout the ship. "All hands . . . remain at battle stations, but you are to keep an eye out for Commander Mackenzie Calhoun. Mr. Calhoun, acting in defiance of Starfleet orders, has attempted to take over this vessel by force. His attempt has been beaten back, but he is at large and apparently has allies in his cause. It is possible that he is under Dufaux influence."

"Oh, terrific," I muttered. "Why not say I'm a disguised Romulan while I'm at it."

"All personnel are to maintain sidearms at all times. If Commander Calhoun is seen, do not hesitate to fire. Phasers on stun unless deadly force is absolutely mandatory."

"This is just getting better and better," Mueller said.

Shemin was studying her board and frowning. "What did you beam to the utility shaft? You couldn't have just activated the beams; it wouldn't have read into the log as a transmission. You'd never have fooled them.

"Air," said Mueller. "Air has mass, weight. I simply sent a chunk of air to the shaft." She turned to me. "Thoughts?"

"All right," I said slowly. "None of the command staff, with the exception of Hash, knows that you're involved, and he can't tell anyone without tipping himself off. So he's in. I think you should proceed as normal at this point."

"As normal? There's nothing normal about the present situation, Mac."

"I know. I need you to, very quietly, get a feel for what's going on out there. We can't let the captain continue in this manner."

"What 'continue'? From what I hear, we're helping to destroy the Dufaux. It won't go on for much longer."

"Trust me . . . it will. Once the desire for vengeance fully gets going, there's no stopping it. Believe me, I know. Find out who, if anyone, is backing up the captain . . . particularly on the command crew. Check with your people especially. Night shift might not have the same attachment to the captain as the day shift does; they work with him so much less. As for graveyard, hell, they might not even know the captain's name."

"What about you? They might come back here once they find you're not where they think you are. They're going to tear apart every square inch inside this ship."

I thought about that a moment . . . and then looked at the storage bin, looked at the equipment that was in there.

"You're probably right," I said. "Which leaves one logical alternative."

As it turned out, Mueller was right once again. Within ten minutes another security team was back at the transporter room. Shemin, however, was one of the more ingenious transporter operators we had, and she'd been able to rig the transporter log so that its most recent beaming transmission had disappeared from the records.

Which left yours truly, Commander Mackenzie Calhoun, in an EVA suit, clinging to the rear of the saucer section of the *Grissom,* watching the demolition of the Dufaux fleet.

THE SLAUGHTER

IF CAPTAIN KENYON thought he had a good seat for the dismantling of the Dufaux fleet, he should have seen mine.

From my position outside the saucer section, I was able to see everything.

What was eerie was the silence of it all. I mean, explosions naturally don't make any noise in space. But when you're on a bridge and you're witnessing a battle, there is at least all the noises one comes to expect from within the starship itself. The talking, the sounds of the instrumentation, even that annoying red-alert alarm. But I was on the ship's exterior, in a Low Pressure Environment Garment, and the only noise I heard was the sound of my own breathing. Oddly, that can be one of the loneliest sounds in the galaxy.

I had magnetic boots on the LPEG, of course, to aid

me in adhering to the hull. Moreover, there were magnetic grasping plates in the palms of the gloves. Normally one did not want to spend excessive time outside in the LPEG. The advantage of the suit was that it was lighter in weight and more easy to maneuver in than the more high-powered Standard Extravehicular Work Garment, or SWEG. The problem with the LPEG was that it provided far less protection than the SWEG, since its simple multilayer construction gave it almost no protection against such hazards of space as micrometeoroids and radiation. But at least at the moment, as long as the shielding remained in place, that would provide me all the protection I needed. Besides, the LPEG was what had been in the storage bin of the transporter room. It wasn't as if I'd had a lot of choice.

High above me the shielding glowed in place around the ship. Naturally nothing could beam beyond that point . . . but there was nothing that prevented the transporter being able to move someone from inside the ship just to the other side of the hull. All in all, it was actually a fairly devious place to hide. It wasn't the type of place that anyone would generally think to look. Moreover, a starship is pretty damned big. Noticing one person against the ship's exterior would be quite a challenge, even if you were looking for them.

So there I clung to the ship and watched the slaughter.

The *Grissom* was still firing on Dufaux ships. I had to admit that Kenyon and Cray made a fairly formidable team. With Cray marshaling the security forces, and Kenyon finding ways to justify his actions, they were virtually unassailable.

The Carvargna forces assumed the bulk of the work and responsibility. They assaulted the Dufaux from all sides, making certain not to let themselves be drawn out of formation. They divided the Dufaux vessels from one another, cutting them off and assailing them individually or as small, easily controllable units.

But helping to herd them all together was the *Grissom.* Sometimes the starship fired warning shots that drove them toward the Carvargna squadrons. Other times they simply opened fire directly on the ships themselves. Space was alive with bursts, like fireflies battling one another in coordinated fury. Every time I saw the *Grissom* responsible for another Dufaux vessel erupting in quickly-snuffed-out flames, my heart would die a bit more.

There were so many ways I wanted to explain what had happened to Captain Kenyon. He had been . . . I don't know . . . possessed. Possessed by an evil free-floating creature. Or perhaps he'd been replaced by an evil twin. A shapeshifter had come aboard the ship, that was it. A shapeshifter who was impersonating the real Kenyon. Even better . . . not only was this not really Captain Kenyon, but evil shapeshifters had impersonated the corpses of Stephanie and Byron as well in order to make the entire charade seem more credible. They weren't really dead, but instead being held captive by the Dufaux, who themselves were part of an insidious plot . . .

And so on, and so on.

How nice that would have been. How gloriously involved, and wonderfully dismissive of the realities of life.

Would that it were that way, or had been that way.

Because that way, you see, I wouldn't have had to deal with the truth of it. And the truth of it is that sometimes good people go somewhat crazy.

We all have the darkness in us. No matter how good, how decent we are, there is the beast residing within us, waiting to get out. I know, because he lurks within me, never far below the surface. The violent, brutal being I tapped into for the purpose of freeing my people. I made extensive use of him for a very long time, and then, when I tried to bottle him away, he did not go quietly or willingly. To this day he rumbles around in my head, spoiling for a fight. I try not to indulge him.

It's not as if he's my personal demon. He's in you. He's in all of us.

James Kirk wrote an autobiography, you know. Much of it was dismissed by critics as a collection of tall tales. Some believed that Kirk had a penchant for exaggerating. Outrageous stories of planets of sorcery, or confrontations with Greek gods or Abraham Lincoln, or the removal of his first officer's brain (which some more waggish commentators claimed was not so extraordinary, considering that there were ostensibly any number of Starfleet officers for whom such a loss would not make any noticeable difference). Many felt that the reason Kirk's legend was so phenomenal was that he himself took great pains to build it. Some referred to him as the Baron Münchausen of space, and the fact that his friends and officers backed him up was written off as simple personal loyalty.

I never believed that. Never believed it for a minute. Because space is vast and unknowable, and it's the height of presumption to consider any aspect of it and toss it aside as unbelievable. Once upon a time, to the people of Earth, the idea of beings from another planet was preposterous. Yet here I am. To some, the very notion of this place, the Captain's Table, would likewise be considered absurd. Yet here we are, telling stories.

Stories.

I'm getting off track. I'm sorry. Why did I start talking about Kirk . . . ?

Oh. Yes.

There was one particular thing that Kirk wrote that stuck with me, that truly hit home for me. He was writing of officers he had met who, as he put it, had "lost the vision." They had forgotten what they were supposed to be, what they were intended to represent. He encountered several of them in his career: Captain Tracey of the *Exeter,* who—not unlike Kenyon—used advanced weaponry to interfere in a planet's local politics. Or Captain Merrick of the *Beagle,* who brought his crew, one by one, down to a planet's surface to fight in an atmosphere reminiscent of Roman gladiatorial bouts. Another man, a historian rather than an officer, named John Gill, who reshaped an entire world into Nazi Germany. One of his own men, Lieutenant Kevin Riley, who attempted to kill a man he suspected to be a war criminal. A commodore—although he didn't name him for some reason, but just described him in general terms—who completely lost his reason and started taking reckless chances when his entire crew was killed in a confrontation with an alien artifact. A few others, I think.

The thing is, Kirk said that whenever he encountered someone like that, he saw something in their eyes . . . that seemed to stare back at him. He would think of all the vast power that was at his command, and the number of times he himself played reckless games with the principle of noninterference in order to suit his own ends. That things turned out well for him oftentimes seemed as much a matter of luck as anything else. I remember exactly what Kirk wrote on the subject:

"I'd look into their eyes and see the choices they made . . . and not only would I be able to understand how and why they made them, but I could also—on some level—see myself doing the same thing. I'd like to tell myself it could never happen. It might have, though. We like to think that we would behave in a consistently moral and worthy manner, and it's only the others, the failed others, who fall by the wayside. I think that's too simplistic, though, and too denying of human nature. Every time I look at one of those fallen from the vision of Starfleet, I cannot help but say to myself: There, but for the grace of God, go I."

I doubt that there is a God, or gods. But if there is, then He exists as a divine spark in each of us. That spark had been lost in Captain Kenyon. He had turned away from it, turned away from himself.

Like Kirk, I knew the feeling. I knew what was going through his mind, knew the tragedy that he was experiencing. There was no alien invasion of his soul, no fiendish doppelgänger. He had instead succumbed to the darkness within us all. His loss . . . was a diminishment to all of us. Darkness and loss, grief pervasive and everlasting. To be so low in one's soul that the light which guides us is forever extinguished, or at least so it seems.

There, but for the grace of . . . whatever . . . went I.

And I was determined to bring him back from that. To pull him out of the abyss. Perhaps because, in a way, to help him would be to help myself.

Cray, on the other hand, I wanted to beat the crap out of. Nobility of motive only goes so far, after all.

I had a lot of time to think on such matters as I clung to the outside of the ship.

One by one the Dufaux fell. In my imagination I could almost hear Captain Kenyon laughing in joy over the disaster that had befallen the slayers of his daughter and brother. I could only hope that the Dufaux leaders—particularly the one called Kradius, who had sent the defiant message to the *Grissom*—had already died in the assault. If they still lived, and the opportunity for further revenge came into Kenyon's possession, it would be a terrible, terrible thing.

The *Grissom* advanced, meter by meter, along with

the rest of the fleet. In short order, we were within range of Anzibar IV. That was when the true horror began.

The fleet started firing upon the surface of Anzibar IV. Whereas before I had fancied that I heard Kenyon's laughter, now I was hearing the screams of those countless millions below. The fleet surrounded the planet, firing from all sides. I lay there helplessly, watching it all. The *Grissom* was not one of those raining destruction down upon the world itself. My suspicion is that even Kenyon knew he couldn't push matters that far. The entire bridge crew would likely rise up in protest if he attempted that. But even though he wasn't attacking the planet directly, his was still the responsibility. He had made it all possible, had galvanized and focused the Carvargna. And so had I, at his instruction. My hands were as red with blood as his own. Unfortunately I was the only one who could see that.

All over Anzibar IV, there was flare after flare as more strikes hit. They had some ground defenses that they were able to launch against the invaders. I can only be grateful that none of them struck the *Grissom,* because that might have given him the excuse he needed to open fire on Anzibar itself.

The bombardment continued forever, it seemed. I lost all track of time, minute stretching into hour, and into what seemed like days. Miles away on the planet below, it seemed like some parts of it were . . . moving. No, not moving. Burning. Entire continents were on fire, shimmering as if black snakes were undulating across them. Madness.

Madness.

Anzibar IV was burning.

I wondered if the Carvargna were taking any joy in it. These had ostensibly been a peaceful people. Yet I knew that, when I had been teaching them about military tactics, they had taken to it with almost gleeful abandon. Perhaps they weren't peaceful so much as they were repressed bullies, cheerfully happy to annihilate an opponent once they had big enough weapons and ships backing them up.

I closed my eyes against the sight, but that didn't stop me from hearing their voices in my head. I could hear them calling. . . .

"Mac . . ."

The suddenness of the voice startled me and it took me a moment to realize that it was inside my helmet rather than in my imagination. It was Mueller's voice. She was remarkably in control, but I could hear the edginess in her tone. "Are you seeing it?"

"Yes."

"My God, Mac . . . what have we done."

"The question isn't whether you're asking that, Kat. The question is whether the rest of the crew is. Where are you? Do they suspect . . . ?"

"No. No, not at all. At least, I hope not. There's all sorts of rumors flying throughout the crew about what happened. The captain made that announcement about you—"

"And people know that it's not true?"

"Well . . . no. There's discussion about it."

"You mean they're not rejecting it out of hand?"

"Some do. A lot . . ." Her voice trailed off.

I shouldn't have been surprised, I suppose. I'd made no effort to really get close to the crew. I liked keeping my distance, wanted to maintain my loner status. Consequently, it had cost me. When it came down to the word of a beloved captain versus the actions of a suspicious newcomer and outsider, one should easily have been able to expect that reaction.

Nonetheless, it hurt. It hurt far more than I ever would have expected.

"Mac . . . are you still there?"

"Yes." I shook it off. "Yes . . . I'm here. . . ."

"Your air supply . . . how's that holding up?"

I checked my on-line systems and realized that I'd been paying no attention to it at all. That was probably not the brightest move on my part. "It's running low. Eighteen minutes before I'm breathing my own carbon dioxide in here. Are you planning to beam me in?"

"That . . . could be a problem."

I suddenly started to feel icy, as if the vacuum of space was seeping through my suit. "A problem . . . how?"

"Lieutenant Cray doesn't want a repeat of your vanishing act. So he has security guards at all the transporter stations until further notice."

"Oh . . . perfect. How am I supposed to get back in? Crawl up a photon torpedo tube?"

There was dead silence.

And she said, "Well . . . actually . . ."

THE TUBE

IT'S AMAZING HOW SLOWLY you can move when you want to go very, very quickly.

Keeping an eye on the time that it took to maneuver in the weightlessness, even as I was being anchored by the magnetized boots, I felt as if it was taking an achingly long time to get from point A to point B. With my air supply ticking down as I went, it wasn't as if I had a good deal of time to waste.

I was closer to the aft torpedo tube than I was the forward, so that was obviously where I wanted to be. The air was already becoming stale in my helmet, my breathing more and more labored as I exerted myself. I knew that the torpedo tube would be wide enough for me to climb through, although it would be a fairly tight fit, particularly with the LPEG suit. On the other hand, I could remove the LPEG suit as soon as I was inside the tube. There was air in the tube, after all . . .

naturally, because the far end of the tube opened up directly into the Torpedo Bay Control. It's not as if everyone at the TBC was in danger of being sucked out into space or losing all their air every time we launched one of the damned things.

The fact that the tube opened into the TBC was one of my major problems. There were always two people on station there, particularly during time of red alert. The tube itself was thirty feet long, with the first twenty-five or so sufficiently obscured by shadows and such that they'd never see me coming. But the last five feet were going to be the trickiest, because they'd see me emerging from the tube and have enough time to alert security as to my whereabouts.

First thing was first, though. Before I could worry myself about what I would do upon emerging from the torpedo, I had to get to the tube first.

Five minutes' worth of fresh air left, and the tubes still seemed miles away. Four, and I was becoming more light-headed. It was requiring greater and greater effort to maintain my focus. Three minutes, and my magnetized feet felt as if iron weights had been attached to them. I heard a buzzing in my helmet, a distant voice, and it sounded like Kat Mueller, but I couldn't be sure. I couldn't be sure of anything except that I felt like lying down and taking a nap. Certainly the rest of the distance could wait for a few minutes. Just a few minutes more so that I could shut my eyes and take it easy . . .

"Mac!" came her urgent voice again, snapping me momentarily out of my fog. I was tired, my lungs felt so damned heavy. Kat's words were racing over me in a torrent, something about a ship, but I wasn't paying attention. I shut off the communications beacon to my helmet because her voice had become so irritating to me. Everything bothered me at that moment. I just

wanted the entire galaxy to go away and let me get some sleep.

I could smell the burning.

It wasn't possible, of course. There was no way that I could possibly smell the conflagration that had consumed the world of Anzibar IV. It was my imagination, my imagination spurring me on. It was enough to prod me forward, to keep me going and think about what had been done and what had yet to be done. And suddenly, just like that, the photon-torpedo tube was just ahead of me.

I looked at my instrumentation and saw that I was out of clean air. The tube was still ten feet away. It felt like ten yards. I came to the realization that I'd stopped moving. I had no idea how long I'd been like that. I shoved myself forward, going to my hands as well as my knees, pulling myself forward foot by foot. The tube drew closer, closer, and then I was right at it. My head was swimming as I pushed my way through the annular forcefield that covered the business end of the torpedo tube. It was the same type of forcefield that was employed in the shuttlebay, the kind that permitted solid objects to pass through it. Objects such as shuttlecrafts, or photon torpedoes, and even the occasional renegade officer were able to move through an annular forcefield with impunity, but air remained within the confined area.

I hauled myself completely into the torpedo tube. The moment I was through, my breathing inside the helmet sounded completely different to me. I disengaged the clamps of the helmet, twisted it, and removed it. I sucked air greedily into my lungs and waited for the light-headedness to disappear. I also tried to keep it as quiet as possible, concerned that any loud noises might echo up the tube and alert crewmen at the other end.

I sat curled up in the tube for a few moments,

composing myself and letting my thudding heart slow to a more normal speed. It was tight inside there; I'd certainly known more comfortable fits in my life. I also knew that I was going to have to move quickly once I got out of the tube. The simple fact was that I was going to have to knock out whatever crewmen were at the other end before they summoned security. I wasn't looking forward to it, but it had to be done. However, if I was clomping around in an LPEG suit when I was trying to do it, I'd never be able to move quickly enough. The LPEG was more formfitting than other, bulkier suits, but it still wasn't going to allow me the full mobility I was going to need.

The rest of the LPEG suit was one piece, gloves and boots all attached. Of course, it was generally designed to be removed in some place that was slightly more spacious than the inside of a photon-torpedo tube. But I didn't see that I had much of a choice. I unlatched the back restraints, slid my torso out, and then shimmied the rest of my body out of it. I took one more deep breath and then twisted around to see the far end of the tube. The way seemed pretty clear. The trick was going to be making the approach with sufficient stealth.

Leaving the suit behind, I hauled myself forward on my elbows. Slowly I made my way forward, the tube running at a slight incline just to make my life that much more exciting. I listened carefully, straining to hear if there was any discussion going on. I wanted to know how many people were going to be waiting for me. I desperately needed more information than I had. Because the less I knew, the more chance there was of something going wrong.

I covered ten feet with no incident. Up the darkened tube I went, fifteen feet, halfway there. I kept my elbows tight, moving forward, ever forward, and I heard the toe of my boot squeak against the interior of the darkened tube. I froze, hoping that the noise hadn't tipped anyone off. I thought I heard someone ahead, at the far end. At least two voices, talking with one another, and I drew myself closer. I'd covered twenty feet. Another five or so, and then we were going to get to the hardest part, because I'd be visible to anyone at the other end. I called upon all my strength, all my speed, hoping and praying that I would be up to the task.

Suddenly the inside of the tube lit up.

There are moments in your life where you should really understand instantly what's happening. But the situation becomes one that is so horrendous, so problematic, that your brain spends a few moments in ignorance or denial or both. In this case, it was definitely denial.

Ten feet ahead of me, a photon torpedo was shoved into place, blocking my intended exit. "Lock and load!" I heard.

"Aw, *grozit,*" I snarled, no longer being quite as concerned whether I was heard or not.

I started scrambling frantically backward. There was no time or space to turn myself around, so I just kept shoving as fast as I could.

The photon torpedo started to roll forward, caught up in the inevitable process that would send it hurtling into space. It wasn't armed yet. If it was employing the standard cycle, it wouldn't go active until just under two seconds after it cleared the ship. But it would still have more than enough power to blast me into space. Granted the shields were up and that would prevent me from spiraling away into the void, but I'd still be sufficiently far enough away from the ship—with no means of propulsion—that I'd never be able to get back before I asphyxiated.

I pushed myself back, faster and faster. As if it were caught up in the spirit of a race, the photon torpedo casing began to build up speed as well. It was gaining on me. I completely lost track of where I was in the tube, or how far I had to go before I was clear at the end. All I knew was that the torpedo was catching up. I was practically nose to nose with the damned thing. I shoved back faster, driven by building panic, and then my feet became entangled in something. It was my LPEG suit. The photon torpedo was practically on top of me, and I grabbed my helmet and shoved it under the torpedo. The obstruction momentarily jammed it. I heard the buildup of energy as the torpedo pushed against the helmet that had been wedged into the clearance area. I grabbed up the rest of the suit but there was no time as the torpedo, driven by the explosive forces of the building energy that was to propel it at near-warp speeds, slammed forward. It ran over the helmet, crushing it, and then the torpedo was coming right at me.

At the last second I suddenly sensed the void directly behind me. My instinct was to take a deep breath, but that would have been exactly the wrong move. The pressure of the vacuum would have tried to equalize the pressure and I would likely have had my rib cage crushed in no time. Instead I blew all the air out of my lungs and hurled myself backward into space, clutching onto the suit for dear life.

I'd seen old vids and such from centuries ago, featuring fanciful depictions of people exploding in a vacuum, their eyes bulging out of their heads, their major organs exploding into a rather impressive rain of red liquid.

Very decorative. Not correct, but very decorative. You don't explode. You don't combust. You simply either freeze to death or you suffocate, and it happens fairly quickly. I'm not entirely certain whether that's any improvement, but it certainly requires far less clean-up.

The cold was beyond anything imaginable. A million knives stabbing into all my pores and twisting couldn't begin to approximate the cold of space. I tried to twist myself around to get back to the ship, my body already slowing down as the frigidity of the vacuum worked its way into my joints, my muscles, and that was the instant that the torpedo blasted out of its tube. The light from the release of the energy was blinding and I closed my eyes against it.

The torpedo just barely grazed me as it passed, but even the slightest impact was enough to send me spiraling. By what easily qualified as the one bit of luck that I was having at the moment, the angle of the sideswipe actually sent me tumbling back toward the *Grissom.* But I was stunned, freezing to death, no air in my lungs . . .

From the corner of my eye, I saw a ship in the distance. It was a small one, a Dufaux fighter. It must have been a straggler, a survivor of the massacre. It was firing upon the *Grissom.* Obviously, rather than be satisfied with simply surviving, the ship's pilot had chosen to attack, as futile a gesture as that might have been. The pilot's blasts bounced off the shields harmlessly, and then the photon torpedo struck home. The ship disappeared in a flash of distant light.

Would that I had been in a position to admire the marksmanship.

I hit the hull about two feet away from the torpedo tube and then bounced off and away. There was nothing to stop me from tumbling off to my death.

Nothing except the suit that I was still clutching in my numb fingers.

My brain sent commands to my arms, trying to get them to function. I couldn't feel any part of my body.

I couldn't get anything to move. *Not like this,* I thought furiously, *not like this! I will not die like this!*

I think I shocked my arms into movement with the vehemence of my anger. I was still clutching the sleeve of the suit. I didn't have a choice; my fingers were frozen in a paralyzed rictus around it. I swung the suit around in an arc, like a lifeline, and the magnets of the boots slammed into the hull . . . and held.

I floated in space, clutching the suit, adhering to the side of the ship through only the slimmest of margins. The nearness of a possible salvation galvanized me. I refused to attend to the fact that my body wasn't responding, and instead forced it to do so through sheer ire. My lungs were beyond airless, and in the deathly silence of space, I heard my heart pounding. It was the single loudest noise I'd ever heard.

Hand over hand, I pulled myself toward the ship. The entire time I was terrified that the magnets would come loose, or that the cloth of the suit would slip through my numbed fingers. I drew closer, closer, and just at the very end I was convinced that I wasn't going to make it. I was positive that I was going to die right there, right then, inches away from my destination.

Then my conscious brain completely shut down. That's the only explanation I can really provide for it. I was functioning entirely on autopilot. I must have been, because I don't even remember hauling myself back into the photon-torpedo tube. It took a minute or two for me to realize that I was safe, jolted back to consciousness by the sting of air in my lungs. My lower legs were still freezing and I realized I hadn't completely pulled myself into the tube. With a low grunt of pain I hauled myself completely in and then lay there for an eternity, just making sure that I was in one piece.

To some extent, all I wanted to do was rest. But I didn't dare take the chance. For all I knew, another ship might show up behind us and the captain would consider it a good idea to blow it to bits with an aft torpedo as well. I might not have any time at all.

Working completely on adrenaline, I clambered back up the torpedo tube as fast as my body would readily let me. I covered the distance faster than I would have thought possible. On the way I grabbed up the scattered pieces of the helmet, since I'd suddenly come up with a quick use for them. When I reached the point where I'd found myself staring down the barrel of a torpedo, I flinched inwardly. But there was no repeat performance. I drew to within the critical five feet where I would be visible and paused a moment.

There were two crewmen, going about their business. They weren't staring straight at me, but from the angle that I was coming and from where they were standing, they would unquestionably see me before I was ready to be seen.

I gathered the crushed pieces of the helmet tightly in my right hand. The edges were sharp and a couple cut my hand. I couldn't even feel it. Lucky me.

I cocked my arm, took a breath (an action for which I had never been quite as grateful before), and threw. The pieces sailed over the heads of the crewmen and bounced off the far wall. The noise immediately distracted them as they moved toward the origin of it to investigate. With only a couple of seconds to act, I hauled myself up and clear of the tube. I rolled off the loading section and the instant my feet hit the ground, they turned with questions on their faces.

Clear astonishment registered in their expressions. Actually, for all I knew, they were sympathetic to my situation. But I couldn't take the chance. Making the element of surprise work for me for all it was worth, I charged, grabbed each of their heads in either hand, and slammed their heads together with all my strength. They sagged to the floor, unconscious. I sagged with them.

To no one in particular, I muttered, "I'm not getting paid enough for this."

THE DEVELOPMENTS

I TENSED AS THE DOORS to the torpedo station opened. I suddenly realized that I was too tired to move, momentarily having given everything that I had to give. If this was a security team, or even a very irate tribble, I was not going to be able to do anything to fight back.

Katerina Mueller walked into the room.

When she entered, she did so looking extremely businesslike . . . and yet she was also determinedly casual. I realized immediately that she was attempting to appear as if she were simply making a routine check on whatever activity was presently going on in there. She knew that's where I was going to wind up . . . if I was damned lucky. But the instant that she saw me, as well as the two unconscious crewmen, she immediately relaxed . . . only to tense up again as she got a good look at me. "My God, Mac, what happened?" she asked. She went to me and touched my hair. "There's frost on it. It's all stiff. Your lips are blue . . . what—?"

I told her, in as quick and unvarnished a way as I could. I tried not to make it sound worse than it was. Unfortunately the facts alone were enough to cause the once-unflappable German XO to turn several shades of pale.

"Are you all right?" she asked when I finished. "I mean, now."

"Do I look all right?"

"Well . . . your lips are starting to turn a lighter shade of blue. How are your extremities?"

I flexed my hand and, inside of my boots, squeezed my toes. "Still numb . . . but they're moving, at least."

"Hold on. Let's check."

And she leaned over and kissed me, slowly and longingly on the lips. It was the single best kiss we'd ever shared. We separated and she nodded in approval. "Recovering nicely, I think. I think that warmed it up a bit."

"My lap feels chilly."

"Don't push it, Calhoun." She moved over to the fallen crewmen and checked them. "They're breathing steadily. Strong pulse. They'll be okay, I think."

"They'll have serious headaches, though."

"You've got your own headaches. So do I. There's been some developments."

Walking out into the corridor would not have been the best idea in the world. Instead we scrambled up a service ladder and, moments later, were crawling through the ship's utility shafts. Once we'd put sufficient distance between ourselves and the torpedo room, Mueller found a fairly secure area for us to hole up.

"Okay . . . here's the situation," she said, getting

down to business. "The Carvargna battle fleet has been, to put it mildly, a success."

"That's no surprise."

"The Dufaux have surrendered unconditionally. That's also no surprise," she continued before I could say anything. "They were outnumbered, outgunned . . . there was nothing else they could do. The Carvargna are hailing Captain Kenyon as a galactic hero."

"A hero." I shook my head in disbelief. "He's a tortured man."

"Don't tell me you feel sorry for him. After everything he's put you through . . ."

"I helped bring it about, Kat. If I'd taken a stronger hand when I should have, I might have prevented all of this. Instead I let it happen. I did that."

"Mac, you can't blame yourself for everything."

"I have to stop him. I have to stop him before it goes any further."

She stared at me in disbelief. "Further? Mac, Anzibar Four is in smoking ruins. The Dufaux are, for the most part, crushed, begging for an end to it. They've been defeated. . . ."

"It may not be over," I warned her. "The leaders. The Dufaux leaders . . . Kradius, and whoever his associates might be . . . do you know if they're dead? If so, then maybe . . ."

"Actually, Kradius is alive. The Carvargna have him in custody on the planet's surface right now. That was part of the terms of the surrender as dictated by . . ."

"By Captain Kenyon."

"We don't know that for sure," she told me.

I shook my head. "Perhaps not. But I wouldn't bet against it. In fact . . . I bet I can tell you how the rest of it is going to go."

"Dazzle me with your knowledge, Calhoun." Despite the seriousness of the situation, the delicacy of our position . . . she actually managed to sound remarkably casual about the entire thing. She was quite a woman, our Katerina was.

"They're putting Kradius on trial," I said. "The trial will be overseen by the Carvargna rulers and the heads of the alliance they've formed. And they've invited Captain Kenyon to take a position at the trial, a position that he's accepted. In fact, he's probably already down there. No reason to delay matters . . . particularly since the longer he delays, the more chance there is that somehow Starfleet will manage to shut this all down and stop him from exacting the full measure of his vengeance."

Despite her faintly sarcastic air from moments before, she actually looked at me with genuine amazement. "I'm impressed," she said. "How did you know all that?"

"Because, Kat, things don't happen in a vacuum . . . well, most things," I added ruefully, touching my lips, which were only at that point starting to have some degree of sensation in them. "I've seen scenarios like this play out, time and again. Some in Earth history, some on other worlds. These things tend to turn out depressingly the same. The wrinkle in this instance is that Captain Kenyon is a part of it."

"Right now I'm less concerned about the captain than I am about you," Kat told me. "We've got a serious problem here. I'd hate to see them put you on trial for court-martial. It'll be your word against the captain's and Lieutenant Cray . . ."

"It's not going to come to that," I said.

"Mac, this isn't the time for false confidence."

"That's not it. Cray isn't going to want to take any chances."

She stared at me as if she couldn't believe what I was suggesting. "You're not saying that he's . . . you think . . . ?"

"He'll try to kill me."

"No." She shook her head vehemently. "No, I don't believe it. . . ."

"Mueller, there's too many ways to get at the truth. Computer readouts, telepathic scans . . . the works. The last thing that Cray is going to want to risk is my living to tell exactly what happened."

"He's a Starfleet officer, dammit!"

"He's an Andorian, first and foremost," I told her. "There are certain traits that are part and parcel of being an Andorian."

"Don't be a bigot, Calhoun."

"It's not bigotry, it's simply observed. Andorians speak quietly on the whole, but when it comes to an opponent they can be absolutely ruthless."

"So can you," she reminded me.

I smiled grimly. "That's true. That's how I know just what it is he's going to do. That's one of the reasons I've been trying to stay out of lockup. Not for a minute do I believe that I would live to get to a starbase for trial if I were in Cray's hands."

"I don't know that I believe it. But for sake of argument, we'll say you're right. In that case, then we've only one choice," Mueller said reasonably. "We have to get to the captain directly. We have to . . ." Her confidence faltered a bit. "We have to . . . what?"

"I don't know," I admitted. "I have to get through to him. To make him realize that what he's done is horribly, horribly wrong. There may be no way that he can make amends. But we can stop him from making it worse."

"You said that before. How could it possibly be worse?"

"That's easy," I said. "He could kill Kradius."

"Kill? You mean . . . murder? He'd . . . he'd never do that. . . ."

"Oh, yes he would. Where his state of mind is at the moment . . . he absolutely would. It's one thing to rationalize firing on the Dufaux vessels that fired upon the *Grissom*. We were acting to protect ourselves. Likewise he could explain away to himself the defense of the Carvargna flagship. But to cold-bloodedly stand there and execute a helpless opponent . . . doing something like that changes you forever. I wouldn't wish that on anyone, least of all the captain."

It seemed to me that she was dissecting me with her eyes. "You did it once . . . didn't you?"

"No."

"No?"

"No. More than once. Many . . . more times than once. Don't you see, Kat? No one . . . should have to be like me. No one."

She said nothing for a long moment. And then, to my surprise, she reached over and hugged me. "Why did you do that?" I asked.

"My own reasons. And they'll remain my own." She considered the situation a moment, stroking her chin thoughtfully. Then she tapped her combadge. "Mueller to Takahashi," she said in a very soft voice.

"This is Hash. Go ahead." His voice was also soft. Clearly they had coordinated earlier.

"I'll need the coordinates for where the captain beamed to on Anzibar Four."

"Hold on." Obviously he was double-checking them off his ops board. After a moment he told Kat, and she repeated them carefully to make sure she had it right.

"That's it."

"Much obliged. Mueller out."

"Okay, we know where he went. Now what?"

"Now we get down there," she said as if it were the most reasonable thing in the world.

"How? We jump?"

"No. We're going to have to get to one of the transporter rooms. It'll probably necessitate overpowering the security guard. If you don't think you're up for that . . ."

I raised an eyebrow. "Is that to be considered a challenge, XO?"

"Whatever you want to call it."

"Kat . . ." I hesitated. "There's . . . there's really no way I can thank you for all this. I—"

"You're right," she said immediately. "So it's probably better that you don't even try."

She moved off down the utility shaft, and I immediately followed her. I had to admit it: It was tough to argue with logic like that. It probably *was* better that I didn't try. We made our way through the utility shaft, approaching the main transporter room. The plan was going fairly well. By sticking to the utility shafts, we were able to stay out of sight. If we were able to get close enough to the transporter room, then we might face minimal opposition once we got there.

In fact, according to Mueller, we might face even less than I had previously thought.

"There's a lot of people who aren't thrilled with the way all of this has turned out," she told me. "Not the majority of the crew, certainly. But enough. Enough to make people wonder whether all of this has gone down properly. It might not just be your word against the captain and Cray. . . ."

"Whether people believe or don't believe is up to them," I said as we climbed down one of the ladders. I took each step slowly and carefully. The last thing I needed to do was slip and break my ankle or something similarly intelligent. "I'll be perceived as the instigator. What we have to do is—"

I didn't get a chance to finish the sentence, because suddenly the utility shaft was filled with a terribly familiar noise. It was the whine of transporter beams, and before we could do anything at all we were caught in their grip. The utility tubes dissolved around us and suddenly we found that we were in the main transporter room.

Lieutenant Cray was standing there with his phaser aimed levelly at us.

THE ANDORIAN

There was no one else around. Just Cray. Cray, Mueller, and me. Kat looked dumbfounded, staring at Cray as if she couldn't comprehend what she and I could possibly be doing there.

As if he'd read her mind, Cray spoke in that same eerie whisper of his, "You and he. Obvious."

"He figured you were the one who helped me, Katerina," I said. I didn't bother to raise my hands. "He's head of security, after all, and he's very thorough. I strongly suspect that he knows just about everyone's business aboard this ship."

He inclined his head slightly in acknowledgment.

"So he locked on to my combadge," she said in slow understanding, "and beamed me and whoever was with me here, on the assumption that it would be you."

He nodded again. His blue lips thinned in a self-satisfied smile.

For a moment, no words were spoken. Then I said, "Cray . . . it's pointless to discuss this further. We're two of a kind, you and I. We both know what needs to be done here. The only question will be whether you do it as a coward . . . or as an Andorian. Oh . . . I forgot. That's pretty much the same thing, isn't it."

The amusement vanished from his face.

"What are you doing?" Mueller said softly out of the corner of her mouth.

I ignored her. "Tell you what, Cray. I'll make it easy for you. This is what your kind prefers, after all." I turned my back to him. "Here. That's your method of operation, isn't it."

"This won't work," he said softly.

I faced him once more. "Cray . . . don't waste my time or yours. We both know you're going to fire the phaser from a nice, safe distance. No stomach for hand-to-hand, to show who's the better man. Finish us off, nice and quick. No witnesses. That's the way you want it, isn't it. You've probably already made adjustments to your log to fake receiving entries from Starfleet, so no one else can find out your deceit as I did. But just out of curiosity . . . how long do you think that's going to last? Once the real investigation starts . . . whatever entries you've cooked up will never stand up to scrutiny. You've totally miscalculated the game, Cray. You thought by cooperating with the captain, doing whatever he wanted, that would be how you'd get ahead. Plus there was certainly no love for me lost on your part. If my career, and I, had to be destroyed, well . . . you weren't going to shed any tears about that. Correct?"

He said nothing. The phaser hadn't wavered. This wasn't a good sign. Cray wasn't going for the taunting, wasn't allowing his advantage to slip away. There was only one thing that could possibly make the situation worse.

Katerina Mueller drew herself to her full height. "Cray . . . put it down. Now. That's an order."

That was it.

Cray turned and fired at Katerina.

I saw it coming about a half second before he fired. I shoved her to the right as I lunged to the left. But Katerina didn't move fast enough as the phaser blast clipped her right shoulder. Kat let out a howl of pain and crumbled to the ground. Cray wasn't screwing around. The phaser was set on kill. If he'd struck a vital area, such as her heart, she would have been dead before she hit the floor.

"Don't move," he said. The order wasn't addressed to Kat, but to me. He had the phaser aimed at her head and the threat was clear. If I didn't make myself a nice easy target, she was dead.

But she was dead anyway. We both were.

I spit at him.

It was the purest means by which I could express contempt, and certainly the most pointed. The wad of spittle sailed across the room and struck Cray on the right side of the face. His eyes went wide with fury as, in silence, he felt the spittle trickling down.

And then, very slowly and very deliberately, he placed the phaser down on the control console.

"You will never . . ." It was as if every section of his sentence was an effort. ". . . insult Andorians . . . again. . . ."

I struck a defensive pose. He matched it. Slowly we circled the cramped quarters of the transporter room. There wouldn't be a lot of room for maneuvering. Despite the fact that he was an enemy, I couldn't help but admire the fluid way in which he moved.

"You will receive . . . what you desired," he said, his hands tracing elaborate patterns in the air. Slowly I paralleled his steps, keeping the console between us. I moved slightly to the left and he already moved in anticipation of it. His eyes glittered with fury. "No weapons, save our hands. We will see . . . who is the coward. We will see . . . who is the better man. We will see . . . who is the . . ."

Calmly, I reached over the console and picked up the phaser that he'd put down and I aimed it at him.

His face twisted in contempt. "Coward!"

"Idiot," I replied, and fired. I hit him squarely in the chest. The impact of the phaser blast lifted Cray up off his feet and sent him slamming back into the far wall of the transporter room. He hit it with a most satisfying thud and slid to the ground, his head slumped to one side, his eyes closed.

I knelt down next to Kat, took her arm gently, and tried to bend it at the elbow. "Does this hurt?" I asked.

"A little. I can handle it." She started to sit up, her teeth gritted against the pain that she was obviously feeling. She glanced at Cray. "Is he dead?"

"I doubt it. Andorians are fairly tough, actually."

And suddenly Cray was sitting up.

There was red-hot fury in his eyes and, without slowing down, he lunged at me. The hole where I had nailed him was still smoking from the blast.

"*Fairly* . . . tough?" he snarled, as if the modifier was the worst insult I could have hurled. His hands were around my throat.

I tried to bring the phaser around but he released one of his hands briefly enough to knock the phaser away, sending it clattering into a far corner of the room. He straddled me, choking me, and Kat tried to throw herself against him to knock him off me.

Without even looking away from me, Cray swung his right fist around and caught Mueller squarely on the point of her chin. Her eyes rolling up, Katerina sank to the ground and Mueller returned to the important business of crushing my larynx.

My hands were gripping his wrists, pulling as hard as I could. It didn't seem nearly to be enough. His powerful fingers, like iron bars, dug deeper and deeper.

I rammed the heel of my hand into his nose.

I felt a satisfying crack beneath my fingers and knew that I had just busted his nose. He was momentarily dazed as I shoved him to one side and got to my feet, facing him.

He didn't look happy.

I wanted to finish it quickly and swung a roundhouse. No chance. He blocked it as if I were moving in slow motion and drove a fist into my gut. I gasped, doubled over, and he spun and slammed a foot into my head. I went down, tried to stand and he was moving so fast that I never even saw the backspin that sent me crashing to the floor when it connected. I tried to roll back out of the way, but he was up and kicking me in the torso, causing me to tuck my legs up as if I were assuming the fetal position. He grabbed me by the scruff of the neck, hauled me to my feet, spun me around and slammed me face first into the wall. The impact expelled air from me, winded me. He released me for a moment, much to my surprise, and I stood there and wavered as I tried to mount a defense. No chance again. Leaping high, he spun in midair for the purpose of crushing the front of my face with his feet. Fortunately enough I managed to block it partly, but that wasn't enough to save me from the full impact. Someone dropped an anvil on my skull as I collapsed again under the superior hand-

and-footwork of Cray. I was getting knocked about so badly that my thoughts were completely tattered. *We should hire this guy, he's good,* I mused. That's how bad a shape I was in.

Cray reached down, snagged my shirtfront in his huge hands, and hauled me to my feet with the very likely purpose of finishing me off. I had been right. Right straight down the line. Why, dammit, why did I have to be right all the time?

"Die," he growled.

I grabbed one of his antennae atop his head, got a firm grip, and pulled as hard as I could. Cray hadn't realized what I was doing until I actually did it. There was a nauseating ripping sound and antennae suddenly tore free of his head and came up, truncated and bloody, in my hand.

Cray was beyond agony. He screamed as loudly as I've ever heard a sentient being scream. He dropped to one knee, clutching at his head, blood pouring out and staining his head of white hair. I leaned against a wall, gasping, observing Cray's discomfort.

"You . . . bastard!" he managed to get out.

"You're still an idiot," I replied, and I hit him as hard as I could.

I knew instantly that something had broken, although whether it was his jaw or my fist was a bit hard to tell. He went down, his eyes rolling up and back, and then he keeled over and thudded to the floor.

I immediately went over to Katerina and shook her gently. Her head lolled a bit, but slowly her eyes opened. "Are you okay?" I asked.

"Oh . . . fine," she managed to get out.

"I need you to beam me down to the planet. Do you remember the coordinates that Hash gave you?"

She grinned lopsidedly and tweaked my cheek. "You're cute," she informed me.

"That's a relief to hear. Get up, Katerina. Can you get up?"

"Why? Is it time for school?"

I realized that the process of bringing her out of it was going to take slightly longer than I had anticipated.

THE SENTENCE

PERHAPS MATTERS MIGHT have been a bit more difficult for Captain Kenyon if Kradius had at least looked repentant. Or, for that matter, had even looked remotely like someone sympathetic.

It didn't help that Kradius had horns.

In point of fact, he looked almost demonic. Kradius was huge, over six feet, and about as wide as a shuttlecraft. He had a huge head of hair that bore a resemblance to the mane of a lion, an impossibly huge brow, and small horns situated just above the hairline. His eyes were dark red, and there was a thin covering of what appeared to be fur on him.

He was surveying his captors with open contempt.

The Carvargna board of inquiry and trial sat in a row of chairs, regarding Kradius with what appeared to be equal amounts of boredom and disdain. To say that they were in a room might be to overstate it.

They were in the burned-out remains of what once had been the central government site of the Dufaux. Now it was smoking ruins, the ceiling gone and the night sky glittering. There was a faint chill wind cutting through, but nobody seemed to be paying much attention.

There were no other Dufaux there aside from Kradius. All of the government officials had either died in the assault or were in a holding facility awaiting their own "trial" . . . much too generous a word, really. Kradius's accusers were arrayed before him, and most prominent among them was Captain Kenyon.

He sat in the middle of the line of judges. He stared at Kradius, his eyes half-lidded, hiding whatever thoughts were going through his mind. Hatred seeped from him like a toxic waste. Barhba was next to him. And Barhba . . .

Barhba seemed tired of it all. It was as if the immensity of their activities, the full weight of the slaughter that they had perpetrated, was starting to weigh upon him. The novelty, such as it was, had worn off. The Dufaux were no threat anymore, and the sooner that this business was ended, the sooner Barhba would be able to return home and put all of this behind him.

Except it was unlikely that he would. Far more likely was that he would lie awake at night, imagining the screams of terror of the Dufaux people as death hammered down on them from on high. He would probably think about his finger on the trigger, his involvement in the eradication of the Dufaux. He would begin to wonder if, indeed, there hadn't been some other way possible. A chorus of imaginary shrieks of despair and death rattles would be the serenade that would sing him to sleep at night and the alarm that roused him in the morning. No, Barhba did not have an enviable life ahead of him.

Kenyon, on the other hand, did not look tired at all. He was completely focused on Kradius. Kradius did not appear to notice him. Either that or he held him in such contempt that he simply didn't bother to acknowledge his presence.

Doc Villers was standing directly behind Kenyon, and there were two security men, Meyer and Boyajian, directly behind her. The guards were armed, and even Kenyon had a phaser on his belt.

Kenyon had no greater supporter aboard the ship than the irascible Doc Villers, but even she seemed a bit daunted by the proceedings. She kept looking at Kenyon as if she were trying to urge him, mentally, to give up his seat on the tribunal and return to the stars. For in truth, he had no business here. Not really.

Yet here he was.

"Kradius," Barhba said, sounding fatigued, "this board has found you guilty of crimes against sentient beings of this sector. You have remained silent during your trial, offering no defense. Would you speak now?"

His gaze swiveled toward Barhba and he appeared to be aware of the Carvargna, as well as the Carvargna's allies, for the first time. When he spoke his voice was surprisingly low. "Why?"

"Why?" The question seemed to puzzle Barhba. "In order . . . to have your side heard. To explain yourself."

"To you?" Kradius dripped contempt. "I do not acknowledge that you have power over me."

"Whether you acknowledge it or not, your life is in the hands of this board."

He snorted derisively. "My life is in the hands of our god. He does with it as he sees fit. You are simply the instruments of his will."

This pronouncement appeared to intrigue Kenyon. He leaned forward, his fingers interlaced. "You have a god?" he asked in clear amazement. "You believe in something greater than yourselves?"

"Greater than ourselves. Greater than you," Kradius replied. "We are his chosen. You . . . are nothing."

"Oh. We are nothing. I see." Kenyon rose from his seat at that point and slowly started to approach Kradius. The huge Dufaux posed no threat, his hands bound in front of him. "Is that how you see it, then? Is that how you justify your actions?"

"We do not need to justify anything," said Kradius. "We do what we will. If you do not like it, that is your problem."

"Ohhhh no," Kenyon said, shaking his head. "It's your problem. It is entirely your problem now, sir."

"Captain." It was Villers who had spoken. She was looking increasingly uncomfortable with everything that was happening. "Captain, please . . . perhaps it would be best to . . ."

"Quiet, Doctor," Kenyon said, cutting her off. There was a demented gleam in his eye, as if he were running a fever. "I want to hear about this bastard's religion. I want to hear what he has to say for himself. To hear him spout about his superiority while he is standing here in chains awaiting his punishment."

Kradius was looking Kenyon up and down, and then comprehension appeared to dawn on his face. "I thought you looked familiar to me," he said at last. "The Federation ambassador . . . he was related to you in some way, wasn't he."

"He was my brother." Kenyon fairly shook with anger. "And the girl was my daughter. They were the last of my family, and you killed them. You did that. I'm now alone in the galaxy. You did that, too."

"Norman . . ." Villers started again.

"Shut up, Doctor."

This was the second time Kenyon had rebuked the doctor. Meyer and Boyajian glanced at each other, looking a bit nervous. The relationship between Kenyon and Villers was well known as one of total respect and genuine admiration. For Kenyon to have cut Villers off at the knees in that way . . . it indicated that something was truly very, very wrong.

But Barhba spoke up at that point. "This is accomplishing nothing, honored Kenyon. We see no reason to continue with it. Kradius, it is the decision of this board that you be executed. Said execution, in the interests of mercy, will be performed in as timely and painless a manner as can readily be devised."

"You are alone in the galaxy?" Kradius was addressing Kenyon as if the others hadn't spoken. "You? I had three mates, human. Three. Nineteen children. They are all dead now. Dead, thanks to the barrage from you and your associates. Do not speak of being alone to me, human. You cannot even begin to grasp the definition."

"You brought it on yourself. You killed . . ."

"I killed trespassers."

"You killed representatives of the Federation that you yourselves gave permission to come to your world!"

He shook his head violently. "I refused permission. It was subsequently granted by a lieutenant of mine who had no respect for my wishes in the matter. Who felt that the attitudes of my government were too extreme. He desired that I speak at length with those whose opinions were different from mine. The moment I discovered his schemes, I had him executed. I gave the Federation representatives the opportunity to leave unmolested. They insisted on trying to speak with me." He had been speaking in an almost conversational voice, but now his tone became louder. "I refused them. They insisted and insisted. Imagine the disrespect, to ignore my wishes in that matter. I am Kradius. *I am Kradius,"* and he sounded indignant over the mere thought of how he had been "treated" at the hands of those he had killed. "They were overconfident. They were certain that I would desire to listen to them. Warning after warning I gave them, and still they would not leave. They desired to talk when I had no interest in doing so. I had no choice in the matter. To treat me with disrespect, before my advisers, before all of the Dufaux, by not honoring my wishes. They had to die for that offense."

"You butcher," Kenyon snarled. "You goddamn butcher."

"They had their opportunities to survive. They had their chances and chose not to take them," Kradius replied. "Those were offered to them by me. What chances did you offer my mate and children, eh?" He looked at all of them then, not just Kenyon. "What chance did you offer? My understanding—from what I hear your soldiers tell—is that I put up a considerable fight when they came for me. The truth is that when your soldiers arrived, I was sitting in the ruins of my house cradling the body of my newborn son. I said nothing to them, did not lift a hand against them. That is the tale of the mighty Kradius at bay . . . but it's not remotely as interesting, is it. So it has to be built up, exaggerated."

"Your crimes are no exaggeration. Your brutality is documented," Kenyon told him.

"I do not care for your opinion of me, human. Perhaps you'd be well advised to save it for those who do."

"Honored Kenyon," Barhba addressed him. He rose from his chair and took a couple of steps in Kenyon's direction. "The anger you bear this man is quite clear. We," and he indicated himself and the council, "feel it right and just that you handle his execution. He has committed crimes against us, of course, but yours are the most personal and therefore it is the most appropriate that the requirement of blood be settled by you and only by you. His life . . . will be in your hands."

"Thank you," said Kenyon, bowing slightly. He turned to Meyer and Boyajian. "Gentlemen."

"Yes, sir?" said Meyer.

"Line up, please."

They did as they were told, still clearly a bit puzzled. But Villers was ahead of them and Kenyon. "Norm," she said urgently, "don't do this. This is crossing a line."

He ignored her. Instead he stepped in close to Kradius and grabbed him by the elbow. With a force that was surprising in the older man, he shoved Kradius back against a wall, or at least what remained of a wall. Carvargna and other allies who were observing made sure to clear away. Kenyon stepped back, leaving Kradius standing there by himself. His huge fists were clenched.

"Norm!" She was becoming more insistent.

"Not now, Doctor. Security team . . . weapons up."

The reality of what they were being faced with slowly began to dawn on Meyer and Boyajian. Acting automatically, they removed their weapons from their belts and gripped them firmly, but there was nothing but uncertainty and even confusion on their faces, as if they were in the middle of a truly demented nightmare.

"Ready . . ." began Kenyon. "Aim . . ."

They didn't aim. They just stood there, holding their weapons but down and at the side. Meyer, who had been all for attending to the captain's wishes back in the transporter room, seemed racked with indecision. "Captain . . . this is . . ."

"Problem, Mr. Meyer?" Kenyon asked icily.

"Captain . . . we're security guards," Boyajian now spoke up. "We're not . . . we're not executioners. We're not acting on behalf of the Federation here. We don't even have a death penalty in the UFP. . . ."

"Yes, but we're not on one of the United Federation of Planets members now, are we," Kenyon said with forced calm. "We're on a world where brutal deaths are apparently part of the standard policy. The death that has been ordered for this . . . person . . . is far more merciful than what he dealt out to the two UFP representatives who were here weeks ago. Now do as you're ordered. Weapons up."

They looked at each other, as if trying to decide what to do.

"My God," Villers said in low astonishment, "Calhoun was right. How could I not have . . ."

"This is not a noninterference question, gentlemen. This thing has been condemned to die!"

"They said it was in your hands, Norman," Villers spoke up. She turned to Barhba. "Does that mean that . . . that if he doesn't . . ."

"If the honored Kenyon shows mercy, I do not see how we could do less," Barhba said. He looked to the others, who nodded in agreement.

"There will be no showing of any such thing. Now I'm not going to order you again!" Kenyon said, his ire mounting. He walked right up to Meyer and Boyajian. Kradius observed the entire scene with cool amusement.

"That . . . is fortunate, sir," Meyer said. "Because I've never disobeyed a direct order before. And I . . ."

"Typical," Kradius said.

"You shut up," Kenyon said sharply.

For someone whose death was being debated, Kradius seemed remarkably detached from the whole thing. "So typical. Your own soldiers cannot carry out a simple execution."

"I'm warning you . . ."

"Would you like to know the real reason that we were not interested in becoming involved with your Federation?" Kradius asked. "It's because we sensed your weakness. Your whining brother came across as an effete, petulant snob rather than someone who should be attended to. His death was inevitable the moment he set foot on our world. He didn't have the strength of character to survive."

Kenyon started to turn a distinct shade of purple. "You . . . heartless bastard," he snarled. "Not enough that you killed him . . . killed my child . . . now you say these things . . ."

"You Starfleet men are seekers of truth, are you not?" said Kradius. "Here is the truth for you, then. I handled his execution myself. I did. He seemed so weak, so insufferable, that I wanted to see how much he could take. To see how much pain he could endure before he cried like a child, begged for his life. It took almost no time at all. Then I continued to beat him so that I could see how long it would take him to realize that begging would do no good. That took a much longer time. Actually . . . he never stopped begging. Right until the end. He died with whimpering and pleading on his lips, or what was left of his lips."

"I'll . . . kill you . . ." whispered Kenyon.

"Yes, by all means, do so," sneered Kradius. "For all your posturing, prove to me at the last that you're no different. Would you like to hear of your daughter's death as well? She had more bravery, I will grant her that. She only begged at the end . . . and I believe she called for you repeatedly, although you of course didn't come. . . ."

Kenyon snapped. His own phaser forgotten, he

grabbed instead the first weapon that he saw, which was Meyer's phaser. He snatched it right out of the hands of the startled security officer, took several steps forward, and brought it to bear on Kradius, ready to shoot him down on the spot.

And that was when I stepped forward.

I had been able to secret myself easily enough in the crowd of onlookers. It wasn't as if Kenyon was particularly looking for me at that point. Mueller had recovered enough to beam me down, and I had stayed out of sight during the entire confrontation, hoping and praying that Kenyon would do the right thing on his own. But that, it was becoming clear, was not going to be the case.

I was holding the phaser that I had taken off Cray, and now it was leveled directly at Captain Kenyon. There I was, first officer of the *Grissom,* with my commanding officer at gunpoint. As I said to you before . . . if one is going to go down, best to go down in flames.

Amazingly, Kenyon didn't seem surprised to see me. "Hello, Calhoun," he said as if I'd happened to wander in during a family picnic.

This didn't seem the time for niceties. "Put the phaser down, Captain."

"You first."

"I can't do that."

"Well, then we have a problem, don't we."

His phaser didn't waver from being pointed at Kradius.

"Meyer, Boyajian . . . back away from him. Doctor, you too. This is between the captain and me."

I was pleased to see that they didn't dispute or debate me. They did precisely as I was ordered. It was entirely possible that it was the last order I was ever going to wind up giving. At least it had been obeyed.

What I found most significant about the moment

was that Kenyon hadn't fired yet. In point of fact, there was nothing stopping him. I wasn't in the way, and even if I fired upon him after he squeezed the trigger, there was nothing I could do about his killing Kradius. I couldn't knock Kradius out of the way, and I certainly couldn't move faster than the beam of light that was the primary discharge of a phaser. But if Kenyon hadn't fired yet . . . then it was entirely possible that something deep within him was stopping him. Perhaps he wanted me to talk him out of it somehow.

"Between you and me?" Kenyon asked with faint amusement, echoing my words. "Calhoun . . . there's nothing between you and me. It's all me," and he gestured with the phaser, "and him. That . . . thing who killed my—"

"I know what he did, Captain. And believe it or not—and I know it's not going to feel like much consolation at the moment—but I know what you're feeling. But I cannot let you do this thing. There has to be a point at which this ends."

"Yes. That point is his death," and he indicated Kradius.

"No, sir. Enough has already happened. Enough is enough. Don't you see? If you turn away from this now . . . turn away from the vengeance that's presenting itself to you . . . there's still a chance for you. Still a chance to—"

"A chance? You mean like the chance he gave my baby . . . my Stephie . . ."

"Captain . . ."

"This tribunal has condemned him to death. I'm simply carrying out their will. . . ."

"This tribunal wouldn't be here if it weren't for you, Captain! You set this entire thing into motion! You made it possible! All of it, possible!" I kept my phaser leveled on him. "My God, Captain, think of all the people who have died thus far! Died because of the guiding hand provided by the *Grissom!* It has to end, sir!"

"It does. It ends with him."

"If that's the will of these people, then let them attend to it. But not you. You're not one of them. You're separate from them, you're . . ."

When Kenyon spoke, it was as if from very far away. "You can't stop me, Mac," he said. "Whether you approve or not . . . whether it costs me my command or not . . . I am going to do this thing. I . . . I can hear them. . . ."

And before my eyes, before the eyes of everyone, Kenyon came completely unraveled. It was the man whom I had seen losing control of himself in the ready room, but this was worse, far worse. He lost it completely, tears pouring down his face. Kradius sneered in contempt at the sight, and I could only be grateful that Kenyon was so much in a world of his own at that point. For if he had seen Kradius's expression at that moment, nothing in the universe would have been able to prevent him from blowing off the Dufaux's head.

"I can hear my brother . . . my . . . my little girl . . . begging me for help, I can hear them in my head . . . begging me, cursing me because I let them down . . . I can't live with that, Mac. . . ." His voice was going in and out, louder and softer, a bizarre mixture of laughing and crying.

"Captain," I said desperately, "I'm trying to save a fine officer . . . a fine and distinguished career. . . ."

I knew I was losing him then. Because I saw his finger starting to tighten on the firing control. "If you want to stop me . . . you're going to have to kill me. . . ."

All the options raced through my mind at that moment.

I could try to shoot to stun or wound. But that might not stop Kenyon in the state of mind that he was in. He might still manage to get a shot off and kill Kradius.

The problem was that I was a practical man. Always had been. And I knew at that point that there was really only one possibility open.

Kradius had to die.

Kenyon was too far gone. Weeks of imagining his daughter's and brother's awful deaths had completely unhinged him. The voices were in his head, voices crying for vengeance that I knew only too well. I had lived with them all my life, and would continue to do so. But Kenyon, he was too new at this, too good a soul to have to tolerate it.

The harsh but inescapable reality of the situation was that, as long as Kradius was alive, Kenyon could never heal. Never be the man that he was. It was possible that it was too late for that anyway. . . .

Possible . . . but not impossible.

I had pledged to watch out for the captain. To support him. He was going to have enough difficulties defending his actions up until that point. Cold-blooded murder would be damned near impossible. It was possibly the difference between being asked to retire after a distinguished career and being brought up on charges, being forced out in disgrace.

There was already so much blood on my hands, so much blackening of my soul . . . what was one more death, really, laid at my doorstep? And if they tried and convicted me, court-martialed me and stuck me in a prison camp somewhere, well . . . so what? Small loss in the grand scheme of things. Just another commander with only a semi-promising future at best. That couldn't even begin to compare to what Kenyon would be giving up.

The answer was obvious, really.

Understand . . . I didn't really give a damn about Kradius. I had killed far less worse than him, with far less provocation. It was what he represented in terms of Kenyon's own life and career that concerned me.

If Kradius's life ended . . . then Kenyon's at least had a prayer of continuing in something vaguely resembling its previous form. If Kenyon were the one who killed him, that was pretty much it for Kenyon. It was going to be bad enough as it was; Starfleet would roast him alive if he took that final step. Plus, I was convinced that Kenyon was in the throes of a temporary insanity, driven there by the trauma of losing those who were so beloved to him. If and when that madness passed, everything that he had done would come crashing down on him. I desperately wanted to avoid homicide being added to the list.

If Kradius lived, however, then the drive for vengeance would continue to eat away at Kenyon. I knew from personal experience what that was like.

That left only one option.

I didn't know what to do. I was completely torn, and the savage within whispered, *Just do it. Get it done.*

Before I had given it rational thought, before I was completely resolved, I had already swung my phaser in the direction of Kradius. All it would take was a quick squeeze and the problems would be over.

And as fiercely as the savage had called to me, the would-be civilized officer within me begged me not to.

I hesitated for a split instant . . .

. . . and then I aimed at Kradius and blew his head off.

Because at the last second, the moment of indecision before I knew absolutely what I was going to do, that was when I had seen the phaser in Kradius's hand. Even though Kradius's hands were shackled, somehow he was holding a phaser in them. As his headless body started to tumble forward, I glanced at the only source I could think of and saw that I was right. The phaser was gone from the captain's belt. When Kenyon had pushed him up against the wall, he had been so irate that he hadn't noticed Kradius palming his phaser.

And Kradius had chosen now, this very moment, when Kenyon and I seemed totally distracted by, and wrapped up in, each other, to try and take a shot directly at Kenyon. His arms were already half raised in Kenyon's general direction when my phaser blast had drilled right through his face and splattered his brains on the back wall. The phaser slipped from his nerveless hands and Kradius, or what was left of him, pitched forward and hit the ground with such impact that the floor shook beneath our feet.

"My . . . God . . ." Villers said in amazement. She looked at me with something that I had never thought I would see in her face: admiration. "You're the fastest shot I've ever seen. You're lightning! I didn't even see the phaser until just now. You saved the captain's life."

I couldn't believe it. I absolutely couldn't believe it. They had thought that I was acting to prevent Kradius from shooting Kenyon, when in point of fact I had been totally unaware that Kradius posed any sort of threat until the very last instant. I was "lightning" only because I was already in motion before I knew Kradius posed a threat.

I said the only thing I could, given the circumstances:

"Thanks."

Kenyon hadn't moved from his position. He still had the phaser leveled at Kradius, or at least where Kradius had been. His eyes were wide, his brow still covered with sweat.

"Captain . . . it's over," I said gently. I took a step

towards him. "Kradius is dead. It's done. So just lower the phaser now . . . and we can all go home. . . ."

And Kenyon turned to look at me with a more haunted expression than I had ever seen in any man . . . including myself.

"You didn't understand me, Mac. I said I couldn't live with their voices in my head. Killing Kradius would balance the scales . . . but it wouldn't stop the voices . . . only one thing can do that. . . ."

I saw it coming an instant before it happened.

Kenyon reversed the phaser, aimed it at himself, and fired.

THE HEARING

I STOOD BEFORE the Starfleet tribunal on Earth and offered no defense whatsoever. I refused to have defense counsel. I refused to utter a word as to why I had done anything that I had done, because I felt that my actions should speak for themselves. The main reason that I did so was that I felt like a total and complete failure.

I was exonerated anyway.

Officer after officer came before the tribunal and testified as to my bravery, to my diligence. Mueller called me the greatest officer she had ever known. Villers blamed herself for not flagging the problem earlier, blinded by loyalty. Takahashi admitted his culpability in the *Grissom* mutiny and wound up getting a commendation, as did Mueller. Cray was tossed into a Starfleet prison camp for a sentence of five years for attempted murder and falsifying Starfleet orders.

And I was hailed as a hero.

When the verdict came down, I sat before the tribunal, disbelieving. Dead center, beaming, looking proud as anything, was Admiral Jellico. Jellico, whose life I had once saved and who was one of my biggest boosters as a result. There in the council room, with the crewmen who had testified on my behalf present, Jellico read the unanimous decision of the tribunal. I had acted in a manner in accordance with Starfleet regulations, and was not to be blamed for any aspect of the unfortunate behavior which had resulted in the mutiny and Kenyon's unfortunate demise. They even held up my shooting Kradius as an example of exemplary behavior.

I sat there, stunned. I simply couldn't believe it. I had failed, failed in every way possible. My sworn duty was to protect Kenyon. I had failed. I might have averted the entire thing if only I'd been firmer, if I'd stepped in when there was still the opportunity. I had refused to do so. And I had been *that* close to shooting a man dead in cold blood . . . probably would have, given another second . . . but it hadn't looked that way to anyone who had been present.

They thought me a hero.

I was a fraud.

I heard them speaking of captaincy, of advancement. Of being a shining example of everything that Starfleet stood for. All I wanted to do was vomit.

I rose from behind the table where I was seated and approached the tribunal. They were smiling, clearly figuring that I would be pleased over their decision. Without a word, I removed my combadge and placed it on the table in front of them.

"I quit," I told them.

"What?" Jellico actually laughed, as if he thought I was joking.

"I quit. I resign my commission. I'm out," I said. I turned away and started to leave.

Jellico was around the table inside of a second, and he grabbed me by the arm, sputtering. "Commander . . . we know this has been a great stress on you. If you give it some time, however, we're sure you'll see . . ."

"You know this has been a great stress? Admiral, believe me when I tell you: You know nothing. Nothing." Inside I was furious, furious with myself, and I took it all out on Jellico. "What you don't know could fill volumes. I resign. I quit. I'm out. You are no longer a superior officer; you're just a man holding my arm. Let go."

Anger started to darken Jellico's face. "Don't talk to me that way, Calhoun. I went to bat for you. You owe me. Now sit down and we'll discuss this in a—"

"Let go of me," I told him, "or I will knock you down."

"Calhoun . . ." he started to say, and he pulled on my arm again.

I never heard the rest of what he was going to say. I'm sure it would have been very interesting. It might even have made a major difference in my life.

My fist swung around and caught him squarely in the side of the head. Jellico went down, landing hard on his rump and staring up at me in open astonishment. The other two admirals were on their feet. If I had suddenly ripped off my head to reveal I was a Regulan blood worm in a man suit, they couldn't have looked more surprised.

"I warned you," I said.

I didn't even look back over my shoulder as I heard Jellico raging, "You're finished, Calhoun! You hear? You're finished in Starfleet! Finished!"

Considering that I had just resigned, that wasn't a threat I was particularly concerned about.

I went back to my apartment to clear out my stuff. What I could carry I simply shoved into a suitcase that would be easy to travel with. What I couldn't carry . . . furniture and such . . . I was going to leave behind.

There was a chime at my door. "Go away," I called.

"Mac," came a familiar voice.

I sighed, knowing that standing there and arguing wasn't going to do any good where she was concerned. "Come," I said.

Katerina Mueller entered. And stood there.

"So?" I said.

I was curious as to how well she truly knew me. Whether she would bother to try and argue. Whether she would give me grief, or tell me how I was throwing away my career, or besiege me with any number of unasked-for and unwanted reasons why I was being an idiot.

For a long moment, no words were spoken.

And then she said simply, "One for the road?"

I smiled and accommodated her. It seemed only polite.

THE END

I LEFT EARTH shortly thereafter and began to wander. After about a year, I was found by one Admiral Alynna Nechayev, who had her own plans and interests for me. I cooperated with her for a time, doing things that were of interest to me and of service to her because it seemed an equitable arrangement. And one thing led to another, and I eventually found myself as a captain once more in Starfleet. Becoming involved in Starfleet, serving on a starship . . . I wasn't particularly anxious to embrace the concept. I'd done it before, and as the old saying goes, once burned, twice shy. Then again, it wasn't such a terrible thing, I suppose, going back. If nothing else, it allowed me to be here at the Captain's Table.

When I took command of the *Excalibur,* I wound up bringing some associates with me. Lieutenants Hash and Gold work the nightside on the *Excalibur.*

Katerina Mueller is likewise along, serving as ship's XO as she did so capably for the *Grissom.* It's an odd situation, really, since my first officer and former fiancée, Elizabeth Shelby, doesn't know about how closely Mueller and I served together before. She probably wouldn't care if she did . . . but then again, on the other hand, it's probably better that she not know.

And then there's Captain Kenyon.

Right there. Seated right there, on the other side of the Captain's Table, obviously having wandered in from an earlier time in his life. He has no idea what's to come, and thanks to the rules of this place . . . I can't warn him. Can't let him know what's to come.

I still have his combadge, tinted with blood. It's right here, in fact. I keep it with me to remind me . . .

. . . to remind me of . . .

. . . to hell with it.

Here.

Here, you take it. Let me pin it on you . . . there. There. It actually looks rather good on you.

I've never spoken of this to anyone. Not in all the detail. No one truly knows all the aspects of it, not even Mueller. I suppose that I was holding on to the badge . . . until I found someone that I could trust with the story. So I've trusted you now. You have the combadge, you have the story. I've opened myself up to someone, as I promised Cap I would. I chose you. Do with the story, and the badge, as you will.

As for me . . . I was just trying to meet my obligations as best as I was able to. Which, in the final analysis . . . is all any of us can do.

Nice talking to you.

* * *

Captain Mackenzie Calhoun stood up, ignoring the Gecko that scurried quickly from under his chair, and looked once more in a forlorn manner across the bar. Then he turned away from Captain Kenyon and started to head for the door.

Cap, the bartender, intercepted him halfway out. He looked at Calhoun with a slightly scolding air. "You cheated, Mac," he said.

"Cheated? You said I owed a story. I did exactly as you said. I sat down at a table and told my story to another captain."

"The purpose is for you to share aspects of yourself, Mac. To open up, to air things out. You, of all people—the most tightly wrapped, the one who is mostly likely to internalize everything and keep it to yourself—you, most of all, could have used that release. Instead you dodged it."

"I told the story. And I figured if anyone could appreciate a story about a disaster, *he* could."

"Yes, but you know damned well he didn't hear a word you said."

Calhoun shrugged.

Cap tried to look gravely at him and ream him out some more, but ultimately he wasn't able to. Instead he laughed. "You know . . . you remind me of an arrogant, disheveled kid who came in here thinking he was smarter and better than everyone else."

"Yeah. Whatever happened to him?"

"He was in here just yesterday."

"Really?" Calhoun smiled. "Seems like ages."

He clapped Cap on the back and headed toward the door.

And behind him, at the table he had just left, a man continued to sit there. A man with a white beard and an old-style naval uniform, circa early 1900s. A man who just sat there as he had for so long, and would continue to do, shaking his head and murmuring over and over, "Damned iceberg. Goddamned iceberg."

And on his chest, hidden among various medals and service ribbons he'd received, a blood-tinged Starfleet communication badge sat unobtrusively and glinted faintly in the subdued lighting of the Captain's Table.

Evening painted the sky orange, and a chill wind off the bay made Christopher Pike shiver as he walked along San Francisco's waterfront. Red and yellow leaves swirled in the air and danced around the other pedestrians on the street. Coming toward him, a young couple struggled to keep control of both their hovercart full of baggage and their exuberant four- or five-year-old son, who called out happily as he passed, "We're going to Affa Centauri!"

"That's nice," said Pike, who had often traveled to Alpha Centauri and beyond. During his ten years as captain of the *Enterprise* he had gone many places indeed, most of them far more distant—and far more exotic—than Sol's nearest neighbor.

History moves in cycles, he thought as the family swept past. The street on which he walked had once been named the Embarcadero because it ran along the wharves, and it was from the wharves that people embarked on sailing ships in their travels around the world. When the age of ships had given way to the age of the airplane, the street had become a commercial center, full of warehouses at one end and tourist shops at the other, but nobody had set out on long journeys from there. Then had come space travel and the need for a good place to launch and land passenger ships. The airport was already too busy, and acreage elsewhere was at a premium for living space, so the fledgling industry had turned to the last open space near the sprawling city: the Bay. Now, four centuries after the Embarcadero's genesis, the same street was once again busy with travelers. They were boarding shuttles to take them into orbit rather than wooden ships that plied the ocean, but the spectacle of families struggling with overpacked bags looked the same no matter where they were headed.

Pike wished them all well, but he was glad to be on solid ground again. He'd done his time in space, and now he was putting that experience to use as fleet captain, assigned to Starfleet Headquarters right here on good old Mother Earth. He had the best of both worlds: an adventurous past and a position of responsibility on his own home planet.

So why did he feel so unfulfilled?

He'd been telling himself for the last year or so that he was just growing restless. It had been five years since he'd brought the *Enterprise* back home for refitting and renovation. He'd originally thought he would resume the conn when the ship was ready to fly again, but it had taken two years to replace all the worn and outdated machinery on board and to increase the crew complement from 203 to 430, and by then Starfleet had already promoted him out of the job and given it to James Kirk. Pike didn't begrudge him the post; Kirk was a good officer, if a bit impulsive. He would do well if he didn't get himself killed in some defiant act of bravado. And Pike had come to enjoy his new position, but he had to admit he sometimes missed the thrill of facing the unknown.

Not very often, though. That thrill usually came hand in hand with mortal danger, and even when Pike survived it, other members of his crew often didn't. He had lost more friends than he cared to count during his decade on the *Enterprise,* and he had no desire to experience that again. Maybe some captains could go on after a crew fatality without blaming themselves, but he had never been able to. Every time it happened he went through days of anguish and self-recrimination. And every time he took the ship into danger again he worried that his actions would lead to more deaths.

No, he didn't envy Kirk the job.

Another gust of wind bit through his light topcoat. He had underdressed for the weather. Mark Twain had often said that the coldest winter he ever spent was a summer in San Francisco—well, he should have tried it in autumn. The western horizon was clear enough to allow a sunset, but the sky directly overhead threatened rain and the air was humid enough that it felt like mist already. Pike looked at the buildings along the waterfront, seeking a store he could duck into to warm up for a moment, and his eyes came upon a sign he hadn't seen before.

It was an old-style wooden sign, with letters carved deep into planks held together with black iron bands. It projected out over a windowless doorway and swung gently in the wind, its iron chain squeaking softly. The orange light of sunset made the words THE CAPTAIN'S TABLE stand out in bold relief on its rough surface.

Something about the place seemed inviting, yet Pike hesitated before the door. He couldn't very well just duck into a bar for a minute. He would have to order something, and it was a bit early in the evening to start drinking. That wasn't what he had come down here for anyway. He had merely wanted to get some exercise and some fresh air.

On the other hand, he didn't have any place special he had to be.

The first few drops of rain on his face decided him. He was willing to put up with cold, but cold and wet wasn't part of the plan. He reached for the wrought-iron handle on the solid door and tugged it open, noting a faint tingling sensation as he touched it. A security field of some sort? Or . . . a transporter? He turned and looked behind him. The Embarcadero was still there. Not a transport beam, then. It sure had felt like it, though.

"Close the door!" someone shouted from inside.

Pike nearly let it swing back into place without entering, but the rain was picking up so he ducked in and pulled the massive wooden slab closed behind him.

He couldn't tell who had spoken. Everyone in the bar was looking at him. There were a dozen or so people, mostly human, seated in twos and threes at tables between him and the bar itself, where a Klingon woman held down a stool and a tall, heavyset man stood on the other side, polishing a beer glass. The glasses were either very small, Pike thought, or the bartender had huge hands to go with the rest of his bulky frame.

Fortunately he also wore a smile to match. "Don't pay no mind to Jolley, there," he said. "That's just his way of saying 'Hello.' "

Pike nodded. He wouldn't. All his attention was on the Klingon woman. Not because of the unusual bony ridges on her forehead, nor her exotic face with wide, full lips and an enigmatic grin, nor even the ample cleavage revealed by her traditional open-chested battle garb, though Pike found the latter alluring enough for a second look. What drew his attention was the fact that she was there at all. The Klingon Empire and the Federation had been in conflict for nearly fifty years. All-out war seemed imminent, yet here sat a Klingon in a bar on the waterfront not a kilometer from Starfleet Headquarters.

She had to be a member of a peace delegation. She had probably snuck away from their hotel to check out Earth without a chaperone breathing down her neck. Maybe she thought she could seduce someone here in the bar and learn military secrets from them.

She had undoubtedly recognized Pike the moment he walked in. A fleet captain would be well known to the enemy. Well, Pike would keep his eye on her, too. One of the other patrons was no doubt a Secret Service agent assigned to tail her, but it wouldn't hurt to back him up.

He looked for a good place to sit. There was a piano to his immediate left, and a single small table wedged in next to the piano. A lizardlike alien with slits for eyes and talon-sharp fingers was sitting at the table, sipping at a glass full of something red. Pike didn't look too closely; he just nodded and stepped past, unbuttoning his jacket.

Most of the tables were to his left, clustered in a semicircle around a large stone fireplace that popped and flared as if it were burning real wood. The ones nearest the fire were obviously the popular places to sit. Pike didn't see any vacant tables there as he approached the bar.

"What'll you have, Captain?" the bartender asked.

Pike wasn't wearing a uniform, but he assumed the bartender called everyone "captain," after the name of the place. He looked to the mirrored shelves on the back wall to see what kind of stock they kept here, and was surprised to see several bottles of rare and expensive alien liqueurs in among the more common bourbons and gins. He was tempted to ask for Maraltian Seev-ale just to see if they had it, but he wasn't in the mood for the green stuff tonight. "Saurian brandy," he said instead. He had picked up the taste for that on the *Enterprise,* and it was still his favorite drink.

The bartender poured a snifterful from a curved, amber-colored bottle. Pike took a sip and smiled as the volatile spirits warmed their way down, then turned away to look for a quiet table. He didn't want to sit at the bar; he would either have to sit right next to the Klingon woman or close to a scruffy-looking fisherman who had taken a stool halfway between her and the wall.

There was a stairway to the right of the bar and two tables in an alcove between that stair and the front door. Neither table was occupied. Pike went over to the smaller of the two and sat facing the rear of the bar at an angle, neither turning his back on the others nor staring at them. He sipped his brandy and examined the decor while conversations started up again at the other tables.

There was plenty to look at. Artifacts from dozens of worlds hung on the walls. Pike saw drinking mugs with handles for nonhuman hands, wooden carvings of unrecognizable creatures, and metallic hardware that might have been anything from engine parts to alien sex toys. A Klingon *bat'leth* stuck out just overhead, its curved blade buried so deeply into the wood that Pike doubted anyone could remove it without a pry bar. A thick layer of dust on it provided evidence that few people even tried. A Vulcan harp hanging from a peg next to it apparently came down more often; there was no dust on it, and the strings were discolored near the fingerboard from use.

That was a good sign. Pike liked music better than fighting, too.

The fisherman belched loudly, then said to the bartender, "Another tankard o' grog." He looked over at Pike while the bartender refilled his stoneware mug. Pike looked away—the guy had a drunk and despondent air about him—but when the fisherman got his drink he stood up and walked over to Pike's table anyway.

"You look like a man who's got a lot on his mind," he said as he pulled out a chair and sat down uninvited. Pike could smell the salt and fish and seaweed on him.

"I suppose I might have," Pike admitted, "but I didn't really come here to talk."

The fisherman didn't take the hint. He leaned back in his chair—the wooden frame and leather seat squeaking under his weight even though he was lightly built—and said, "What then? To drink yourself into oblivion? I've tried that. It doesn't work."

Pike laughed softly. "I came in because it was cold outside and starting to rain."

"An admirable reason for a drink," said the fisherman. He took a gulp of his grog—Pike could smell the rum from across the table—and belched again.

How could he make this guy go away? "Get lost" would probably do it, but for all Pike knew this was the bar's owner. Or the Secret Service agent. "I'd really rather not—" he began, but the fisherman waved a hand in dismissal.

"Now me, I drink because my wife and son were killed on a prison colony."

His statement hung in the air between them like a ghost. The short, brutal intensity of those few words and the deep sadness with which they were spoken left Pike gasping for breath even as he tried to think of a response to them.

"I—I'm sorry to hear that" was all he could manage.

"Tortured to death," the man went on. "Right in front of me. A place called Rura Penthe."

What had Pike gotten himself into now? He looked

up toward the bar, saw the Klingon woman flinch as she heard the name of the place, but he had no idea why. It meant nothing to him.

"They damned near killed me, too," his unwelcome companion went on. "Forced me to work in the mines, digging nitrates and phosphates for gunpowder while I held the secret that would make their puny chemicals obsolete overnight! I held it, too. Never told a soul. Saved the world, I did."

"I'm sure you must have," Pike said. "But perhaps you shouldn't be talking about it now, if it's such a dangerous secret."

The man laughed, a single, quick exhalation. "Ha! What do I care now? It's apparently old news. Nuclear power! Splitting the atom! The most elemental force of the universe—only two hours ago in this very bar someone told me it was nothing compared to antimatter annihilation. And that's apparently nothing compared to zero-point energy, whatever that is." He looked at Pike with eyes red as cooked shrimp. "I held my tongue for *nothing.*"

Who *was* this guy? Talking as if the secret of nuclear fission was something new. Pike looked at him more closely. His clothing was rough, coarse cotton and wool dyed in drab brown and blue, and he wore a red bandanna around his neck. He had a high forehead and wide-set eyes, and he sported a two- or three-week beard that hadn't been trimmed since he'd started it, but his features underneath it were fair. And young. His general appearance had made him look older, but his hair was still coal black and his skin smooth. He couldn't be much over thirty-five, if that.

"Who are you?" Pike asked him.

"A fool, apparently," he replied. "One who's seen and suffered more than should be required of any man." He slurped noisily at his grog, then said softly,

"At first I tried to serve humanity, then when I realized what I had discovered I tried to protect it, but now I find that I despise humanity and all it stands for." He looked Pike directly in the eyes and said, "And a man who despises humanity must needs despise himself as well. Many's the day I've wondered if I should put an end to it all."

Pike heard the sincerity in the man's voice, and his experience as a ship's captain raised the hackles on the back of his neck. Just his luck. He'd come out this evening to dwell on his own problems, and now it looked like he might have to talk someone out of suicide.

"Come now," he said. "Whatever your past, you're safe now. You're a free man, warm and dry with a drink in your hand and a roof over your head. Your future can be whatever you make of it." *Especially with a little psychiatric help,* he thought, but he left that unsaid.

"Oh, aye, I'm aware of that," said his unwelcome visitor. "I'm clever enough to make a go of it if I choose. I *have* made a go of it, come to that."

"Oh?" asked Pike. That sounded promising.

The fisherman took the bait. "Well, sir, not to brag, but I masterminded an escape from the prison island. I and twenty men stowed away in empty powder casks and let the stevedores load us on board a warship. It was cramped, but no worse than what we suffered in our barracks at night. And there was no worry of being mistreated in a powder cask!" He grinned, then took a drink. "We waited until the ship was at sea, then rose up in the night and took her. The men pronounced me 'captain,' and we became pirates of a sort, preying on our former captors until they brought in too many ships for us to match. We eventually took damage too heavy to repair ourselves, so we withdrew and set sail here for refitting." The glint faded from his eyes and he shook his head sadly. "It may not be worth the effort. Even if we return to Rura Penthe, no amount of battle has yet managed to vanquish the memory of what I have suffered."

The man told his story with the air of someone who believed every word. Yet how could any of it be true? A prison colony, in the twenty-third century? Mining nitrates for gunpowder? And transporting it by sailing ship? This guy was about four hundred years out of phase with the rest of the world.

Yet he was so convincing that Captain Pike actually looked around the bar again for confirmation that *he* wasn't somehow in the wrong time. He found it in abundance: the Klingon woman on her stool, the Vulcan harp overhead, the Saurian brandy in his glass. He took a sip of it and savored the tart, smoky explosion of flavor.

His gaze fell on the alien by the door. He had seen a few lizardlike humanoids in his travels, but never one like that. It was from an entirely new species. And its kind had to be fairly common for one to be here on Earth, unescorted, in a hole-in-the-wall bar in San Francisco. Pike wondered how he had missed hearing about them before this.

The fisherman—if that's what he was—noticed where Pike was looking. He shook himself out of his reverie and said, "Yes, strange things are about. But I've seen stranger."

"Have you now?" Pike asked, interested despite himself.

"Aye, that I have. Under the sea. Even a single fathom below the surface, everything is different."

"So I've heard," Pike said. He had grown up in Mojave, and even after he'd moved away he'd never felt comfortable in the water.

"So I've *seen,*" the seaman said. "Manta rays bigger than sails, fish with lanterns dangling before their noses so they can see in the black depths, pods of whales all the way to the horizon, making the sea boil as they breached and dove."

Now Pike knew the man was having him on. There hadn't been a whale on Earth for two centuries.

Well, if he was just telling tales then Pike had a few of his own to share. And maybe he could get this guy's mind off his troubles for a while. "I saw some whales once," he said. "But these weren't in the ocean."

His companion considered that a moment. "I've heard there are lakes in China where—"

"Not a lake, either. These were in space."

The man snorted, but when he spoke there was an air of sophistication that hadn't been there before. "Sir, you force me to express doubt."

Pike laughed out loud. "I didn't believe them myself when I first saw them, but they were real enough." He took a sip of brandy and settled back in his chair. "It was back when I was captain of the *Enterprise.* We were out in the Carrollia sector, mapping subspace anomalies and looking for new sources of dilithium, when we received a distress call from a planet called Aronnia. They had a problem with their interstellar fleet. Seems all their starships had run away. . . ."

To be continued in
Star Trek: The Captain's Table
Book Six: *Where Sea Meets Sky*
by Jerry Oltion

Captain Mackenzie Calhoun
by
David Mack

Captain Mackenzie Calhoun was well known as the leader of the planetary revolution that freed the planet Xenex from Danteri control before he entered Starfleet Academy.

During Calhoun's tenure in the Academy, he earned a reputation for being high-energy and quick with his fists, and for never backing down from any confrontation.

Calhoun is never afraid to say precisely what's on his mind; nor does he suffer fools gladly. Although he understands and appreciates the chain of command, respect and loyalty are not commodities he gives to superior officers simply because they are of higher rank. He feels those privileges must be earned.

Captain Calhoun's given name on his homeworld of Xenex was M'k'n'zy. When he joined Starfleet he changed it to Mackenzie, the closest Terran equivalent, and adopted the name of his home city, Calhoun, as his surname.

Calhoun has an older brother, D'ndai, who conspired with Thallonian Chancellor Yoz to overthrow the Thallonian royal family.

—from the Star Trek: New Frontier Minipedia

An excerpt from
Star Trek: The Next Generation
Imzadi II: Triangle
On Sale Now!

Deanna Troi sat in the *Farragut*'s lounge, looking out at the stars as they hurtled past, and for the first time in a long time she felt adrift. She was now faced with the inescapable: The time with her extended family was ticking down. It bothered her that it bothered her. She was, after all, a Starfleet professional. She went where she was told, and served the needs of Starfleet to the best of her ability. For that matter, as a counselor, she was obligated to maintain a professional detachment at all times. She should not be letting herself get so close to the crew of the *Enterprise* that it would hurt when she left them. Yet that was precisely what had occurred. She had let them get too close, let them get to her, get under her skin. There was something to be said for that, she supposed. It was a measure of her compassion and her empathy. But now there was going to be a price for that empathy.

There was irony to it as well, for she realized that

they would very likely not be dwelling on her as much as she would be on them. To all of them, she was simply one individual. But she had come to think of them as one great whole. Her crew. Her people. It was the height of egocentricity, she decided, to become as possessive as all that. It was inappropriate, and not in their best interest, and it sure as hell wasn't in her best interest.

She had to detach herself. Had to separate, had to be alone with herself . . .

"May I join you?"

She turned in her seat and looked up at Worf standing behind her. "You should not," he continued, "be seated in that fashion."

"What fashion?"

"With your back to the door. It is wise to have a clear view of the door at all times, in the event that there is an unexpected threat."

"You'll protect me, Worf," she said with exaggerated breathlessness, as if she were the heroine of some romantic melodrama.

Worf didn't so much as crack a smile. "Of course I will," he said matter-of-factly. He stepped around to the other side of the table and sat down opposite her.

"How is Alexander?"

"He is resting comfortably. I am appreciative of the aid that you extended to him. I shall not forget it."

"It was nothing."

"No . . . it was most definitely something." He leaned forward, his scowl deepening. "There is a matter I need to discuss with you."

She quickly discerned that it was something of a very grave nature. One didn't need to be an empath to figure it out; his overall demeanor was more than enough to signal to her that there were very dire matters waiting to be discussed. Was there more to Alexander's condition than Worf had been willing to admit? Or was there some political crisis with the Klingons that would need to be attended to? "What is it, Worf?" she asked worriedly.

"It has to do with . . . an arrangement."

"An arrangement?" She was lost. "You mean, like . . . a flower arrangement?"

"No. An arrangement having to do with us."

"Oh." She was no closer to understanding what he was talking about than she had been when he first sat down. "What did you have in mind?"

"It has to do with life and war."

"It does?" Her eyebrows were so high in puzzlement that they were bumping up against her hairline. "Does this have to do with a last will?"

"No . . . not that at all. Deanna . . ." He interlaced his fingers, and the depth of his glowering was Deanna's tip-off that he was thinking extremely hard. ". . . life is very much like a war. It has to be approached with planning and strategy. You have to anticipate that which may be thrown into your path, make optimum use of your resources and . . . most importantly . . . you must have solid allies and a firm army at your back."

"All right," she said slowly. "I'm with you so far. I don't especially pretend to understand where this is going, but I'm with you."

"I consider you a most valuable ally. You . . . you anticipate my concerns. You understand my strategies. You support me . . . even if you feel that my plans are wrongheaded or inappropriate. But you are not afraid to let your sentiments be known if you feel that I am acting in a counterproductive manner. I do not intimidate you."

"It takes all my self-control," Deanna said. "Normally one look of disapproval from you makes me weak at the knees and I just want to crawl under a chair and expire."

For a moment he was rather pleased to hear it, but

then he said after due consideration, "You were being ironic."

"Actually it was more like sarcastic, but ironic is close enough."

She laughed softly, and he noted that her shoulders shook slightly as she did so. He realized that even the most casual movement of her body seemed like poetry to him.

"Worf"—and she placed a slender hand on his—"what is this about?"

"Alexander likes you."

"I like him, too," she said. "He doesn't have it easy. He's trying to stride two cultures, and I know from personal experience how difficult that can be. You should be proud of him."

"I am. And I believe that you have been a very positive influence on him. You listen to him."

"So do you."

Worf shook his head. "Not always. Not at first, certainly. You taught me how. You taught me to realize when he was not saying what was on his mind, rather than accepting his words at face value. You taught me to probe. And even now . . . it takes me tremendous effort to listen patiently to the boy. Frequently I find myself frustrated. But you do it so effortlessly. He knows that. I believe that is part of why he feels so affectionately toward you."

"As I do with him. And with his father," she added.

"Indeed. And how his father . . . that is to say, how I . . . feel about you." He growled angrily to himself. "I am doing this very badly."

"Doing what? We're having a very nice conversation about feelings. I know that's not necessarily the thing you're most comfortable discussing, but I'm proud of you for the effort. It's sincerely made."

"It is not simply a matter of discussing things. It is . . ."

"War?" she prompted.

"Yes. That is right. And I would like to . . ." He searched for the right words. "I wish to formalize our alliance."

She stared at him for a long moment, completely clueless as to what he could possibly be talking about. And then it hit her like a ten-ton anvil. Her eyes went wide, her jaw slack. "Worf, are you . . . are you asking me to . . . ?"

"If you laugh . . ." Worf cautioned her.

"No! No, I . . . I wouldn't think of laughing! I'm . . . I just, I don't know what to say. . . ."

"The preferred response to a marriage proposal is 'Yes.'"

She sat back in her seat as if rocked. "A marriage proposal. Worf, I . . . I won't lie to you. I never could lie to you, really. I love you, you know that, and I think you love me. . . ."

"Yes." He didn't sound particularly loving. It was more matter-of-fact. But it was enough that he'd said it.

"Still, for all that . . . Worf . . . may I ask what prompted this?"

"More self-examination?"

"If you hope to be married to me, you'd better get used to it."

"A valid point." He still had one hand tightly wrapped in hers. The other he drummed thoughtfully on the table. "I have been observing families . . . seen what they have to offer one another. Mother, father, child . . . I consider it a reasonable and intelligent situation. Not the only viable one, but it may very well be the ideal one. We complement each other well, Deanna. We function well as a team. And Alexander deserves . . ." He took a deep breath. ". . . he deserves better than for me to be his sole influence."

"Oh, Worf . . . don't sell yourself short. . . ."

"I do not. In fact, quite the opposite. I have a rather high opinion of my abilities as an officer and as an individual. I have my failings, Deanna, but false modesty is not one of them."

"Yes, so I've noticed."

"More sarcasm. It does not suit you."

"Sorry." She kept her lips pursed and a determinedly serious expression on her face.

"It is my opinion that whatever qualities I have are due to the exposure I had to a multiplicity of backgrounds. The galaxy is too small for isolationism. The more Alexander knows, the better he will be able to serve others and himself. And I . . ."

"Yes? What about you? Thus far we've spoken almost entirely about Alexander. What about you, Worf?"

"I . . . do not wish to be without you. Deanna," he said, looking her levelly in the eyes, "I know that I am not exactly the sort of mate that the average Betazoid dreams of. Has nightmares of, perhaps, but does not dream of. But I am stronger with you than without you, and I would like to think you feel the same way about me."

"I do feel that way, Worf. But it's such a major commitment . . . and everything is so much in flux right now . . ."

"Precisely my point. At a time when matters are in flux, that is the moment when security should be grabbed. A security that we can offer one another . . . and, together, offer Alexander."

"I . . ."

"I do not need an immediate answer," Worf told her, "but it would be preferable. For I know that an answer given now would be one given by your heart . . . and I would find that much easier to accept, no matter what the answer was, than one that required overintellectualization."

What he said struck a cord. She remembered when she had first met Will Riker, years ago, and how he had accused her at the time of overanalyzing things to death. Of being incapable of acting on impulse or with emotion, which was peculiar considering that she was someone who was supposed to understand emotion so thoroughly. . . .

Riker.

My God, she thought, *I'm in the middle of a marriage proposal . . . and I'm still thinking about Will.*

This was madness. All the time that they had spent together on the *Enterprise,* all the back-and-forth, and the suggestions, and the one step forward, two steps back . . . all of it, really, amounted to nothing except pleasant memories of a relationship that had long ago cooled. Yet she realized, with startling clarity, that she was still holding on to it in some measure, deep down, for one of the simplest and most obvious of reasons:

Imzadi.

They were Imzadi.

They were Imzadi, and they were supposed to be together.

But life, as an Earth musician had said several centuries earlier, was what happened to you while you were making other plans. Life for Riker and Troi had taken them in other directions, and although there had been some dalliances and some rekindling here and there, the fire had never been fanned once more into full blaze.

With Worf, though, love burned very hot indeed. Worf did nothing in half measures, and although he had obvious trouble discussing things such as feelings, he nonetheless loved her with the type of all-consuming passion that she had once thought Riker felt for her, and she for him. The very thought of it made her heart pound, made her realize just how much she was missing.

And he was right. They were about to be cut adrift. Who knew where Starfleet would send them? Who knew if they would be reunited or sent in different directions? Requests could be put in, strings could be pulled, but in the final analysis no one knew anything for sure. Deanna had felt as if everything was slipping through her fingers, and here was an opportunity being given her to have something permanent, something real.

It's crazy, an inner voice cautioned her. *Marry for the right reasons, not because you're scared of being alone.*

But she was not afraid of solitude, of that she was quite positive. Being on her own, being alone with her thoughts . . . these were not things that held any trepidation for Deanna Troi. She was an independent, secure, self-sufficient woman. She had nothing to prove.

Why marry Worf?

She loved him, and he loved her. And she loved Alexander, too, or at least was reasonably sure she did. They had good chemistry, he was dependable and brave and would willingly lay down his life for her, although heaven forbid it would ever come to that; it was simply an indicator of the depth of his feelings for her. From a purely social growth point of view, he was an up-and-coming officer in Starfleet. They would be able to be assigned to the same ship.

Why not marry Worf?

It might still be too soon, the relationship too young.

But she had known him for so long. He wasn't a stranger. He wasn't . . .

Imzadi . . .

The word came unbidden to her once more, and with almost physical effort she pushed it away.

"Yes." She didn't say it so much as blurt it out, and a look of surprise crossed her face.

"Did . . . did you say, 'Yes'?" Worf asked, leaning forward and tilting his head slightly as if he needed to hear her better.

"I . . . I did, yes." Now that she had made the reply, she instantly felt as if a weight had been lifted from her. "Yes. Yes, Worf . . . I will marry you. . . ."

Worf leaped to his feet, slapping the table with enthusiasm, and shouting, "Yes! She said yes! We are engaged!"

And that was when Worf saw Commander Riker.

Riker was at a table halfway across the room. He was half standing, clearly in the act of rising from the table at which Geordi La Forge was also sitting. And he had frozen in position, his face completely inscrutable.

It was at that moment that Worf abruptly realized, at the most rudimentary of levels, that his engagement might well be the most short-lived on record.

Look for STAR TREK Fiction from Pocket Books

Star Trek®: The Original Series

Star Trek: The Motion Picture • Gene Roddenberry
Star Trek II: The Wrath of Khan • Vonda N. McIntyre
Star Trek III: The Search for Spock • Vonda N. McIntyre
Star Trek IV: The Voyage Home • Vonda N. McIntyre
Star Trek V: The Final Frontier • J. M. Dillard
Star Trek VI: The Undiscovered Country • J. M. Dillard
Star Trek VII: Generations • J. M. Dillard
Enterprise: The First Adventure • Vonda N. McIntyre
Final Frontier • Diane Carey
Strangers from the Sky • Margaret Wander Bonanno
Spock's World • Diane Duane
The Lost Years • J. M. Dillard
Probe • Margaret Wander Bonanno
Prime Directive • Judith and Garfield Reeves-Stevens
Best Destiny • Diane Carey
Shadows on the Sun • Michael Jan Friedman
Sarek • A. C. Crispin
Federation • Judith and Garfield Reeves-Stevens
The Ashes of Eden • William Shatner & Judith and Garfield Reeves-Stevens
The Return • William Shatner & Judith and Garfield Reeves-Stevens
Star Trek: Starfleet Academy • Diane Carey
Vulcan's Forge • Josepha Sherman and Susan Shwartz
Avenger • William Shatner & Judith and Garfield Reeves-Stevens

#1 *Star Trek: The Motion Picture* • Gene Roddenberry
#2 *The Entropy Effect* • Vonda N. McIntyre
#3 *The Klingon Gambit* • Robert E. Vardeman
#4 *The Covenant of the Crown* • Howard Weinstein
#5 *The Prometheus Design* • Sondra Marshak & Myrna Culbreath
#6 *The Abode of Life* • Lee Correy
#7 *Star Trek II: The Wrath of Khan* • Vonda N. McIntyre
#8 *Black Fire* • Sonni Cooper
#9 *Triangle* • Sondra Marshak & Myrna Culbreath
#10 *Web of the Romulans* • M. S. Murdock
#11 *Yesterday's Son* • A. C. Crispin

#12 *Mutiny on the Enterprise* • Robert E. Vardeman
#13 *The Wounded Sky* • Diane Duane
#14 *The Trellisane Confrontation* • David Dvorkin
#15 *Corona* • Greg Bear
#16 *The Final Reflection* • John M. Ford
#17 *Star Trek III: The Search for Spock* • Vonda N. McIntyre
#18 *My Enemy, My Ally* • Diane Duane
#19 *The Tears of the Singers* • Melinda Snodgrass
#20 *The Vulcan Academy Murders* • Jean Lorrah
#21 *Uhura's Song* • Janet Kagan
#22 *Shadow Lord* • Laurence Yep
#23 *Ishmael* • Barbara Hambly
#24 *Killing Time* • Della Van Hise
#25 *Dwellers in the Crucible* • Margaret Wander Bonanno
#26 *Pawns and Symbols* • Majiliss Larson
#27 *Mindshadow* • J. M. Dillard
#28 *Crisis on Centaurus* • Brad Ferguson
#29 *Dreadnought!* • Diane Carey
#30 *Demons* • J. M. Dillard
#31 *Battlestations!* • Diane Carey
#32 *Chain of Attack* • Gene DeWeese
#33 *Deep Domain* • Howard Weinstein
#34 *Dreams of the Raven* • Carmen Carter
#35 *The Romulan Way* • Diane Duane & Peter Morwood
#36 *How Much for Just the Planet?* • John M. Ford
#37 *Bloodthirst* • J. M. Dillard
#38 *The IDIC Epidemic* • Jean Lorrah
#39 *Time for Yesterday* • A. C. Crispin
#40 *Timetrap* • David Dvorkin
#41 *The Three-Minute Universe* • Barbara Paul
#42 *Memory Prime* • Judith and Garfield Reeves-Stevens
#43 *The Final Nexus* • Gene DeWeese
#44 *Vulcan's Glory* • D. C. Fontana
#45 *Double, Double* • Michael Jan Friedman
#46 *The Cry of the Onlies* • Judy Klass
#47 *The Kobayashi Maru* • Julia Ecklar
#48 *Rules of Engagement* • Peter Morwood
#49 *The Pandora Principle* • Carolyn Clowes
#50 *Doctor's Orders* • Diane Duane
#51 *Enemy Unseen* • V. E. Mitchell
#52 *Home Is the Hunter* • Dana Kramer Rolls
#53 *Ghost-Walker* • Barbara Hambly

#54 *A Flag Full of Stars* • Brad Ferguson
#55 *Renegade* • Gene DeWeese
#56 *Legacy* • Michael Jan Friedman
#57 *The Rift* • Peter David
#58 *Face of Fire* • Michael Jan Friedman
#59 *The Disinherited* • Peter David
#60 *Ice Trap* • L. A. Graf
#61 *Sanctuary* • John Vornholt
#62 *Death Count* • L. A. Graf
#63 *Shell Game* • Melissa Crandall
#64 *The Starship Trap* • Mel Gilden
#65 *Windows on a Lost World* • V. E. Mitchell
#66 *From the Depths* • Victor Milan
#67 *The Great Starship Race* • Diane Carey
#68 *Firestorm* • L. A. Graf
#69 *The Patrian Transgression* • Simon Hawke
#70 *Traitor Winds* • L. A. Graf
#71 *Crossroad* • Barbara Hambly
#72 *The Better Man* • Howard Weinstein
#73 *Recovery* • J. M. Dillard
#74 *The Fearful Summons* • Denny Martin Flynn
#75 *First Frontier* • Diane Carey & Dr. James I. Kirkland
#76 *The Captain's Daughter* • Peter David
#77 *Twilight's End* • Jerry Oltion
#78 *The Rings of Tautee* • Dean W. Smith & Kristine K. Rusch
#79 *Invasion #1: First Strike* • Diane Carey
#80 *The Joy Machine* • James Gunn
#81 *Mudd in Your Eye* • Jerry Oltion
#82 *Mind Meld* • John Vornholt
#83 *Heart of the Sun* • Pamela Sargent & George Zebrowski
#84 *Assignment: Eternity* • Greg Cox

Star Trek: The Next Generation®

Encounter at Farpoint • David Gerrold
Unification • Jeri Taylor
Relics • Michael Jan Friedman
Descent • Diane Carey
All Good Things • Michael Jan Friedman
Star Trek: Klingon • Dean W. Smith & Kristine K. Rusch
Star Trek VII: Generations • J. M. Dillard
Metamorphosis • Jean Lorrah
Vendetta • Peter David
Reunion • Michael Jan Friedman
Imzadi • Peter David
The Devil's Heart • Carmen Carter
Dark Mirror • Diane Duane
Q-Squared • Peter David
Crossover • Michael Jan Friedman
Kahless • Michael Jan Friedman
Star Trek: First Contact • J. M. Dillard
The Best and the Brightest • Susan Wright
Planet X • Jan Friedman

#1 *Ghost Ship* • Diane Carey
#2 *The Peacekeepers* • Gene DeWeese
#3 *The Children of Hamlin* • Carmen Carter
#4 *Survivors* • Jean Lorrah
#5 *Strike Zone* • Peter David
#6 *Power Hungry* • Howard Weinstein
#7 *Masks* • John Vornholt
#8 *The Captains' Honor* • David and Daniel Dvorkin
#9 *A Call to Darkness* • Michael Jan Friedman
#10 *A Rock and a Hard Place* • Peter David
#11 *Gulliver's Fugitives* • Keith Sharee
#12 *Doomsday World* • David, Carter, Friedman & Greenberg
#13 *The Eyes of the Beholders* • A. C. Crispin
#14 *Exiles* • Howard Weinstein
#15 *Fortune's Light* • Michael Jan Friedman
#16 *Contamination* • John Vornholt
#17 *Boogeymen* • Mel Gilden
#18 *Q-in-Law* • Peter David
#19 *Perchance to Dream* • Howard Weinstein

#20 *Spartacus* • T. L. Mancour
#21 *Chains of Command* • W. A. McCay & E. L. Flood
#22 *Imbalance* • V. E. Mitchell
#23 *War Drums* • John Vornholt
#24 *Nightshade* • Laurell K. Hamilton
#25 *Grounded* • David Bischoff
#26 *The Romulan Prize* • Simon Hawke
#27 *Guises of the Mind* • Rebecca Neason
#28 *Here There Be Dragons* • John Peel
#29 *Sins of Commission* • Susan Wright
#30 *Debtors' Planet* • W. R. Thompson
#31 *Foreign Foes* • David Galanter & Greg Brodeur
#32 *Requiem* • Michael Jan Friedman & Kevin Ryan
#33 *Balance of Power* • Dafydd ab Hugh
#34 *Blaze of Glory* • Simon Hawke
#35 *The Romulan Stratagem* • Robert Greenberger
#36 *Into the Nebula* • Gene DeWeese
#37 *The Last Stand* • Brad Ferguson
#38 *Dragon's Honor* • Kij Johnson & Greg Cox
#39 *Rogue Saucer* • John Vornholt
#40 *Possession* • J. M. Dillard & Kathleen O'Malley
#41 *Invasion #2: The Soldiers of Fear* • Dean W. Smith & Kristine K. Rusch
#42 *Infiltrator* • W. R. Thompson
#43 *A Fury Scorned* • Pam Sargent & George Zebrowski
#44 *The Death of Princes* • John Peel
#45 *Intellivore* • Diane Duane
#46 *To Storm Heaven* • Esther Friesner
#47 *Q Continuum #1: Q-Space* • Greg Cox
#48 *Q Continuum #2: Q-Zone* • Greg Cox
#49 *Q Continuum #3: Q-Strike* • Greg Cox

Star Trek: Deep Space Nine®

The Search • Diane Carey
Warped • K. W. Jeter
The Way of the Warrior • Diane Carey
Star Trek: Klingon • Dean W. Smith & Kristine K. Rusch
Trials and Tribble-ations • Diane Carey
Far Beyond the Stars • Steve Barnes

#1 *Emissary* • J. M. Dillard
#2 *The Siege* • Peter David
#3 *Bloodletter* • K. W. Jeter
#4 *The Big Game* • Sandy Schofield
#5 *Fallen Heroes* • Dafydd ab Hugh
#6 *Betrayal* • Lois Tilton
#7 *Warchild* • Esther Friesner
#8 *Antimatter* • John Vornholt
#9 *Proud Helios* • Melissa Scott
#10 *Valhalla* • Nathan Archer
#11 *Devil in the Sky* • Greg Cox & John Gregory Betancourt
#12 *The Laertian Gamble* • Robert Sheckley
#13 *Station Rage* • Diane Carey
#14 *The Long Night* • Dean W. Smith & Kristine K. Rusch
#15 *Objective: Bajor* • John Peel
#16 *Invasion #3: Time's Enemy* • L. A. Graf
#17 *The Heart of the Warrior* • John Gregory Betancourt
#18 *Saratoga* • Michael Jan Friedman
#19 *The Tempest* • Susan Wright
#20 *Wrath of the Prophets* • P. David, M. J. Friedman, R. Greenberger
#21 *Trial by Error* • Mark Garland
#22 *Vengeance* • Dafydd ab Hugh

Star Trek®: Voyager™

Flashback • Diane Carey
Mosaic • Jeri Taylor

#1 *Caretaker* • L. A. Graf
#2 *The Escape* • Dean W. Smith & Kristine K. Rusch
#3 *Ragnarok* • Nathan Archer
#4 *Violations* • Susan Wright
#5 *Incident at Arbuk* • John Gregory Betancourt
#6 *The Murdered Sun* • Christie Golden
#7 *Ghost of a Chance* • Mark A. Garland & Charles G. McGraw
#8 *Cybersong* • S. N. Lewitt
#9 *Invasion #4: The Final Fury* • Dafydd ab Hugh
#10 *Bless the Beasts* • Karen Haber
#11 *The Garden* • Melissa Scott
#12 *Chrysalis* • David Niall Wilson
#13 *The Black Shore* • Greg Cox
#14 *Marooned* • Christie Golden
#15 *Echoes* • Dean W. Smith & Kristine K. Rusch
#16 *Seven of Nine* • Christie Golden

Star Trek®: New Frontier

#1 *House of Cards* • Peter David
#2 *Into the Void* • Peter David
#3 *The Two-Front War* • Peter David
#4 *End Game* • Peter David
#5 *Martyr* • Peter David
#6 *Fire on High* • Peter David

Star Trek®: Day of Honor

Book One: *Ancient Blood* • Diane Carey
Book Two: *Armageddon Sky* • L. A. Graf
Book Three: *Her Klingon Soul* • Michael Jan Friedman
Book Four: *Treaty's Law* • Dean W. Smith & Kristine K. Rusch

Star Trek®: The Captain's Table

Book One: *War Dragons* • L. A. Graf
Book Two: *Dujonian's Hoard* • Michael Jan Friedman
Book Three: *The Mist* • Dean W. Smith & Kristine K. Rusch
Book Four: *Fire Ship* • Diane Carey
Book Five: *Once Burned* • Peter David
Book Six: *Where Sea Meets Sky* • Jerry Oltion